Employed at a luxurious villa in the South of France by a glamorous couple – famous playwright, Nicholas Forrest, and his rich and beautiful German wife, Magda – Annabel is fascinated by her employers, and startled by their strange (and sometimes sinister) assortment of guests. She is also repelled by the ruthless streak which she detects in Nicholas Forrest. Meanwhile, from an old trunk, she is unearthing her own parents' extraordinary secret history. Can anything, she wonders, be what it seems?

MARINA WYLIE

This Kingdom by the Sea

PANTHER
Granada Publishing

Panther Books
Granada Publishing Ltd
8 Grafton Street, London W1X 3LA

Published by Panther Books 1984

First published in Great Britain by
Granada Publishing 1983

ISBN 0-583-13689-3

Printed and bound in Great Britain by
Collins, Glasgow

Set in Baskerville

For George Greenfield

Acknowledgements

Warmest thanks to R, to M and B, to I and P, to the members of the OCA, and of course to A.

PART ONE

{1}

I sank back with a sigh into the softness of the well-upholstered seat, and leant my head against its snowy antimacassar. My feet rested on the thick pile carpet - even the corridor of this train, I had noticed, was carpeted. My eyes traced the elaborate designs in various woods that were inlaid in the panelled walls.

When I made that journey on the twenty-fifth of July 1938, it was not the first time I had been to the South of France, but it was the first time I had travelled on the Blue Train. After the austerity and greyness of the past months, and the dark hell that had preceded them, there was something almost dreamlike about such luxury - unreal, but, as a happy dream is, soothing and relaxing. I closed my eyes for a moment, letting myself be lulled by the rhythm of the train.

How wonderful it was to have a compartment to myself. That, I decided, was the best thing of all: not to have to adjust to the presence of strangers, and at such close quarters. I would have to face a world of strangers soon enough - on the following morning, in fact.

I hoped that I would be met at Nice by a silent, impersonal chauffeur - the journey to the villa allowing me a further respite on my own. The worst thing I could imagine was that, on the train, there might be others destined for the same household - hard, glittering people, wondering who on earth this girl was whose company had been thrust on them in the motor. That could soon be explained, of course: the new secretary – that would account for her off-the-peg clothes, her lack of smart chatter. They would have found it hard to imagine that Nicholas and Magda Forrest could be entertaining such a person as a guest. Odd, even so, that she should have been accommodated on the *Train Bleu* – surely the ordinary *Exprès du Sud* would have done quite well enough?

Indeed I myself had thought the same. I had been astonished when I collected the ticket, together with a lavish allowance of francs for dinner on the train, at Thomas Cook's. I had almost asked if there were not some mistake. But then an explanation had occurred to me. I had been booked on the Blue Train *because I was my father's daughter.*

Soon it would be time for dinner. A steward would come along the corridor, announcing the *premier service.* I felt limp. I did not relish the prospect of making my way through the train to the dining-car, of getting settled at a table, which I might have to share. I felt that even choosing what to eat from the menu would be a strain. But, if I did not go to dinner, then I would be in my compartment when the steward came to prepare it for the night. I would have to talk to him – I didn't want to talk to anyone. He might ask me why I was not dining. It would all be awkward and tiresome. No, it would be better to make the journey to the dining-car, in spite of the effort involved. And besides – I was hungry. I had eaten nothing since the croissant that had accompanied the *café-au-lait* which the chambermaid had brought me that morning in my small room in the quiet little hotel in Montparnasse.

All day I had wandered about Paris, and almost every street had seemed to awaken some echo of memory. The sun was shining brightly, and how lively every aspect of the town appeared after my sojourn in London. Surely, people even trod more lightly in Paris, with more of a spring in their step. They conversed in sharp, clear voices, instead of muttering to each other as if it were 'not done' to be overheard. While the Thames had flowed sluggish and sullen, the Seine sparkled. I went into Notre Dame, and it made me think of a forest of Christmas trees, lit by candles, where people wandered to refresh themselves, or knelt down to pray. How unlike St Paul's Cathedral, which I had visited on one of my long solitary walks about that other city: a magnificent building, but so cold and formal - more like a great public hall than a church; I had not seen anyone praying there.

Yet, in spite of all its pleasant aspects, Paris, for me, was pervaded with the griefs and horrors of the past. When I had arrived in London, six months before, the impersonality and the aloofness of the English people had come to me as a positive relief. Despite the all-pervading greyness, the shabby mustiness of the boarding-house where I had stayed, the long days at the secretarial college, I had found balm for my bruises in the fact that no one knew me - or wanted to know me. One thing I didn't desire to be again was 'conspicuous' - I had that, if nothing else, in common with the English.

'Such a mouse!' my mother had exclaimed to me, in one of her more lucid moments, not long before she went away for the last time. 'Who'd ever have guessed that two tigers would give birth to such a little mouse?' But I was glad to be what she called a mouse. The last thing I wanted to be was a tiger. Tigers were dangerous - and, like the ones in the poem, could become shabby too, even if not tamed.

For tamed and shabby tigers
And dancing dogs and bears.

When I was small, my father once found me crying over that poem. He had been wonderful - as he could still very often be wonderful in those days. He told me that the poem had been written a long time before, and that nowadays people hardly ever made dogs and bears dance. 'Except in circuses,' he said, 'and there are fewer and fewer of them, anyway. People are going to the movies instead. And as for the tigers

– well, they may be shabby, but they aren't tamed. I can promise you that tigers are never, never tame.' Of course, the time when he told me that had been long before I stopped believing in his promises.

Now I could hear the steward coming along the corridor with his little bell. '*Premier service!*' I must prepare for the ordeal ahead. But, after all, it wasn't much of an ordeal. The real ordeal would come next day.

At dinner, a kindly steward looked after me well. From the many dishes, the numerous courses on the menu, I chose a meal that I enjoyed – chilled consommé, then *noisettes de veau* in a creamy sauce, accompanied by *pommes Anna* and a purée of spinach. I decided to complete my dinner with a compôte of fruit, followed by coffee.

'Mademoiselle would care for some wine?'

'No, no wine.' A trace of sharpness in my voice obviously surprised the steward, and I smiled as I added, 'Just a bottle of mineral water, please.'

Though there was a flock of chattering people in the dining-car, I had a table to myself. I found myself relaxing again, as I had in the compartment, and felt able to appreciate the good food and the novelty of my surroundings: the glowing lamps, the gleaming cutlery and glass on the snowy tablecloth, the deft movements of the steward as he served me. The rhythm of the train gave me a sudden feeling of being on vacation. How different this was from eating with my parents – eating out with them had always been an agony for me.

I could picture with what a disdainful look my mother would have cast her eyes down this splendid menu, and how she would have ended by demanding something that did not appear on it at all – a stuffed tomato or a breast-of-chicken-and-lettuce sandwich. She had a horror of what she called 'sluck', a word of her own invention which could loosely be defined as anything elaborate or much cooked – though at times its meaning was extended to cover anything at all that was available. Despite what she described as her 'simple tastes', she often made impossible requests – insisting on strawberries or asparagus in November at places where such out-of-season delicacies would never possibly be obtainable. And my father, although he had lived in France for so many years, remained obstinately American in his preferences – petulantly demanding, at some *brasserie* in the early hours of the morning, clam chowder, chipped beef with hard-boiled eggs, or corned-beef hash. Sometimes – though by no means invariably – he could be distracted by the offer of a steak with a baked potato, which however, when it arrived, he seldom did more than toy with.

In fact, in spite of all the fuss they made about it, neither of my parents was really at all interested in food. It was drink which was their constant, over-riding preoccupation. Here in this train, whatever they might ultimately have selected from the menu – how the champagne would have flowed! The pop of the champagne cork – to many people such a festive sound – would always be, for me, an alarm signalling the approach of disaster.

Lying on my berth that night – comfortable, if narrow, though it was – I could not sleep. The train rattled across France – Seine et Marne, Yonne, Saône-et-Loire. I tried to lull myself into slumber by repeating the names – fitting them to the motion of the train – of the provinces we must pass through before reaching Lyon in the middle of the night. *Seine et Marne, Yonne, Saône-et-Loire* – but sleep would not be summoned. Sometimes the steady rhythm would be interrupted by a blast on the whistle – a sound which had a place among the memories of my American childhood, which had been a brief one, for we had sailed for Europe when I was six.

I remembered being awakened by loud voices, by the breaking of a glass violently hurled – sounds which were far from unfamiliar to me, but which always left me trembling with fear. A silence followed, almost more frightening than the shouts and crash of glass, for I had no idea what might be happening in it. Then, far away in the distance, as I lay rigid in the darkness, I heard the whistle of a train. It had sounded extraordinarily lonely - had made *me* feel lonely, as I recalled later when my father became fond of a song called 'I hate to hear that lonesome whistle blow'.

Restlessly, now, I turned over, lifted the corner of the window blind, saw only silent, greyly moonlit country. How I longed to sleep. Feeling and looking tired and washed out, would be an extra burden with which to face the challenges of the day ahead of me.

What would they be like - Nicholas and Magda Forrest? Shortly before I left London, I had seen, in a dentist's waiting room, a picture of them in an old copy of the *Tatler*. 'The popular playwright and his beautiful wife, who is the daughter of Herr Otto von Kronenberg, the well-known German industrialist.' Hers had been a face fair, regular and smooth as a madonna's - I wondered if the Forrests had children. Looking at the photograph - only the presence of two other prospective patients in the waiting-room had prevented me tearing it from the magazine - I had thought that Nicholas Forrest's features (he reminded me of someone, but I could not think whom), dark, almost brooding, did not match the cool sophistication and brittle wit of the only play of his I had ever seen. Or, rather, partly seen, for I had gone to it with my parents, and their rare visits to the theatre seldom outlasted the interval, by which time the call of bar or café had acquired, especially for my father, an insistence not to be denied.

It was in the London *Times* that I had come across the Forrests' advertisement. My father had once told me that this was the 'only' English newspaper, and - as I always accepted his opinion where this sort of information was concerned - I had, during my stay in London, solemnly bought a copy twice each week, on Monday and Friday.

My aim was to 'keep in touch', but I found most of the news rather dry, and the editorials were too pompous for my taste. What I really liked was the personal column which occupied the front page - how typically English, I thought, to bury the news inside, and have only a page, in tiny print, of births, marriages, deaths, expensive objects for sale, and so forth, to attract the prospective purchaser's attention. But doubtless *The Times* felt it had no need of anything so showy as 'attractiveness'.

Anyway, it was in the 'personal' section that I had seen the advertisement: 'Writer and his wife, resident in the South of France, require qualified and experienced secretary to undertake literary and social duties.'

It was a Friday evening. I was in my gloomy little bedroom in the boarding-house. It was the words 'South of France' that captured and held my attention, made me consider the advertisement more closely, beckoned by a vision of sunshine, blue sea, palm trees and brilliant flowers.

I wondered what 'social duties' involved - they sounded somewhat intimidating. And while in three weeks' time I would be qualified, I was certainly not experienced. However, I did have experience of writers - well, of one writer at least. The South of France! What a delightful idea it was in this damp Summer that - slowly and reluctantly, it seemed - was edging into the place of the cold, wet Spring. Why not be bold? I had nothing to lose.

I wrote off to the box number given at the end of the advertisement. I described how I was just completing my secretarial training, and mentioned that my late father had been a writer. I wondered, waiting for a reply, who *this* writer could be. His answer came within a week.

Of course I knew of him. He was very successful, very famous. I cast my mind back to that half play of his I had seen. I hoped that he didn't talk in the same clipped, witty dialogue as his characters – I didn't feel I would be able to cope with that.

In his letter he briefly described the duties a secretary would have to undertake: typing out his current work and dealing with his correspondence. His wife ('My wife leads an extensive social life,' he wrote) would also require assistance – settling accounts, sending out invitations, preparing seating plans for dinner parties, and so on. If these were the 'social duties', they were certainly not as alarming as I had feared, being essentially 'behind the scenes'.

The letter ended: 'You tell me that your father was a writer, and that he died very recently. Is it possible that, as your surname suggests to me, he was Delaney Lee whom, in defiance of the idiotic fact that his works aren't fashionable at present, I regard as one of the finest novelists of our time? I'd be delighted to become acquainted with his daughter. If that is what you are, you must be a girl of intelligence – which, in my eyes, would more than compensate for your lack of experience. My last secretary was experienced, but I found her stupidity quite intolerable.'

In a postscript, he had added: 'I met your father many years ago, at a party, when I was a very young man, and I'll never forget the impression he made on me. What magical charm he possessed!'

I passed my shorthand and typing exams with flying colours – the prospect of the job with the Forrests certainly gave a spur to my final efforts. I wrote to tell Nicholas Forrest of my success and confirmed that Delaney Lee had indeed been my father. A few days later, I heard that the job was mine, and that I should collect my tickets – London to Paris, and Paris to Nice – at Thomas Cook's main office in London.

One thing I knew I liked about Nicholas Forrest – that he appreciated my father's work. There indeed we were on common ground. In spite of everything that had happened, I could still pick up one of my father's novels and be instantly entranced by his particular spell. Life still sprang, freshly coloured, from each page, and, I believed, would always do so. I felt certain that a magic aura would always surround even the most twilit of his characters, despite the fact that, as Nicholas Forrest had written, his work was not currently fashionable. I was sure that this was because it did not carry the 'social message' which, at that time, seemed obligatory. The critics complained that he wrote about 'worthless' people. Well, that didn't bother me! In his writings he created a world that was entirely his own, and I believed that he would survive when a thousand earnest hacks had been forgotten. Yes, I believed that, would always believe it of Delaney Lee – my dear, deplorable, dead, defeated father.

At that point, in the swaying train, I must have fallen into a kind of uneasy sleep – a half-sleep in which scenes and figures from the past rose like objects tossed up by the waves during a shipwreck: glimpsed, lost, sighted again, vanished forever.

We are on the porch of a big old house. It is crowded with people, who are all talking and laughing loudly. I am very small, for the noise they are making comes from far above me, and I am chiefly aware of feet. So many feet – ladies' feet in high-heeled shoes and thin stockings, men's feet in socks and polished brogues. I see my mother's feet – I recognize her white shoes with the straps across the insteps, her slim ankles, the hem of her pink dress. I tug at her skirt, but she takes no notice. I am cross, and I make my way to the edge of the porch. Sitting on the tall steps, I edge myself down from one to the next. When I reach the bottom, I am on the garden path, and I head for the gate with a definite sense of triumph. The gate is open. I go out into a dusty lane, and set off down it. I stumble on a stone, and nearly fall. I look back, and there is nobody in the lane. Why has no one come to find me? I hear a low growling sound, and look ahead again. There is a big dog, black and brown, with pointed ears, standing in front of me in the middle of the lane. It shows its teeth, and makes the growling noise. I am so frightened that I cannot move. The dog takes a step towards me. But then there is a shout, and a man with a stick comes running down the lane. The dog hears the shout and turns its head. The man shouts again, and the dog slinks back to him, its tail between its legs. 'Bad dog,' the man says now. Then he picks me up. I start to cry. He asks me where I live, and I point back towards the gate. He carries me into the garden, making the dog sit down in the lane. My father comes running down the steps from the porch. The man says something to him that he doesn't like. His face goes red, but then he smiles. He asks the man if he would like a drink, but the man puts me down now, shakes his head, goes away. People gather around me on the porch, but I am still crying, and soon I am handed over to the maid who takes me through to the kitchen. The noise dies away as she closes the door. I feel safer now, but whenever I think of the dog, I begin to cry again.

We are in a great square, someplace in Europe. In the middle of it is a vast fountain, crowned by a tall iron goddess, reining in a trio of plunging horses. My mother climbs over the rim, and wades in the basin of the fountain. My father, who is laughing loudly, puts a hand on the rim, jumps on to it, then vaults on to the back of one of the horses. He circles the waist of the goddess with his arm.

A moment before, the square had seemed almost empty. Now people are gathered all over it in little clusters. They are all staring at my parents. A policeman detaches himself from one of the clusters, and starts to walk towards the fountain. I am terrified. I gaze beseechingly at my parents, but they are utterly caught up in their game, in their laughter. I feel completely alone: deserted.

We are driving up the circling Corniche road – my parents have rented a villa at Antibes this summer. I am alone in the back of the car. My father is driving, and my mother, sitting next to him, is muttering in a low, angry voice. Suddenly she leans across him, and grabs the steering wheel. He fights with her for possession of it. The car swerves across the road. I have a sudden dizzying glimpse of blue depths, of cruel rocks, far below. There is a hideous screech of brakes.

I awoke - though had I really been asleep? - with a loud hissing in my ears. The train had stopped. In the silence that followed the release of steam, I heard doors being slammed, and someone shouting - the words indistinguishable - in French. Had there been an accident? In sudden panic, I sat up, and tugged at the edge of the blind. I saw an iron sign on a dimly lit station platform. *Lyon.* A normal halt on the train's journey south.

I was trembling. My forehead was hot and damp, and I wiped it with my handkerchief. The past still possessed me. There was more slamming of doors, then a shout, a shrill blast from a whistle. As the train moved off, I switched on the light. How reassuring the softly lit compartment looked - the dazzlingly white sheets, the blue monogrammed blanket, my old brown travelling bag. (My only other luggage, the old tin trunk containing my father's papers, was in the baggage compartment.)

I swung my feet on to the floor. The carpet was soft under my toes. I wished that I had something to read which would put me in the mood for sleep. But there was nothing except, at the bottom of my travelling bag, my father's copy of Keats' poems in its worn leather binding, his name - the ink faded to brown now - on the flyleaf: *J. Delaney Lee, 1912.* He had been sixteen then. It was eight years before my own birth.

I lacked the energy, I found, to take my bag down from the rack, and forage in it for the poems. And, anyway, I wasn't really in the mood for poetry. I opened my pocket-book, and took out Nicholas Forrest's first letter. It had a worn, crumpled look, and there was the circular brown mark of a saucer on it. I had read it over and over again, trying to form a picture of the household of which I would so soon be a member.

Now I read it once more, lingering on the points which interested me.

'My last secretary was experienced – but I found her stupidity quite intolerable.'

I was afraid he might be disappointed in me. *'Quite intolerable'* – perhaps he was not a very tolerant man. Though I did not consider myself stupid, impatience had always brought out the worst in me. My hands would start to shake. I would drop things. My mind would become a blank. I knew why – it was because my mother had so often reduced me to that state – but knowing why didn't necessarily help, as I had noticed when my London shorthand teacher once snapped at me.

In the last years, when her skin had coarsened, and her face had developed the thickened, blunted look which Dr Zeiss had told me was often associated with her illness – her beauty almost gone, only glimpsed occasionally in a quick turn of her head, or a flash of what someone had once called 'that eagle's swift regard' – and when all her attempts at achievement, in rivalry with my father, as actress, painter, writer (yes, she was even bold enough to do battle with him on that field where he was an acknowledged champion) had failed, my mother had striven, with a sudden intense passion, to fulfil her ambitions through me. I was subjected to ballet classes, to singing lessons, to attendance at a well-known artist's *atelier*. How she had raged at my unsteady arabesques, my uncertain scales, the feebleness of my drawings. And, even though I didn't really believe that I was stupid, to *her* my 'stupidity' had been 'quite intolerable'. Anyway, I thought defiantly, Nicholas Forrest would not expect me to practise at the *barre*, to sing scales or to sketch the Mediterranean. Such activities, thank heaven, would not be among my duties.

'My wife leads an extensive social life.'

My wife – I noted that he did not include himself. Did that indicate that he, as opposed to her, was a recluse? And I wondered in what Mrs Forrest's social life consisted. Would this be a return to life with my parents, to the old days of drunken parties ending in a general collapse at dawn?

I hoped not, and – recollecting the smooth madonna face which I had seen in that photograph – I felt that Magda Forrest's entertaining was unlikely to take such a form. Rather, I saw her at the foot of a great dining-table, nodding and smiling graciously at the guests on either side of her, her eyes alert to anticipate their slightest requirements. Then a nod to the butler, and the need at once silently satisfied. A different scene indeed from the kind of thing which had been apt to happen at my parents' parties, which were always subject to dramatic mishaps! Food that had been ordered would not arrive, or a manservant, hired for the evening, would depart after some escapade of my father's. I remembered a whole cold salmon on a bed of cucumber being hurled across the room by him because he had suddenly decided that pink and green were an insipid combination of colours. Such events usually necessitated a transfer of the entire party to an expensive restaurant – where the cost was often literally doubled by my father's habit of giving preposterously lavish tips. No, I could not imagine such events taking place at the Forrests' home – the Villa Aurore.

I wondered now on what occasion it had been that Nicholas Forrest had been so captured by father's 'magical charm'. Although, even towards the very end, that charm could still make brief appearances – just as my mother's face could flicker into a momentary approximation of its former beauty – I found it hard to imagine its appeal surviving the course of a whole party. But then, of course, Nicholas Forrest had written that the party had been held many years before, and that he had been a very young man at the time. Now he must be in his middle thirties, at least, I imagined. So the party had probably taken place in the Twenties. At that time, my father's 'magic' would still have retained all its natural power.

Cocktails and laughter,
But what comes after?
Nobody knows.

I knew.

A sudden tremendous yawn engulfed me. With relief, I realized that, at last, I would be able to sleep. I put the letter back in my pocket-book, and switched off the light.

{2}

It turned out as I had hoped. There were no other passengers destined for the Villa Aurore. When I got out of the train at Nice, the spacious, airy station, with its iron columns and glass roof, reminded me of a giant conservatory. A chauffeur, wearing a linen coat and a peaked cap, found me quickly. He was English. His name was Edwards. He was small, ginger-haired and, to my delight, taciturn.

We drove along the Moyenne Corniche. Had it been on this road, or on the Grande Corniche above it, that my mother had made her terrifying intervention at the wheel? I could not remember – it had happened seven years before. What I could remember was the pounding of my heart when my father had finally managed to bring the car to a halt, right on the brink of the precipitous drop. 'Oh my God, Vanna,' was all he said. He turned to look at me, gave me what was meant to be a reassuring smile, but his mouth trembled. She, for the remainder of the journey, lapsed into a sullen and immobile silence.

Firmly, I put the memory behind me and it was not too difficult to do so, for I could not help feeling my spirits rise. It was as I had imagined in London. After those cold, grey months, there was something positively festive in the brightness of the sun and sea, in the abundance of the Mediterranean trees and flowers. Yes, it did give me a holiday feeling – quite ridiculous and illogical, since I was on my way to my first job. Suddenly I felt a hollow sense of dread in my stomach at the prospect of arriving at the villa.

How I wished that the chauffeur, Edwards, would drive more slowly, but remorselessly the big car gobbled up the miles, effortlessly negotiating the numerous bends in the road.

After Cobbé, we turned right, on the last lap of our journey to Cap-Martin. Soon we were passing magnificent villas, set among pinewoods and olive groves. We climbed a slope with a high stone wall on its left. The car slowed down, and my spirits plummeted. *Let's not be there* quite *yet.* But my silent plea went unanswered – or, rather, was denied. The car drew up by a great iron gate.

'Well, here we are, Miss,' Edwards said. 'If you get out now, and go up the steps, I expect you'll find Mrs Forrest on the terrace. I'll take your luggage around to the back.'

He came to open the door for me, touched his cap. As he returned to the driver's seat, my wistful glance followed him. I wished I could also go 'around to the back'. But after all, I told myself, I was a secretary, not a domestic servant. What was this timidity? In the past, hadn't I always approached villas by the front entrance? I remembered the Sprotts, my parents' rich friends at Antibes. Surely the Forrests could be no more smooth, polished, sophisticated than they had been? Suddenly I remembered the occasion when my father had been banished from their villa for two weeks, after pouring a glass of wine down the back of a French countess's evening dress. Of course, when I had visited the Sprotts, I had not been alone; I had accompanied my parents. But that had sometimes proved to be a doubtful blessing.

I climbed the three shallow marble steps that led to the gate. Now I peered between the curlicues of its elaborate ironwork into the Forrests' domain.

Twelve more marble steps – postponing my arrival at the villa, I actually counted them – ascended to a terrace with a marble balustrade on which stone urns of trailing, brilliantly coloured begonias stood at regular intervals.

The villa, silhouetted against the sky, seemed enormous to

me; it loomed. It was built of limestone, with a slate roof, and its solidity was massive. The central block had three storeys. At the top of the steps, beyond the terrace, I saw a mahogany front door, crowned with a shell-shaped structure of bronze struts and glass panels. On either side of this door, tall, shuttered french windows - the shutters open now - led on to the terrace.

On the second floor, the windows had individual balconies with squat stone pillars. Above each window, a plaque of two Cupids, holding a cornucopia, was set into the wall.

On the third storey was a row of mansard windows with, in the centre, and directly above the front door, an ornamental pediment on which Aurora, goddess of the dawn - it was she who had provided the villa with its name - lounged amongst clouds, sunrays emerging from her body.

At ground level, there was a wing on either side of the central block. The one on the right was topped by a stone balustrade with the same square pillars as those on the balconies. Above the left wing rose a stone belvedere - tall classical columns open to the air on all sides, but topped by a flat roof of graduated stone slabs.

As, reluctantly, I put my hand on the hasp of the gate, I found time to wish that the shutters had not been painted such a bright, ugly yellowish brown. I thought how much nicer they would have looked if they had been grey, or better still a French blue, faded by at least one hot summer.

Decisively I pressed the hasp. I pushed, and the gate swung open without a creak. Everything was perfectly cared for, I noticed, as I closed the gate behind me, and started to ascend to the terrace. On either side of the steps was a large formal bed of red and yellow roses.

As I climbed, I became aware of a buzz of voices, coming from the section of the terrace that was on my left. Reaching the top, I found myself in what was, to me, the worst situation imaginable. A whole party of people was gathered around a table, evidently eating a late breakfast. As I stepped on to the terrace, they all looked up.

They were drinking coffee from gold-and-scarlet cups. In the centre of a heavy white damask cloth was a great dish on which glowed a giant pyramid of fruit – almost unnatural in its perfection, and proudly independent of any season. Peaches, nectarines and apricots, with bloomy skins of rose, cream and gold, rested on a base of small, striped melons, and were entwined with heavy bunches of pale green hothouse grapes. From the peak of the pyramid jutted the palm-like stem of an enormous pineapple. Another pineapple, peeled and sliced, was arranged on a plate.

There were six people seated around the table. I saw an aquiline blonde, with pale protuberant eyes, thin as a reed in white, bell-bottomed pants and a blue-and-white striped fisherman's jersey. Next to her sat an equally fair and aquiline man, who could have been her brother. Beyond him was a dumpy, elderly woman in a dirndl skirt and embroidered peasant blouse, next to a paunchy, bald man with a jowly look, and bags under his eyes. A plump, pretty little woman, with smooth dark hair, wearing a printed silk dress, sat composedly with small neat hands folded in her lap.

Nicholas Forrest was not present on the terrace – one glance had assured me of that. But rising to meet me now, very tall and upright, was a woman. At that instant, however, my eyes were distracted from her by the dog which had been lying at her feet.

It rose as she did – large, lean, narrow-headed, coal-black. A Dobermann. It bared its teeth as it looked at me, and gave a low, menacing growl.

My pocket-book fell from my hand, and I shrank back against the terrace balustrade, possessed by the blind, uncontrollable terror which I had felt ever since childhood, ever since I had encountered that German Shepherd in a Connecticut lane. Shyness, nervousness – these were stupid, childish failings I was determined to overcome. But would I ever be able to conquer my old, blind terror of 'the dog'?

The aquiline, pale-eyed woman in the striped jersey gave a little laugh, but the woman who had risen to greet me frowned. 'Karl, sit!' she exclaimed sternly, and the dog slowly sank down. Now she moved towards me - how smoothly dignified was her slightly swaying walk.

At once, I recognized her from that photograph in the *Tatler.* It had been a very good likeness and yet, I thought now, the impression she made, in the flesh, was entirely different.

The large blue eyes, the narrow mouth, the straight nose, the high wide forehead, the hair - yellow as corn - parted in the centre and drawn down, smoothly, tightly over her ears, to form a heavy coil at the nape of her neck - such thick, strong, obedient hair, not a single rebellious tendril escaping: all these the photograph had shown. What it had failed to capture was her particular quality, her essence. For this was no modest madonna. This was a noble ice-maiden from the Norseland, a goddess of the snows.

Her skin was thick and smooth, and as white as skim-milk. Whereas the other members of the party were, to varying degrees, tanned by the sun, it was obvious that she never surrendered herself to its rays. Indeed, even here, at ten o'clock in the morning, on this shady section of the terrace, her face was shielded by a broad-brimmed hat, and the white dress she wore had full sleeves that covered her wrists. As she came towards me, she fingered, with her left hand, a crystal apple with diamond leaves, which hung from her firm neck on a silver chain. Crystal, diamonds and silver - how appropriate to her they seemed.

I stooped to pick up my pocket-book, stood up awkwardly just as she reached me. She smiled, showing even, dazzlingly white teeth.

'Ah,' she said, 'you must not be frightened of my Karl. Dogs do not like people who are afraid of them.' Her English pronunciation was almost perfect, but her speech had a slightly guttural sound; her 'ah' bordered on an 'ach'.

'So you are our Miss Annabel Lee.' When she said this, I could not avoid glancing at the company assembled around the table, behind whom a manservant in a tailcoat silently hovered (a butler, I supposed, though, squat and stout, with close-cropped hair, he was not the traditional idea of one). I was so used to – so tired of – the smiles which often greeted my name, the jokes about 'sepulchres by the sea' and 'the bright eyes of the beautiful Annabel Lee'. Anyway, my grey eyes are not shiny, and I am not a beauty.

Evidently, however, none of these people was acquainted with the poem by Edgar Allan Poe which bore my name. My parents' drunken jest – by their own report, they had both been drunk at my christening, and had chosen the name, with peals of laughter, in the church porch – was wasted on this gathering. Their expressions – all faintly contemptuous, or so it seemed to me, at my reaction to the dog – did not change.

Magda Forrest took my tentatively extended hand in her strong fingers. Her other hand still toyed with her pendant. I noticed that it was as white as her complexion – the nails slightly broader than oval, and buffed to a rosy sheen.

Still smiling, she turned toward thes table, releasing my hand. 'I must introduce you to my guests, Annabel,' she said, and added, 'I shall call you "Annabel" because you are so young. You do not mind?'

'Oh not at all,' I said sincerely. Looking from one to the other of her visitors, though, as she introduced me to them, I was sure my smile was becoming fixed and unnatural.

'The Graf and Gräfin von Eisenspach' – the dumpy woman and the jowly man nodded like two squat Buddhas. 'Mr Paul and Lady Sarah Cressingham' – the fair man jerked his head; his wife – evidently, from her title, she was his wife, not his sister – merely raised her pale, plucked eyebrows in what could have been interpreted as a gesture of acknowledgement. 'Madame Marèchal' – the plump, pretty woman returned my smile amiably.

'Annabel – Miss Lee – is Nicholas's new secretary,' Magda Forrest continued, 'and she will also be assisting me.' She paused, then she said, 'You will be interested to hear that she is the daughter of a famous American writer, Delaney Lee. Nicholas has much admiration for his books.'

The Germans and the Frenchwoman looked blank. Mr Cressingham's face acquired a faintly puzzled expression, as if my father's name was vaguely and distantly familiar to him. Lady Sarah spoke, in a harsh, arrogant drawl like the rasp of a saw on wood.

'What, poor old Delaney? She's not a bit like him, I must say. And Nick still enjoys his books, does he? The Gay Twenties and so on? I would have thought all that was a bit old hat nowadays.'

I felt an angry flush rise to my cheeks. What entitled this unpleasant woman – for I was immediately sure that I disliked her intensely – to patronize my father? Controlling myself, I cast my eyes down to the terrace floor, then looked up at Magda Forrest.

I thought I saw an expression of annoyance on her face, and I wondered if it had been caused by Lady Sarah's rudeness. But it was gone in an instant.

'Nicholas has much admiration for his books,' she repeated firmly. 'And who are we to dispute Nicholas's judgement? I myself am not well acquainted with the English – or should I say American? – novel. I find that our German literature more than occupies my time.'

How pleasantly she was attempting to smooth things over. I felt that I myself must say something. Why, I had hardly opened my mouth since my arrival on the terrace. 'Oh yes,' I said. 'Thomas Mann. My father loved his books. He gave me *The Magic Mountain* to read, and I thought it was wonderful . . .'

My voice died away in a silence. A sudden chill,

unaccountable to me, had descended on the terrace. Then I saw that the paunchy Graf was positively scowling, and his wife was angrily shaking her head.

Had I said something wrong in praising this famous German writer, who was now living in exile in Switzerland? The Nazis, I had heard, had deprived him of his German citizenship. Could the Graf and Gräfin be Nazis? I looked towards Magda Forrest. Was it puzzlement or distress that clouded her features? I felt it was with an effort that she shrugged her shoulders, said lightly, 'Ah, I am not so fond of the modern writing. I prefer our great classics. Goethe, Schiller—'

'But what a wonderful picture!' It was a new voice that suddenly broke in. I turned - as everyone did - towards the figure now framed in the front doorway.

He strolled toward us. 'I simply love it,' he continued. 'Magda burning the midnight oil as she pores over the pages of *Faust* and *Wilhelm Tell*. Whoever would have guessed it if she hadn't told us herself?'

His tone was light, and the surprise in his voice so natural, that I would almost have accepted what he said at its face value. But Magda Forrest's mouth gave a little twitch. She closed her eyes tightly, though for hardly longer than a blink would have lasted, and turned her head aside. Then she gave her crystal apple a small, desperate tug. She smiled.

'Nicholas will always have his joke,' she said.

Yes, this new arrival on the terrace was Nicholas Forrest. I recognized him, as I had her, from the photograph, though he was even darker than he had looked there, his skin burnt to a deep coppery glow by the sun. Suddenly I realized what it was that the photograph had reminded me of: the picture of Victorio of the Apaches which I had once found in a book on the old West. Here were the same thick, dark brows, the same strong, short nose, the same two deep lines graven between nostrils and lips. *Victorio.* When I had said how extraordinary I thought his appearance was, my father had laughed and said, 'He looks as fierce as a wolf to me.'

Studying Nicholas Forrest, I was somewhat tempted to concur in this verdict. His face had such a hard expression – like Victorio's. But Victorio wouldn't have had those deep blue eyes – in comparison with them, Magda Forrest's eyes were a soft, pale colour and Lady Sarah's were positively grey. And no Indian would have had that thick hair of a brown far lighter than his skin, as bleached by the sun as his complexion had been darkened.

'So you're Annabel,' he said. 'I take it that that's what people call you? Not Anna or – dreadful thought – Belle?'

I shook my head, smiling politely, though I couldn't help thinking how unfortunate his remark would have been if I *had* been known as 'Belle'.

'Most of my friends call me Nick,' he went one. 'Though some people call me Nicholas. My wife does, as a matter of fact. Don't you, my dear Magda?' he asked her, but did not wait for an answer. He turned back to me. 'I think my wife feels that abbreviations are undignified, rather vulgar, you know. She attaches great importance to dignity, of course.'

I could not possibly answer, certainly could not have looked in Magda Forrest's direction. I was embarrassed, and I felt repelled by his cold tone. At that moment Lady Sarah gave a caw of laughter. '*I* call you Nick, don't I – Nick?' she said.

'Yes, indeed you do, Sarah. Of course you have known me for a very long time.' And he did make it sound a very long time, I thought, but she seemed impervious to any such implication.

'As you say, I'm an old friend,' she drawled, although he hadn't said that at all. Her eyebrows were raised again, but not superciliously this time; in a kind of challenge. She had pinched in her nostrils and her lips pouted. I thought her horrible, but suddenly I could see that a man might find her attractive, though Nicholas Forrest gave no sign of doing so. Since his appearance, the attitude in which she sat had altered. She had been lounging; now she almost sprawled. Suddenly I could imagine her, returned from a hard day's fox-hunting across muddy country, slumped loosely like this in a chair, her arms hooked over its back, while a groom pulled off her riding boots.

Nicholas Forrest did not respond to her last remark – in fact he ignored it, and her, absolutely. He was now regarding me, from head to toe.

I was conscious of how stiffly I was standing. I wondered if my cotton dress were crumpled. The inexpensive new shoes I was wearing were too tight, and I shifted from one foot to the other. I was sure that my hair was hanging in limp, untidy strands. Nervously I smoothed it with my hand.

'You look tired after your journey,' he said. 'Magda, haven't you even offered this poor girl a cup of coffee?'

He spoke drily. I did not detect sympathy in the way he said 'tired' or 'poor girl'. I suddenly felt a suspicion that he had raised the subject only in order to criticize his wife.

Hastily, I said that I had only just arrived, that I wasn't tired or thirsty. But Magda Forrest had quickly beckoned to the hovering manservant. 'Emil,' she called him, and spoke to him in German.

Nicholas Forrest moved over to the balustrade, beside which an unoccupied chair stood. He picked it up. There was a space between Mr Cressingham and the Gräfin. Placing the chair in it – the Gräfin had to shift an inch or two, and gave a little sigh as she did so – he gestured to me. 'Sit down,' he said.

Hesitantly, I went around behind Lady Sarah and her husband, and sat, giving the Gräfin a polite smile. She did not respond to it. Perhaps she was offended that a mere secretary should be seated next to her. She looked like a toad, I thought. Her skin was yellowish, and mottled with brown spots.

'Would you perhaps like some fruit?' Magda Forrest asked, but I refused. The peaches tempted me, but I could not face preparing one: peeling it, cutting it, raising a slice of it to my lips - the juice, perhaps, would run down my chin.

Mr Forrest leant against the balustrade. with his back to the view. As his eyes travelled leisurely over us, I saw that his presence on the terrace had affected everyone, not only Lady Sarah. The Graf and Gräfin sat, if that were possible, even more stiffly in their chairs. The Frenchwoman had crossed her knees, extending an elegant ankle, a tiny foot in a beautiful lizard-skin shoe. Even the languid Mr Cressingham raised his head, sniffed the air, like a horse scenting something strange. As for Magda Forrest, I could feel her tension. Round and round she twisted her crystal apple.

A tray arrived, set with a silver-gilt coffee jug, cream jug and sugar bowl, and with one of the scarlet-and-gold cups. When Emil had poured out my coffee, Magda Forrest came around the table, and stood behind me. She put a finger under my chin, tilted my face up, shook her head, smiling.

'My husband is right,' she said. 'You are looking tired. Yes, there are blue shadows underneath your eyes. When you have drunk your coffee, I think that you should go to your room and rest until luncheon - you will hear the gong. We have decided,' she went on, 'that you shall eat with us, except when we have many people to dine.'

The thought of some time alone was delicious, and I had spent a restless night. All the same, I said, 'But isn't there some work you'd like me to get on with, Mrs Forrest?'

Again she smiled. 'That can wait until tomorrow. Today is a day for settling down.'

Nicholas Forrest said, 'Yes, you had better get used to the place.' He paused, then asked, 'Do you walk?'

'Walk?' I repeated stupidly.

'Yes. Take exercise. Move one foot in front of the other.' He saw me flush. He smiled, and I realized that it was the first time he had done so. When he smiled, he looked younger - but not any kinder, I decided.

'My question isn't a foolish one,' he went on. 'Nobody

here walks, except myself. The Graf and Gräfin do not care for it.' The glance he gave them brought me a sudden vision of those two stout figures toiling up a slope. Perhaps they saw it too, for red patches appeared on the Gräfin's neck, and her husband scowled as deeply as he had done when I mentioned Thomas Mann.

'Madame Marèchal, too, only travels by limousine,' he said. She seemed to take this as a tribute, for she smiled and ran a hand over her hair.

'As for the Cressinghams, when *they* take exercise it must always be on the backs of great slobbering animals. I've recently decided that I can't stand horses,' he added. 'Those long, stupid, upper-class faces of theirs depress me.'

I thought at that moment how very much like horses the Cressinghams themselves looked but no such reflection seemed to cross their minds. 'Oh Nick,' Lady Sarah exclaimed. 'And you used to ride so well. Why, I remember—'

But he went on as if she hadn't spoken. 'My wife, of course, has a great enthusiasm for Nature. The clean fresh air, the sunlight ripening the crops to make the good bread, and so on. But really she prefers such delights at a safe distance. She swims, but otherwise she prefers passive, indoor exercise.' I thought I saw a glint in his eye. 'I mean,' he added, 'on the massage table. You will have noticed what care she takes to protect her famous complexion. And how right she is – great works of art should be preserved. Oh, I'm all in favour of that.'

He made her a little bow, as if he had just paid her a compliment, but she turned her head away and tugged at her pendant again. Now I felt quite certain that his intention was to hurt her feelings. No, I definitely did not approve of Nicholas Forrest.

'But you still haven't answered my question,' he said to me.

'You haven't given me a chance to – I've forgotten what it was.' The words came spontaneously to my lips, and the minute I had spoken them I felt slightly nervous. After all, he was my employer.

But he gave an abrupt laugh. 'Quite true,' he said. 'Well, I'll repeat it. Do you walk?'

I replied truthfully: 'Oh yes, I love it. I used to walk for miles and miles in Paris. And in London too,' I added.

The Gräfin pursed her lips. I could see how 'unbecoming' she thought it for a young girl to walk 'for miles' in a great city.

'I see,' Nicholas Forrest said. 'You're a town walker, not a country one. But that could be the result of necessity, rather than choice. Anyway, I shall take you for a country walk this afternoon. We'll leave after tea, when the day's cooler.' Without another word, he turned, crossed the terrace, and went back into the house.

There was a pause in which I noticed an immediate change of atmosphere. The Graf and Gräfin perceptibly relaxed. Madam Marèchal uncrossed her knees. Paul Cressingham hummed a little tune. Lady Sarah, I saw, was studying me with an insolent, assessing glance. She didn't like me any more than I liked her – I wondered why, and suddenly it occurred to me that it might have something to do with the walk to which I had just, so peremptorily, been summoned. Well, as far as I was concerned, she was welcome to Nicholas Forrest's company.

Magda Forrest spoke. 'You have finished your coffee, little Annabel?'

'Yes, thank you, Mrs Forrest.'

'Ah. Well, I will send for a maid to show you to your room.'

'Thank you,' I said again. She was beckoning to Emil. Off he went, and a few minutes later, a uniformed maid appeared in the doorway. I stood up. As I crossed the terrace, I was conscious of the eyes of the party following me.

I was just inside the hall when I heard Lady Sarah say, 'Rather a pathetic little creature, really.' She gave her cawing laugh.

I heard no more. The dark coolness of the hall enveloped me. I had an impression of great looming objects lining the walls – a vast, glass-fronted cabinet, full of elaborate china, a huge inlaid table, dark, carved chairs with crimson velvet seats.

At the far end of the hall was a life-sized marble statue of a togaed Roman. Behind this rose the stairs, also of marble, with short pillars supporting a banister – marble, needless to say. I followed the maid up to a landing where tall Corinthian columns surrounded a central area. It contained potted palms and a few small gilt chairs, but I could not imagine anyone at ease in this stiff setting. Behind the columns were doors, and corridors led to right and left. We took the left-hand one, walked for some distance, and then turned right down another passage. There were doors all along it. The maid opened one that faced us, at the very end.

'Your room, Mademoiselle,' she said.

'Oh!' I exclaimed involuntarily. For, dramatically viewed through the open french windows, was a jagged range of mountains, brilliantly illuminated by the sun and extending along the horizon. I could distinguish a village, perched on a mountain spur.

'Mademoiselle has everything she needs?' the maid was asking.

I glanced around. My luggage had been brought up, and I thought how shabby it looked, particularly the old tin trunk. The room, though not large, was quite big enough, and comfortably furnished. There was a cream-coloured carpet, patterned with festoons of flowers, on the floor. The bed was of gilded cane. There was a wardrobe against the wall alongside the door, and a dressing-table on the right. Otherwise, the furnishings consisted of a bedside table, a small chintz-covered armchair, and a little writing-desk with a tapestry stool.

'It's lovely,' I said.

The maid smiled. 'The bathroom is next door, on the left. Mademoiselle will hear the gong for luncheon at one o'clock.'

I thanked her. As soon as she had gone, I went out on to the balcony.

Behind the house was a big courtyard. I looked down into it, through the branches of orange and lemon trees. Beyond the trees glittered the blue water of a large rectangular swimming-pool. On the left, over the wall of the courtyard, was a grove of orange trees, and on the right was a grove of olives.

Beyond all this, the towering presence of the mountains was almost overpowering. There are, I have often thought, two kinds of people in the world: those who love the mountains and those who love the sea. I am definitely of the latter.

All the same, the mountains were beautiful - as indeed was everything that I could see from the window. An earthly paradise - surely I should be happy here? Happy? I turned the word over cautiously in my mind. Happiness wasn't something I was very familiar with.

Now my thoughts turned to the gathering on the terrace, and I tried to assess it. About Mr Cressingham and Madame Marèchal I felt neutral. I had disliked the Graf and Gräfin on sight - and I disliked Lady Sarah even more. 'Pathetic little creature', she had called me. I might not be tall but, I thought indignantly, I certainly wasn't 'pathetic'. Hadn't I organized a new life for myself, almost at once, after my father's death? And now I was earning my own living. So much for Lady Sarah! But what about the Forrests? What mattered was my opinion of them.

She was kind - I remembered her smile, her finger tilting up my chin. I wondered, though, if I would get to know her well - there was something remote about her. Perhaps it was a defence she had erected against her husband's cruelty. For I was sure he was cruel - he had directed barbs at her as picadors plant darts in a bull. I saw again Magda Forrest's twitching lips, her averted head, the hand perpetually twisting her crystal apple. My father had once told me that Greek men controlled their anxieties by playing with strings of loose beads - 'worry beads' he had called them. Perhaps Magda's apple was her equivalent. No, I did not like her husband.

I yawned. Suddenly I realized how tired I was. I had gone to sleep so late, and I had woken very early, when the train halted at Montélimar. Montélimar! I had recognized the name at once, remembering how, when my parents had taken me south seven years before, my father had stopped to buy me a box of the nougat for which the town was famous - extravagant as ever, he had returned to the car with six. I could still recollect the candy's chewy texture, the cherries and nuts embedded in it. I could even visualize the curly lettering on the box: *Nougat de Montélimar.*

I hadn't liked the nougat particularly, yet it had assumed a special quality when my father told me how wonderful it was, and that it was sent all over the world.

I yawned again. But before I lay down, there was one thing I had to do. Living in the villa, I couldn't carry my pocket-book with me everywhere. And though Magda Forrest's servants were probably all perfectly honest, I wouldn't be happy unless I found a safe place in which to bestow my little hoard.

'My little hoard' - that was how I always thought of it. I had a funny, superstitious feeling about it. For it had been after everything was settled, and either paid for or financially planned - my father's funeral, my mother's expenses, my secretarial course, my London accommodation - that I had found those seven hundred dollars.

I had been sorting out my father's clothes, to give away to charity - a gloomy task - when I had felt a bulge in a pocket of a suit he had hardly ever worn. I opened the pocket, pulled out the money that was screwed into a crumpled ball

– typical of my father – smoothed it out, counted it. Seven hundred dollars! A gift from heaven or a surprise present from my father – whichever way I saw it, it was unique, and I determined that I would treat it as such. I would not spend it and would only use it in some quite extraordinary emergency. It would be my little hoard.

Now my eyes travelled around my bedroom. A drawer? No, too obvious. The top of the wardrobe? No, in such a well-ordered household, the maid would surely dust even there.

I noticed that the flowered carpet was fitted wall to wall, and fastened down. Presumably the maid's activities would not involve disturbing *that*.

Taking the money, and a nail-file, from my pocket-book, I edged into the small corner beyond the wardrobe, levered up two tacks with the nail-file, and pushed the money under the carpet, which I then smoothed over with my hand. I hammered the tacks in again with the heel of my shoe, stepped back into the room, and could see no trace of what I had done.

Now, my mind at rest, I removed the heavy, wine-coloured shot-silk cover from the bed, and lay down. The pillow, cased in stiff linen, was cool against my cheek.

3

I was awakened by a dull booming sound, and started up, not knowing, for a moment, where I was. Then my eyes lighted on the mountain peaks in the distance, and I remembered everything. The sound that had awoken me must have been the gong announcing luncheon. I would have to hurry.

I glanced at myself in the large oval mirror that was set into the door of the wardrobe. Whether or not my dress had been crumpled earlier, it certainly was irrevocably so now. I should, of course, have taken it off before lying down.

Hastily I unfastened my travelling bag, and scrabbled inside it, emerging with another dress. This too was crushed - I have never been good at packing - but much less so than the one I was wearing. Quickly I washed in the bathroom next door, and returned to change, to put on powder and lipstick, and to comb my hair.

My hair has always been a trial to me - so fine that I can never get it to stay in place for long. How I wished that I had smooth, thick hair like Magda Forrest's, and that it was golden yellow instead of pale brown.

I almost always felt dissatisfied with my appearance. Now I tried, as I often did, to concentrate on the good things, the things my father had occasionally commented on favourably in the past: the texture of my skin, my small, straight teeth, the neatness of my features. But secretly I longed to blaze, to be 'striking', to have brilliant colouring and 'presence' - *that* was something Magda Forrest certainly possessed. My mother's words echoed in my mind - 'such a little mouse'. Shaking my head vigorously, to banish them, I hurried along the corridors and down the stairs. When I reached the hall, the house party was making its entrance from the terrace - I was just in time.

The dining-room was on the right of the front door - a vast room with dark, heavy furniture. An enormous Jacobean dining-table, surrounded by velvet-seated chairs, like the ones in the hall, stood in the centre of the room. However, as we were only eight, a smaller table, covered with a white cloth, had been set for luncheon by the french windows.

Nicholas Forrest sat at the head of the table. On his right was the Gräfin, on his left Madame Marèchal. Facing him was his wife, with the Graf on her right, and Mr Cressingham on her left. Lady Sarah, who, I thought, was looking sullen, sat between the Graf and Madame Marèchal, I between the Gräfin and Mr Cressingham.

During the meal, Mr Cressingham addressed a few remarks to me. The Gräfin did not speak to me at all. So, for most of the time, I was free to study the company. I observed them as they ate the courses served by two footmen under the watchful eye of Emil - hors d'oeuvres, fish, an entrée of quenelles, roast meat, a rich dessert. The hors d'oeuvres alone, I thought, would have made a satisfying meal - a multitude of dishes of tiny, dressed vegetables, fishy delicacies, stuffed eggs, chopped meats.

The Graf and Gräfin guzzled steadily - 'guzzled' was the only word I could find for what they did. Eating was obviously an activity of supreme importance to them; they abandoned themselves to it. Their little eyes lit up, and their jaws moved rhythmically. It was an obvious effort for them when they had to disengage themselves, even momentarily, to join in the frivolity of conversation.

Lady Sarah and her husband also ate tremendously, but with apparent indifference to what they consumed - which somehow prevented their being disgusting, as the Graf and Gräfin were. All the same, they had the bad table manners which had surprised me before in English people of the upper class – I would have expected all those nannies to have had a better influence. But no, the Cressinghams lounged with their elbows on the table, and talked with their mouths full of food.

Madame Marèchal, in contrast, ate daintily, and little – until the dessert, of which she had three servings.

But I spent more time studying the host and hostess than their guests – to me, the Forrests were bound to be the most interesting people at the table. And, apart from my situation in relation to them – my first employers – they both possessed those good looks which inevitably draw the eye.

He ate very moderately, but I saw that his wine-glass was more frequently emptied than anyone else's – and so, of course, more frequently refilled. (Three wines were offered: white with the fish, red with the roast, and champagne with the dessert.) In my eyes, that was a black mark against him – and I waited for him to become noisy, argumentative or hilarious.

However, what he drank seemed to have no effect on him at all. He spoke courteously to his neighbours, even managed a perfunctory smile occasionally for Madame Marèchal – *she* was all sparkle and little trills of laughter – though I did not see him produce one for the lady on his right. I sensed that he felt a distaste for the Gräfin – well, that was something I could not blame him for.

Magda Forrest smiled and was gracious, was, in fact, the perfect hostess whom I had imagined the night before. But something I hadn't imagined – how could I have? – and which struck me as rather odd was that, throughout the meal, she ate, at the most, two or three mouthfuls. She took a minuscule helping of each course proffered to her by the footman, but I noticed that she merely pushed the food round and round on her plate, with her fork. She was also the only person, apart from me, who did not take wine. She sipped constantly from a tall glass of Vichy water with ice in it, and all the time her left hand toyed with her crystal apple or fingered its chain. What a nervous goddess, I thought – for now, without her hat, she looked more goddess-like than ever.

The meal seemed to me to go on for ever. Though the food was excellent, there was too much of it. I was perpetually busy refusing things. I was also concerned to find answers to the questions which Mr Cressingham occasionally shot at me. I tried hard not to reply in monosyllables – 'Never say just "yes" or "no"; it's so boring and silly,' my mother had enjoined me. But to such queries as 'Do you ride?' 'Do you play tennis?' and 'Are you keen on sailing, at all?' I found it difficult to respond at any length – particularly since the answer, in each case, was a negative one.

At last Magda rose. We were to have coffee on the terrace. To my surprise, Nicholas Forrest waylaid me in the hall.

'I notice that you look refreshed,' said. 'Will you sleep again this afternoon?'

'Oh no, I don't think so.'

'The others will,' he said. He added, in a lower tone, 'The Graf and Gräfin will need to have a thorough rest if they are to do justice to their tea.'

I almost smiled, then changed my mind. How malicious he was – and anyway, was it my 'place' as secretary to mock his guests, even if he seemed to be inviting me to do so? 'I wonder,' I said hastily, 'if I might borrow something to read?'

'Ah, you read, do you? Well, I suppose that was to be expected.' He gestured to a door at the back of the hall, on the left of the stairs. 'The library is there. You won't be disturbed. Nobody but me ever goes inside it. Feel free to borrow anything you want. I presume, of course, that you know how to treat books, that you don't crack their spines, or turn down the corners of pages to mark your place. How furious you look – I've got my answer! Anyway, you should be able to find something to appeal to your taste – whatever that may be?' His voice had a questioning inflection.

'Oh,' I said, 'I like novels best.'

'Ah yes, of course. All young girls do, I believe. Well, please browse among the books when you've had your coffee. I have mine in my study. I usually find that luncheon exhausts my conversational resources – such as they are. And I don't have tea – which, by the way, is at half past four, on the terrace. I'll collect you there at five.'

Magda Forrest was wearing her hat again, though the whole terrace was now deep in shadow. Lady Sarah gave me one of her insolent looks as I joined the party.

As I drank my coffee, I thought how somnolent they all seemed. In spite of the shade, the heat was tremendous. Drops of sweat rolled down the Graf's forehead, and he mopped them up with a large handkerchief.

It was not long before they all dispersed to their rooms, Magda Forrest giving me a nod, a smile. Karl, the Dobermann followed her with, I thought, a hostile look in my direction – but then I expected fierce hostility from all dogs. This one seemed to accompany Magda everywhere. At luncheon it had lain at her feet.

As they mounted the stairs, I slipped into the library. The shutters were closed, and the room, lined with bookcases, was dark and cool. I switched on the light, and was subjected to the brilliant glare of a heavy chandelier like others which I had noticed in the hall and dining-room. I saw a small lamp on a table, and turned that on instead.

Wandering along by the shelves, running a finger along the books, I saw that most of the titles were in English, although some were in French. Only one case was occupied by German books – heavy volumes, uniformly bound in leather. Were these Magda Forrest's 'great German classics'? I had to admit that they didn't look as if anyone had ever opened them. But then, there was no law that forced her to read. When she had referred to these books, it had only been to bridge an awkward gap in the conversation - and the acid way her husband had taken up her remark had been unnecessary and unkind.

In spite of Nicholas Forrest's other sneer - about young girls' reading habits - there were plenty of novels in the library. Amongst them I found all my father's books, in a row: his four novels and his two collections of short stories.

One bookcase was devoted to plays. Here I ran my employer's works to earth: five slim blue-covered volumes from which I selected two - *Monday's Child*, the play which I had half-seen with my parents, and another called *Meringue Chantilly.* I also borrowed a new novel by a young American of whom I had heard my father speak well. His literary standards were unvaryingly high. Though his judgement of people could be erratic, he never allowed personal feelings to influence his assessment of books. I remembered how he had continued to praise the work of an unpleasant contemporary who had made some slighting reference to him in a magazine. My mother had told him he was a fool to do so, and that it showed he had no pride. *I* thought that it showed quite the opposite.

I took the books up to my room, and sat down in the little chintz-covered armchair. Before I opened *Monday's Child*, I looked at my watch. The time was half after three - what an age that luncheon had lasted! The thought of having to sit through such meals every day was certainly tedious. Why, in an hour's time, I was due at the next one. I sighed. But at least tea - anyway as far as I was concerned - would be brief, for Nicholas Forrest was fetching me at five. Though that, I reflected, wasn't something to look forward to. I started to read his play.

How clever it was. What skill must have gone into producing such light, sparkling dialogue. I remembered how quickly it had passed on the stage - even if not quickly enough for my parents. It was about two married couples who by the end of the play had changed partners. They drank a lot of cocktails, and made many witty remarks.

I tried to connect the impression that it made on me with my first impressions of its author. I saw those hard lines between his nostrils and the corners of his mouth. I heard in my mind the cold way he spoke. There was, it seemed to me, a harshness in him which was not to be found in his play. I would have expected him to have written something - darker. Although his malice was evident in the dialogue, there it seemed witty, almost charming.

Before going down to the terrace, I changed into low-heeled walking shoes, and I took my straw hat with me. Though the sun was lower in the sky now, the day was still very hot.

Magda Forrest was alone when I appeared - except for her dog, which, this time, did not stir at my approach, merely opening one gleaming eye. Mrs Forrest had changed into an afternoon dress of blue chiffon. I noticed, though, that she still wore her crystal apple. Her fingers nestled round it. I wondered if she ever took it off. It seemed almost a part of her.

'You have been sleeping?' she asked me, smiling.

'No,' I said. 'I was reading.'

'Ah yes, reading. I also love to read. How I wish that I had more time for it.'

My father used to joke about people who produced this remark - there were many of them. 'If one enjoys reading, one *makes* time for it,' he said. This slid across my mind as I nodded in reply to Magda Forrest.

'What was it you were reading?' she now asked me.

'I was reading one of Mr Forrest's plays.'

'Ah, what a good secretary! I myself am not very fond of *reading* plays, although, of course, I love to watch them, when they are well performed. You enjoyed it?'

'Oh yes, it was very amusing,' I said.

'My husband is much praised for his wit and humour. He

has a great sense of humour, wouldn't you say?'

Another of my father's remarks now sprang to mind. 'People who talk about "a sense of humour" usually don't have one.' I felt that my picture of Magda Forrest was becoming clearer: she was kind, earnest - and perhaps rather humourless. Anyway, I was delivered from the need to comment on her husband's possession of a quality she probably lacked by the arrival of the Graf and Gräfin.

Mrs Forrest poured out tea from a great chased-silver teapot. Now I saw a third variety of the gold-and-scarlet cups. There had been the breakfast cups that morning, and little demi-tasses after luncheon. The teacups had curly gold rims and twisted gold handles.

To eat, there were tiny pâté and cucumber sandwiches, two large cakes and some small ones. There were even muffins in a silver dish with a spirit-lamp underneath it.

Lady Sarah strolled on to the terrace. 'The English tea!' the Gräfin said to her approvingly. 'What an excellent institution is the English tea!'

Lady Sarah nodded in a bored way. I myself felt that 'the English tea' was not a meal I cared for on a hot Mediterranean afternoon but, out of politeness, I took a cucumber sandwich. As I drank my lemon tea, I noticed that the Graf and Gräfin laced their tea heavily with cream and sugar.

They ate with the same dedication they had shown at luncheon. Madame Marèchal appeared next, and settled down to an éclair. Paul Cressingham was the last to arrive, and joined his wife in demolishing the muffins - it was surprising, I thought, that the Cressinghams were both so lean. Again, Magda Forrest ate nothing, sipped lemon tea and played with her jewel. I wondered how she kept alive. Though she was not at all plump, she was not skeletal, was not, indeed, as thin as Lady Sarah.

Listening to the party's desultory conversation, I suddenly felt stifled. The quantities of food, the elaborate tea service, the munching people - all seemed to me oppressive.

I started. Magda Forrest was speaking to me. 'We have a large party for dinner tonight,' she was saying. 'I thought that perhaps you might like something brought to your room on a tray.'

'Oh yes,' I said eagerly – too eagerly perhaps, delighted as I was at the prospect of missing yet another ceremonious feast.

But she did not seem to be offended by my alacrity. She smiled. 'Tell Emil what you want when you return from your walk. See – here is my husband, come to fetch you.'

He was bare-headed. He carried a walking-stick. 'Well,' he said to me, without preamble, 'are you ready?'

I stood up.

'Are you sure that you would not like another cup of tea?' Magda Forrest asked. 'My husband is always so impatient.'

Politely I refused, before following him down the marble steps. He unfastened the gate, and held it open for me to pass through, ahead of him. Yes, it was definitely a relief to have left the gathering on the terrace. I sighed.

'Are you depressed by the prospect of our walk?' he asked.

'Oh no,' I said. 'No, not at all.'

We went along by the wall, and turned left at the end of it. A dusty path led upward. We passed the villa. Above the wall enclosing the courtyard, I could see the tops of the citrus trees that grew there. Beyond the walled courtyard, we came to an open yard, with garages and outbuildings, topped by a second storey of rooms, around it. Edwards, the chauffeur, was in this yard, whistling as he polished the car in which I had been fetched from Nice that morning.

Nicholas Forrest opened a gate into the olive grove. It was cool and shady there. I admired the ancient trees with their gnarled trunks. Amongst their ashy leaves, the olives were still small and hard.

We walked in silence. I was sorry when we left the grove, and emerged in open country, bleached, dusty and scattered with stones. Here the sun, though it was sinking, was still quite hot. I was glad of my hat.

'You're wearing sensible shoes, I see,' my companion said. 'Once – and only once – that ridiculous woman, Madame Marèchal, insisted that she wanted to accompany me on a walk. She wore the most absurd high-heeled shoes. We had to stop after only a few minutes. She sank down exhausted on a bench in the orange grove, and I was forced to make conversation to her for half an hour. Never again!'

'I think she looks quite nice,' I said.

'Nice? Oh well, not as bad as some others, I suppose. But interested in nothing but clothes and amusement. Really very stupid – and greedy, too. Did you see her tucking into that chocolate mousse at luncheon?'

I didn't answer. How morbidly critical he was! Once more I remembered that phrase he had used about his previous secretary: 'I found her quite intolerably stupid.'

The soil beneath our feet was parched. Between the bare outcroppings of rock, pale grasses grew in tufts, and here and there were squat, stunted bushes. I picked a sprig from one of these, and rubbed its leaves. The harsh tang of rosemary was powerful.

'I'm fond of this country,' Nicholas Forrest said. 'There's something austere about it that appeals to me, but there isn't much of it left. Soon this whole coast will be one vast resort for trippers – unless, of course, a worse catastrophe intervenes.'

'Catastrophe?' I said.

'Yes. To be specific – a war.'

'But why should there be a war?' I asked.

'A rather silly question,' he said. 'You'd do better to ask how there can fail to be one.'

I was annoyed by his rudeness, but said nothing. I glanced at him. The expression on his face was sombre. War? It was something I never thought about, although my father had sometimes teased Frenchmen by telling them that the Germans would 'make mincemeat' of them 'next time'. I remembered feeling sorry for a waiter who had been white with rage as he struggled desperately to keep his feelings under control. But the idea of an actual war seemed quite unreal to me. I gazed up at the brown irregular face of the mountain ahead of us, at the village perched on its spur.

'What is that village called, Mr Forrest?' I asked him, and saw him dragging his mind back from wherever it had wandered - miles away, it seemed.

'For heaven's sake, don't call me "Mr Forrest", Annabel. Call me Nick not Nicholas, which I can't stand either. That village? Oh, it is Roquebrune, named after the brown rock it's made from. The village is medieval - fortified against the Saracens who terrorized the coast in those days. Worse than the tourists today - more violent, anyway. There's a legend about it, or -, who knows? - perhaps it's true. They say that, long ago, there was a nunnery on the very point of Cap-Martin.' He gestured back in the direction we had come from. 'The nuns at the convent had an arrangement with the men of Roquebrune that, if the Saracens were sighted, they'd ring their convent bell, and the villagers would come down to their defence. Well, one night the bell rang out, and all the Roccabrunesques tumbled out of their beds, grabbed their weapons, and careered down the mountain to the nunnery. But the Saracens weren't there - and the nuns laughed and said they'd rung the bell just to see if the villagers would really come. As you can imagine, the villagers were pretty fed up. Then, a few nights later, the bell pealed out again, but this time the men stayed comfortably in bed - they weren't going to be made fools of a second time. But the next day they found that the Saracens *had* come. In the covent were the corpses of the oldest and ugliest nuns - with their throats slit. The rest were on their way to the harems of Algiers. That's what comes of crying "Wolf", you see.' He laughed.

'Oh, poor nuns,' I exclaimed.

'Poor nuns?' he said. 'You're soft-hearted are you? How

refreshing!' Though he sounded, I felt, as though he found my reaction merely naïve. 'Soft hearts are extremely rare,' he went on, 'and especially in women - although, for some strange reason people call yours the gentle sex.' He laughed again.

'Perhaps I'll take you to Roquebrune some time,' he said. 'There's a procession they have each year. Although the nuns didn't escape the Saracens, later the village escaped the plague. They celebrate every year, on the fifth of August. That's next week - a Friday.'

'Oh, I'd love to go,' I said.

'Well, why not? I haven't been for several years. I got tired of it - but possibly I might enjoy seeing it through fresh eyes.'

I couldn't help thinking that he sounded far from convinced of this. We walked on in silence, towards the mountain. I thought what a steep slope it must have been for the villagers, scrambling down, clutching their weapons, on a fruitless errand. No wonder they'd been sceptical the next time.

'You've not visited the South of France before?' he asked me.

'Oh yes, Mr Forrest.' He raised a hand. 'Nick, I mean,' I corrected myself, although I didn't feel natural calling him that. 'But I haven't been to this part of it. One year, my parents rented a villa at Antibes, next door to some great friends of their, the Sprotts.'

'Oh,' he said. 'Yes, of course. The famous Sprotts. So very rich, so very chic, so devoted to *the art of living.* When they went back to the States, it was the end of an era - or so people told me. I met them once or twice, but can't say I was very impressed by them. Devotees of *the art of living* have never much impressed me. Life should be more than an elaborate series of small perfections.' He sounded almost serious, but no, I still detected that chill, underlying irony in his tone. All the same, what he had said interested me.

'I see what you mean,' I replied. 'In a way, my father

thought the Sprotts were wonderful – but in another way he didn't think so at all. He used to rebel sometimes, and do things like smashing their best glasses. Venetian glasses, they were – I remember him tossing them, one after another, over a wall. Mrs Sprott was very angry. She could be as cold as ice. And then there was the time he poured wine down a French countess' dress.'

His laugh was different, this time, from the cold, abrupt one I had heard before. He sounded genuinely amused. 'How perfectly splendid,' he said.

I hesitated. 'Yes,' I said, but doubtfully, 'I suppose it was.'

He glanced at me. 'Hmm,' he said, and then, 'I've been meaning to ask you – what's happened to your mother?'

'She's in hospital,' I answered. 'In the Zeiss clinic in Zurich.'

'I see. I'd heard she'd been ill, but I didn't know that. It's an expensive place – the Zeiss. You can afford it?'

His detached tone, in combination with the intimacy of the question, offended me, but what could I do except answer?

'Oh yes,' I said brightly. 'There are the royalties from my father's books, you know.'

'I see,' he said again. 'And what about visits? Will you want to visit her often?'

Was he afraid that I would be neglecting my 'duties', making requests for frequent absences? Well, I could certainly reassure him about *that*.

I spoke brusquely. 'No,' I said. 'I don't visit her. The doctors don't think it is wise. Seeing me has a bad effect on her. Last time—' I broke off, sternly repressing a shudder at the memory which assailed me.

However, his question answered, he said no more, which I was thankful for.

We had now reached an outcrop of rock which was higher than any we had passed before. Suddenly he stretched out his hand, and took mine. His fingers were warm and dry.

'Come,' he said, and started to climb the rock, using his stick and helping me after him. When we had reached the top, he released my hand.

'Look,' he said. Beyond the stretch of ground we had crossed, the olive grove was a haze of silver grey. We looked down over it, over the slate roof of the Villa Aurore, to the darkening blue of the sea. Evening was coming down fast now.

'It's beautiful,' I said. 'I love the sea.'

'So do I,' he said. 'I swim in it each morning, all the year round, although many people don't like to bathe at Cap-Martin. The coast is very rocky. My wife and her guests far prefer the swimming-pool.'

He glanced at his watch. 'Probably time we were starting back,' he said. 'My wife is having a dinner party tonight – which you, I gather, are to be spared. You're fortunate, I can assure you.'

Not knowing what to answer – what bad taste it showed, I thought, to talk about his wife and their guests to a stranger, in such a tone – I said nothing. He jumped down from the rock, landed lightly, turned and extended his hand to me. The rock was steep, so I took it, and stepped boldly forward, but a loose stone slithered from under my foot. I fell forward, put out my other hand to grasp at his shoulder, and found myself resting against his chest.

He was looking down into my face. Up went his eyebrows suddenly. A little smile which I could only have described as cynical fractionally stretched his lips. He almost shrugged – I could have sworn it. But instead, down came his mouth on mine, and his arms went around my shoulders.

Back I sprang – nearly stumbling again. 'Oh,' I exclaimed, 'oh!' And then, inadequately, 'Really!'

Again he raised his eyebrows. A look of faint, quizzical surprise replaced the earlier cynical smile. 'I do apologize,' he said. 'I had no intention of offending you. What shall I say? That the provocation – I mean the temptation – was irresistible?'

Never, I thought, could anyone have sounded less overcome by 'irresistible temptation'. And then I grasped the implication of his original choice of word - 'provocation'. He had imagined that I had slipped on purpose. I wanted to swing at his face with my hand - might have done so - but he had turned, and was setting off in the direction of the villa.

Neither of us spoke another word on our walk back in the rapidly gathering dusk. When we reached the terrace, it was deserted. I supposed that everyone was getting ready for the dinner party. We went into the house, and I lagged behind him, but he halted and turned.

'Would it suit you to start work early in the morning?' he asked me in a perfectly natural tone. 'At about half past seven, after I've had my swim? In this climate, I find it's best to make an early start.'

'Of course,' I answered - my voice, I hoped, sounding as normal as his.

'Very well. Good night,' he said. Then - eyebrows raised again, faint smile - 'Sleep soundly.'

When he had gone, Emil appeared from the back of the hall - how ugly he was, I thought, almost as ugly as the Graf, whom he rather resembled. He asked me what I would like to eat that evening. Collecting my thoughts, I ordered an omelette, fruit, mineral water and coffee.

Upstairs in my room, I went out on to the balcony. The mountains were a vague shadowy mass, the courtyard almost dark. The moon had not yet risen.

I tried to sort out my feelings. One thing was certain. That insulting kiss of Nicholas Forrest's - Nick, as apparently I must call him - had more than reinforced my existing dislike of him. *Provocation* - I felt a flush of anger rise over my face. But I must be realistic, sensible, clear-headed.

Of course I had no intention of rushing away from the Villa Aurore like some shrinking Victorian heroine. I would,

I determined, proceed just as if nothing had happened. After all, a secretary didn't *have* to like her employer. To do so would make things pleasanter - but that was all. And Mrs Forrest, for whom I would also be working - for how much of the day? I wondered; more than for her husband, I hoped - was kind. I felt a pang of sympathy for her. How intolerable it must be to be married to a man who made advances to every woman he met. For I did not delude myself for a moment that it was my unique attractiveness which had led to that kiss. His expression, his words had made it absolutely clear that that was not the case. Poor Magda Forrest, here was yet another reason for her to twist her crystal apple round and round. I wondered why she stayed with him.

Anyway, there was one thing I was sure of. Having been rebuffed, 'Nick' would make no further approaches to me. I remembered his cool, bored 'apology', how he had instantly turned away afterward, and how naturally he had spoken to me later, in the hall. No, he would make no more 'advances'. So why shouldn't it be easy to behave as if nothing had happened, particularly since nothing of any importance had?

Of course I could do so - and of course I would. I needed this job - needed it badly - and now I vowed to keep it.

A maid brought my tray. When I had finished my supper, I went out on to the balcony again. In the quiet of the evening, I could hear a faint hum of voices coming from my left, and I supposed that the guests were having their *apéritifs* on the belvedere.

I waited for a long time for the maid to return for my tray, only reflecting when she had done so that I could have put it outside the door. Then I took a bath and went to bed. I started to read Nicholas Forrest's *Meringue Chantilly.* The name suited it, I thought, for it was as light and insubstantial as a meringue. All the same, I had not finished it when I switched off the bedside lamp. I fell asleep at once - awoke much later, to find the room flooded with brilliant moonlight. I looked at my watch. The time was half after two.

Suddenly I felt restless. I got up, and went out on to the balcony. Now the trees cast dark mysterious shadows on the brightly illuminated flagstones of the courtyard. I saw that the moon, high overhead, was almost full.

It was just then that I became aware of a murmur of voices coming from below. I stepped quickly back. The low murmur continued. After a moment, my curiosity got the better of me, and I tiptoed forward, to peer over the edge of the balustrade.

Three men were standing in the courtyard. I could see them clearly, for the moonlight shone full on their faces. One of them was Nicholas Forrest. Another was the ginger-haired chauffeur, Edwards. The third man was slim, taller than Edwards, but not quite as tall as Nicholas Forrest. He had a long face, a crooked nose, narrow eyes, and I had not seen him before.

They stood close together. Their murmured conversation looked vigorous, urgent. I wondered what on earth could have brought them together, like this, in the middle of the night. I found it strange, almost creepy.

How awful it would be if one of them (especially if it were Nicholas Forrest) looked up and saw me spying there – the word 'spying' came involuntarily to my mind; their gathering had such a conspiratorial appearance.

Quickly I stepped back into my room. I got into bed again. From there I could no longer hear their voices, but after a few minutes had passed I thought I heard footsteps. Then there was complete silence.

{4}

Drowsily I raised my wrist, looked at my watch, and at once was fully awake. It was a quarter of seven. In three-quarters of an hour, I must present myself in Nicholas Forrest's – Nick's – study, wherever that might be. I would have to ask one of the servants.

I got up, stretched, went out on to the balcony – to which I felt almost magnetically drawn whenever I was in my room. The courtyard was deep in shadow, and I heard the cool sound of running water – a gardener was hosing down the flagstones. The sound, combined with the blue glimmer of the swimming pool, gave me a sudden desire to bathe. I imagined Nick plunging into the sea, an image which was immediately replaced by two others: that kiss – but I was going to forget all about that – and then the gathering I had witnessed in the middle of the night. As I looked down at the gardener, swishing water around the courtyard, I could hardly believe those three men had clustered there so mysteriously. Anyway, even if I'd wanted to think more about that, there wasn't time now.

I dressed in one of my three remaining cotton frocks, which were hanging in the wardrobe. On the previous evening, when I came upstairs, I had found my bag unpacked, my dirty clothes spirited away. There was even a flounced chintz cover on my father's old tin trunk, which had been placed at the foot of the bed. I wondered what the maid had thought of my meagre possessions, as I gave a rueful glance at my two evening dresses. How tired of them everyone would become – I was sure that, whether there were guests or no, the members of this household 'dressed for dinner' every night.

How different things had been ten years before. I remembered innumerable party dresses, and a fur coat with a matching hat. That had been when my father's success was at its peak, and for several years my wardrobe had been extensive – even after the collapse of the dollar in the Wall Street crash. It had been then that my father had embarked on the killing grind of highly paid short-story writing for magazines like the *Saturday Evening Post.* Writing a short story of this kind, almost always unworthy of his talent, was exhausting for him – was almost the equivalent of the drinking bout which inevitably succeeded the story's completion: a bout from which he would emerge pale, limp, puffy-faced, his nerves quiveringly on edge despite his lassitude. I had a sudden picture of him picking up a cup of black coffee, his elbow resting on the table, his left hand grasping his shaking right wrist as he raised the cup to his mouth. There were other days when the trembling had been so bad that he would not attempt even this – I early learnt to gauge a particularly intense hangover from his refusal of his morning coffee.

I met no one on my way downstairs, and the hall was empty. I peeped into the dining-room. No trace of the previous evening's dinner party was to be seen there. The long table, a great silver bowl of fresh roses at its centre, gleamed darkly, and I thought of our dining-room in the Paris apartment after one of my parents' carousals. I remembered smashed glasses, dirty plates, full ashtrays, empty bottles. Our servants, following my parents' example, were never early risers.

I went out on to the terrace, and found a maid – a girl of about my own age, not pretty but sweet faced – sweeping it.

'Bonjour,' I said, and she smiled shyly, and responded, 'Bonjour, Mademoiselle.'

It was now a quarter after seven, and I asked her where Mr Forrest's study was. I spoke in French – a succession of governessess, though none of them stayed long in our household, had seen to it that my French was fluent. Neither of my parents, even after many years in France, had spoken more than a few words of the language. They had, I reflected now, always been aliens in the country they had chosen to live in.

The maid propped her broom against the balustrade, and asked me to follow her. We went along a passage at the back of the hall, behind the stairs. She pointed out a door to me, smiled, and departed.

I wondered if he were back yet from his swim. I hesitated for a moment before I knocked on the door.

'Come in,' he called.

He turned around as I entered. He was sitting at a table of scrubbed, unvarnished oak, facing a large window which looked out on to the courtyard.

I paused for a moment in the doorway, amazed by how different this room was from any other I had seen at the villa. Its walls were whitewashed. The two big windows, their shutters fastened back, were uncurtained. The furnishings were few. There was a filing cabinet between the windows. There was the table at which he was sitting, in a straight-backed chair. An identical chair stood at another, smaller table, also of scrubbed oak, with a typewriter on it, under the second window. The far wall incorporated a fitted cupboard. Against the wall facing the windows were a low white bookcase and a narrow divan, with a blue-and-white-striped cotton cover, on which lay two plain red cushions. There was no carpet on the tiled floor. There were no pictures except, over the divan, a tiny oil of a woman in a red hat, standing on a beach, and looking out to sea. A Boudin, as I recognized at once – for Boudin was my favourite painter.

'You like my room?' he asked, standing up. His tone was

easy. Yes, the previous day's episode was obviously to be completely forgotten. I was relieved, feeling certain that I too could behave quite naturally.

'Yes I do,' I said. 'It's so cool and peaceful - and I love your Boudin,' I added.

There was that characteristic lift of the eyebrows. 'So you know something about pictures!' (Why should he sound so patronizingly surprised?) 'My wife does not care for Boudin. She finds his pictures too insignificant. Too trivial - and, perhaps, too French. In fact she altogether abominates this room. "Why do you wish to write at a kitchen table?" she asks me, and she longs to cover the floor with a carpet. But I have resisted all her pleas to "do the room up". She has stopped trying, at last, I think, but she still feels that it isn't dignified, isn't at all what a writer's study ought to be.'

That cold tone and now his cold, abrupt laugh. Poor Magda, I thought again, although I liked the room - she was obviously just trying to make it nice according to her lights.

He glanced at his watch. 'You're punctual, I see. An excellent quality in a secretary. Do sit down. Will you have coffee?'

As I sat down at the other table, I saw that there was a tray in front of him, on which were a brown earthenware jug, two green pottery cups and a pottery sugar basin and milk jug.

'Yes, please,' I said, and he poured the steaming coffee into the cups. He raised the milk jug, gave me a questioning look. 'Only if it's cold,' I said. 'It most certainly is,' he replied. 'There is nothing I loathe more than the taste of hot milk.'

Well, we had two things in common, I thought: Boudin and cold milk in our coffee - which was strong and delicious. I ran a finger over the rough glaze of the big cup - what a contrast to the thin scarlet-and-gold china I had drunk from the day before.

'We'll have breakfast at nine,' he said. 'Do you mind

having it in here? I find it interrupts my morning if I join that gang on the terrace.'

'Whatever suits you,' I said.

'Ah, the perfect secretary. What do you like for breakfast?' Ham and eggs? Kedgeree? A juicy steak perhaps?'

'Oh no, I never have more than a roll and perhaps some fruit.'

'Just what I have. How convenient. I'll tell Emil.'

He pushed a bell by his desk and when, a minute later, Emil appeared, curtly gave him the breakfast order. I thought he should have been more polite - even to Emil whose appearance I found so unprepossessing.

When Emil had gone, taking the coffee tray with him, Nick said, 'Well, I suppose we had better start work. First of all, I'd like to dictate one or two letters.'

On my table, next to the typewriter, were a shorthand pad and a few pencils. I turned my chair to face him, picked up the pad and a pencil. My first professional letter - I felt just slightly nervous. I raised the pencil to my lips, and nibbled at the end of it.

'Do you chew pencils, Annabel?' He was lighting a cigarette. 'I'll have to break you of that - a disgusting habit. In a few minutes, I suppose you'll be spitting wood shavings on to the floor.'

I had snatched the pencil from my mouth. 'Far better to smoke,' he said, and offered me his cigarette case.

I shook my head. 'I don't smoke,' I said stiffly, remembering the stuffy smell of my parents' parties, and the brimming ashtrays.

'*You*, perhaps, think that smoking is a disgusting habit?' he said.

'As a matter of fact, I do.'

The eyebrows were raised. 'Well,' he said. 'I'm afraid you'll have to put up with it here. You really can't expect me to sacrifice it for your convenience.'

Of course I hadn't meant that *he* must stop smoking. I

floundered. 'I had no intention . . .

He ignored my attempt at an explanation. 'I noticed at luncheon that you don't drink, either,' he said.

'No, never.'

'What a puritan we have in our midst! When I was a boy, my father told me that one should never trust a teetotaller.'

'Mrs Forrest doesn't drink either, does she?' I said.

'For such a young girl, you have a very sharp tongue.' But then he continued quite calmly, 'You're right. You'll never see my wife indulging in the base pleasures of the table. But enough chatter. To work!'

The first letter was to a theatrical manager in London.

'Dear Bernard,' he dictated, in a flat monotonous tone. 'It is really no use your pressing me on the subject of *Summer's Lease.* I'm progressing as rapidly as I can. As I told you before, the first act is finished, but I'm still having problems with the second. Let me assure you again that no one could be more anxious than I am for the whole thing to be completed as quickly as possible. Yours, Nick.'

As he finished speaking, he gave an exasperated little sigh. 'Perhaps that will keep the damn man quiet for a little while,' he said. He was holding a sheet of paper in his hand – perhaps the 'pressing' communication from 'Bernard'. Now he screwed it up into a ball, and threw it across the room. It hit the wall above the bookcase, and dropped to the floor. I felt an impulse to go and pick it up and put it in the wastebasket under my table, but I decided he would probably make some biting comment, and stayed where I was.

The second letter was a cool, formal acknowledgement of an enthusiastic letter received from some admirer. The third was to an actress who had evidently been angling for a part in his new play. To her he repeated, practically word for word, what he had said to Bernard, adding that he did not feel disposed to think about casting until the play was finished.

He was just about to dictate the addresses to which the letters should be sent, when a bright voice called 'Good morning'. He started violently. I turned, and there, framed in my window, was Magda Forrest. She was wearing a long, loose, white towelling robe, and she carried a big white towel over her arm. A bathing cap dangled from her hand.

'Good morning, Mrs Forrest,' I said.

She smiled at me warmly. 'Is my husband working you very hard, Annabel?' She did not wait for an answer, but went on: 'I go to swim before the sun is too bright. I shall see you later.' She turned from the window, and set off across the courtyard.

After that first violent start, Nick had sat quite still while his wife was speaking. Now, his chin resting on the palm of his hand, his eyes followed her.

She reached the pool. Through a gap between the citrus trees, I saw her taking off her white robe. Beneath it she wore a white swimsuit – its whiteness was almost that of her skin. Now she was putting on her bathing cap, tucking her great coil of hair inside it. I had always hated bathing caps – but I realized that, with as much hair as she had, it would be tiresome to get it wet every time one swam.

'Mrs Forrest's hair must be very long,' I remarked.

'Hmmm?' He blinked, then said, 'Oh yes, indeed. She is a positive Rhine maiden. It hangs below her waist. When she brushes it – although it is usually her maid who does that – one can imagine her perfectly on a cardboard rock in some interminable Wagner opera.'

Helmeted, she was poised on the edge of the pool. I observed her full bosom, her slightly rounded hips, her long firm legs. She dived smoothly, breaking the water without a splash.

'How well she swims,' I said, as she appeared in another gap between the trees, striking out with a swift, powerful crawl.

'Yes, she's a strong swimmer. She swims twenty lengths of

the pool each morning. To and fro. Up and down. Afterwards, her maid will give her a massage, and then she will have her bath, with oil of jasmine in the water.'

He had recited all this in a voice as expressionless as that in which he had dictated the letter to Bernard. Now he said, 'In her way, my wife is a very industrious woman – which is more than I can say for you, as you sit there, making conversation.' The coldness was back in his tone with a vengeance.

'I'm sorry. Could you give me those addresses?' I said quietly.

He did so, and I turned to the typewriter. I found that my hands were shaking, and I made a mess of the first letter, and had to start it again. As I pulled the spoilt sheet of paper out of the typewriter, I gave him a sideways glance, but he didn't appear to have noticed anything. He was frowning at the large pad of lined foolscap which lay in front of him on the table. There was nothing written on it, but he was doodling in the red-ruled margin with his fountain pen.

How rude he was, I thought. How much I disliked him. But, all the same, what a bad start I had made. I pictured myself, elbows resting on the table, gazing out of the window, making my inane comments about his wife.

I had typed two of the letters when Emil arrived with the breakfast tray and placed it on the table in front of Nick.

'Thank you. You can go. We shall help ourselves,' Nick said.

As Emil left, I started to type the third letter, but Nick remarked firmly, 'Come on – stop working now. You must be hungry.'

'Oh, not very,' I said, but it wasn't true. Turning around, I thought how tempting the meal looked. There were golden croissants, with butter and pale honey, and a bowl of peaches and grapes, as well as a fresh supply of coffee.

'Do come and take what you want,' he said.

We ate our breakfast in a silence which I certainly did not

find companionable. I became intensely conscious of the sound of my coffee cup clinking against its saucer, of the movement of my hand as I picked a grape from the cluster on my plate.

Through the window, I saw that Magda Forrest was coming back across the courtyard in her bathrobe. She had taken off her bathing cap, and again her hair looked smooth and tidy.

Somehow I found myself hoping that she wouldn't stop at the window – I felt a sort of dread that her husband, in what was surely a bad mood, might say something cutting – but again she paused, resting one hand on the windowsill.

'So, you are sharing my husband's breakfast,' she said. 'I hope he is giving you enough to eat.'

I nodded dumbly, and she smiled and passed on.

'More coffee?' Nick asked me.

'No thank you,' I said, picking up my plate and cup and saucer. I put them on the tray without looking at him. He rang for Emil, and I returned to my typewriter, and embarked on the third letter. Emil appeared and left again. I found it hard to concentrate. Suddenly I felt that Nick gave me the same sense of awkwardness that my mother had often aroused in me. I frowned as I tapped the keys.

The letters finished, I typed the envelopes, then took the completed mail and put it beside him on the table.

'Thanks,' he murmured. Back in my chair, I realized I had nothing to do. I watched him read the letters – there didn't seem to be any mistakes – and sign them. Then he started to fold one up.

Mindful of my secretarial training, I leaped to my feet. 'I'll do that,' I said.

'Sit down. Don't fuss.' So I had to watch as he folded the letters, not very neatly, pushed them into their envelopes, and licked the gummed flaps.

Now he stretched across the table, and picked up a pile of the same lined foolscap – this time, though, covered with writing – that he had been doodling on.

'This is the first act of my new play,' he said. 'I'd like you to type it out. Don't hesitate to ask, if you can't read my writing – I'm told it's difficult. My last secretary never asked me anything – just used to type it all wrong, which was much more irritating.'

Perhaps she'd been afraid to ask, I thought, as I took the papers back to my table. I decided to read the whole thing through before I started typing it. Then I could ask everything I wanted to at the same time.

Summer's Lease was – weren't all his plays? – a comedy. By chance, two married couples rented summer cottages next door to each other, only to discover that one wife had formerly been married to the other's husband. Sparks began to fly – or were meant to, I thought suddenly. For, as I read the dialogue, I couldn't help thinking that the 'touch' for which Nicholas Forrest was so famous was missing. But perhaps I was wrong. I knew so little about the theatre. Probably the dialogue would sound quite different on the stage. And yet I hadn't had this sense of flatness with the other two plays. I glanced at him. Frowning, he was staring at the lined pad in front of him. Again he was doodling restlessly in the margin. Suddenly he looked up, turned, met my eyes, looked away again, dropped his pen on the table, and sighed.

'Have you ever been in love, Annabel?' he asked.

The question took me completely unawares, absolutely astonished me. I was staring at him when he looked round at me again.

'Why . . . no,' I faltered.

'Why do you look so horrified?' he said – I could hear irritation in his tone. 'I'm asking you a perfectly sensible question. Most girls of your age have been – or perhaps I should say have imagined that they were – "in love". I was just hoping that you might be able to remind me of what it was like. I find it quite impossible to write a convincing love scene nowadays. Well, I'm sorry you can't be of any assistance.'

He picked up his pen again, and I returned my eyes to the manuscript in front of me. My eyes, but not my mind – for my thoughts were in confusion. *I was just hoping that you might be able to remind me of what it was like.* Surely he could hardly have stated more clearly that he was not in love with his wife?

Of course I knew that people fell out of love – though my parents, I thought, with a sudden fierce rush of loyalty and affection, had always loved each other, even when things were at their worst. He, then, had fallen out of love with Magda. Well, perhaps he couldn't help that – obviously he had a fickle nature – but . . . he needn't have told me about it.

That, of course, was what had really shocked me: that he should have so lightly confided something so personal, so terrible, to a girl he had met only the day before. That was inexcusable, contemptible – and treacherous. Unforgivably treacherous to Magda, whether he loved her or not.

I realized that my eyes had travelled over a full page of his play without my having taken in a single word. I started at the top again, but once again, after a second or two, my wandering thoughts betrayed me. *Have you ever been in love, Annabel?* I had said 'No' – but had my answer been strictly true? Surely it had, really? Now it was not the Forrests and their relationship that was distracting me. Into my mind had come the image of Tom Storey.

Of course one couldn't be in love at thirteen. (Though Juliet had been around that age when she met Romeo, hadn't she?) No, I must have, as Nicholas Forrest would have put it, 'imagined' that I was in love with Tom. After all, there had been no one else around for me to direct my youthful romantic longings towards.

Certainly, like all solitary girls who read a lot of novels, I had wanted to be in love. I knew no one of my own age – none of my parents' expatriate friends seemed to have children. I was lonely, and just beginning to realize it. Until recently my father had been everything to me. Now, suddenly, I had begun to see him more clearly, and my feelings towards him were changing. Sometimes, when he was drunk, I felt an actual revulsion for him. At other times, I felt an urge to protect him which verged on pity. Neither of these emotions was consistent with idolizing him – which was what I had done in the past. I found a new idol in Tom Storey.

He and his elegant wife, Giselle, quite often came to our apartment at that time. I didn't like Giselle. She was one of those people for whom children simply don't exist – she just didn't *see* anyone under sixteen. But Tom always noticed me.

'How is the Little Silent One today?' he would ask. Or, 'Annabel, what strange secrets are you brooding over?' Such remarks embarrassed me, of course, but at the same time they thrilled me. They turned my failings – my shyness, my quietness – into something *interesting*. When, after he had left the apartment or when I was in bed at night – it was nice to have somebody to brood on as one fell asleep – I thought about the things he'd said, I would feel mysterious and fascinating, like the heroine of a novel.

My father called Tom a dilettante, and did not care for him – but at that particular stage of my development, this only made him more attractive to me. He was very rich. His father was a banker whose Paris office he had desultorily worked in until he suddenly threw the job over. Tom and Giselle edited a literary magazine, and had their own private printing press. Tom also wrote free verse which my father said was terrible. I read some of it – every issue of his magazine contained several of his poems – and thought it exotic and romantic. It was almost all about death, usually mixed up with love.

Tom always dressed in black - black suits, black socks, black shoes, black tie. He even wore a blatantly artificial black rose in his buttonhole. His shirts, in contrast, were dead white. His handsome face was pale, and his hair was blond.

One morning, he and Giselle called at our apartment when my father was out. They sat talking with my mother for a while. Suddenly Tom jumped up from his chair - he was always restless, and hardly ever sat still for more than a few moments.

'How about coming for a drive with me, Annabel?' he asked. The prospect thrilled me, but it was also alarming. I wondered what we would talk about. I had noticed how easily he became bored.

I gave my mother a doubtful glance. She and Giselle were gossiping about the people they knew - mostly Americans living in Paris - as they always did when they were together. Who had gone off with whom, and the scenes they'd made. Though the characters changed, the stories always sounded the same.

'Now wouldn't that be nice, Annabel?' my mother said. 'But are you sure you won't be bored, Tom?' Though she was voicing my own anxiety, I didn't like *her* saying it.

'You know I never do anything that bores me, Vanna,' he replied.

Giselle didn't even glance at me, just said to Tom, 'Remember we're meeting those Spaniards. Don't be too late.'

Putting on my hat and coat in front of the mirror in my room, I thought I looked pale, and pinched my cheeks to make them pink. Then I hurried back to the salon, where Tom was standing by the mantelpiece, restlessly drumming on it with his fingers.

We ran down the stairs, and past the cross old concierge in her glass box in the vestibule. She scowled. I knew she hated my parents - she was always complaining about how much noise they made - and I always felt that I was automatically included in her disapproval.

Tom's car was parked by the kerb outside our building. Jet black, with a long, rounded bonnet, it was beautiful, I thought. He helped me to step up into the passenger seat; then, in a moment, he had turned the starting handle, and was in beside me – how quickly he moved. We were off. It was a fine, crisp April day. Tom never wore a hat, and the wind ruffled his hair as we roared along. I was sure that all the passers-by were watching us, and I didn't mind at all, although when I felt that with my parents, I hated it.

As we turned into the Boulevard St Michel, I held on to my hat, in case it blew off. I glanced sideways at Tom. There was no expression on his face. Was he bored? Perhaps he was already regretting his invitation to me. 'What kind of car is this?' I asked him.

'What?' he shouted, above the wind and the roar of the engine. I wished I hadn't spoken.

'What kind of car is this?' I heard myself yell in a sudden silence. We had screeched to a halt in response to a signal from a traffic policeman on the corner of the Boulevard St Germain.

'It's a Bugatti,' he said. 'It's the best car in the world.'

He started to tell me about Bugattis. I didn't take in a word he was saying. A barrage of horns behind us made him aware that the policeman was impatiently beckoning us forward. We leapt ahead.

'Where shall we go?' Tom said.

I was dumb, my mind a complete blank.

'We'll drive right across Paris, and out on the other side,' he said now, 'and then we'll drive in the country – faster and faster. This car can go one hundred and twenty miles an hour. After that, perhaps it will just take off into the sky. We'll see.'

Suddenly he took his left hand off the steering-wheel, and put it on my knee. A strange sensation ran up my body – a sort of blush, but not quite that. I started violently. The prospect of the drive into the country now filled me with a mixture of excitement and fear. What would happen there? Might he *kiss* me? I felt defiant; my father was always so protective of me. Well, he couldn't protect me now!

I felt free and wild as we crossed the Seine. Soon we turned into Place Vendôme. Napoleon glittered on the top of his column. Suddenly Tom braked abruptly by the kerb.

'I need fuel,' he said. 'We'll have one drink in the Ritz bar.'

I had never been into the Ritz before, although my parents were always meeting people there. I felt nervous at the prospect. About the postponement of whatever might 'happen' in the country, I didn't know what I felt. As for drink . . . but he *had* said *one* drink.

The doorman greeted Tom as a familiar patron. He held a side door open for us. But Tom waved him away, plunged into the revolving door. I plunged after him. He had pushed so vigorously that I was nearly carried around on to the sidewalk again, but just managed to extricate myself in time, feeling flustered.

My feet sank into the thick carpet as we passed clusters of people in the foyer. We went down a passage, and into a long rectangular room, rich brown and gilt. There was a smell of fur, of perfume and leather, of Abdullah cigarettes, but under all these odours I could distinguish the smell I hated, the smell my parents had when they'd been drinking.

Some people were sitting at tables. Others were standing. To me, they all looked rich and old. I tried to make myself invisible – a usually unsuccessful mental trick I sometimes adopted with my parents – as Tom made his way through the crowd with me hurrying behind him.

We reached the bar counter, at which there was one empty stool. Tom helped me to perch on it. My legs dangled, and I felt uncomfortable.

'Two glasses of champagne,' he said to the barman. Was one of them meant for me? Surely it couldn't be? Surely Tom was only joking, but now the barman, with no change of expression, was pouring two glasses of the frothing liquid, placing one of them, unmistakably, in front of me.

'*A votre santé*, Mademoiselle.' Tom raised his glass. Unlike my parents, he spoke beautiful, French-sounding French.

I shook my head.

'You don't like champagne, Annabel? Come, come. I can't believe that Delaney's and Vanna's daughter doesn't like champagne.'

Couldn't he understand, I thought, with a sudden impatient insight, that my parents were the reason *why* I didn't like it? I shook my head again.

He smiled. 'Perhaps you'd prefer a Dry Martini?'

'No,' I said. 'I don't drink any of those things.' What would he offer me next? I determined to forestall him. 'I'd like a *citron pressé*.'

He shrugged good-humouredly. 'A *citron pressé* you shall have.'

The champagne replaced by the delicious fresh-lemon drink, I felt a sense of relief, smiled at Tom.

'As soon as you've finished that, Annabel, we'll go for our drive. I love driving. Though it's not quite as exciting as flying. I'm taking flying lessons now. My mother keeps writing to me, telling me how dangerous it is. But I love danger. Anyway, I intend to die young.'

That was nonsense, I thought, for he was already quite old. Why, he must be nearly thirty. At that moment, a voice behind us said, 'What the heck!'

It was, I knew before I turned my head, my father. From my first glance at him, I realized that he was drunk. His hair was dishevelled. His eyes had the glazed look I dreaded. They were fixed on Tom in a belligerent stare.

'What the heck,' he said, 'do you mean by bringing my daughter here at her age?' He spoke with that drunken assumption of dignity which is probably the most undignifed thing in the world. Tom was looking at him with an expression of polite surprise. 'Just what do you think you're doing?' My father's voice was loud.

I could sense people turning around to look at us. I took a gulp of my *citron pressé.*

'And what's that you're drinking, Annabel?'

'Just a *citron pressé*, Delaney,' Tom interjected.

'I wasn't speaking to you. Is it a *citron pressé*, Annabel?'

'Yes, Dad, of course it is.' Surely he knew I couldn't stand alcohol?

'Hmmm.' And he picked up my glass, and sipped from it, as if he suspected me of lying. How *could* he? Though he was drunk. I must 'make allowances' for that, as I'd heard people say, though I never knew why one must. Tasting the drink, he grimaced. Like most heavy drinkers, he didn't like fruit, especially citrus fruit. The grimace was succeeded by a look of disappointment. He'd wanted to have a fight with Tom, I realized, and he was sorry to lose the pretext for one. But how thankful *I* was - and thankful that the barman had taken away that glass of champagne.

'Vanna said I could come out, Dad,' I said. That was what I called him, though my mother always insisted that I should call her Vanna. She couldn't bear the idea of being called 'Mother' or 'Mom'.

Now I glanced at Tom - and he was looking bored. Very bored. It was quite unmistakable. He finished his glass of champagne. 'Well, Delaney,' he said, 'can I give you a lift home?'

'I'd like a drink first,' my father said aggressively.

'What will you have?' Tom asked. His voice sounded extremely weary - I half resented that, half sympathized. I waited anxiously to hear my father's choice.

'A Dry Martini,' he said, and I sighed. That was one of the strongest, the worst.

'What are you drinking?' my father asked, as Tom gave the order for the Martini to the barman.

'I don't think I'll have anything right now,' Tom said.

'I never drink alone,' my father exclaimed indignantly, although I knew that wasn't true.

Tom shrugged. 'Oh, well then - a glass of champagne.' He was humouring my father, I saw - something I'd learned to do, too.

The barman mixed the kind of Martini my father always had - gin, barely touched by vermouth, with an olive in it, which he never ate. I loved olives, so sometimes he would offer it to me, but I always refused, after the first time, because of the clinging taste of gin.

My father drank his Martini in one swallow, like a glass of medicine. As he put down the glass, he looked towards the barman. I knew that he was planning to order another, and glanced at Tom in mute appeal. He responded instantly.

'Well, Delaney, we'd better be on our way now. I have to hurry,' he said, glancing at his watch. And somehow he swept us from the bar, through the hotel, into the Bugatti on Place Vendôme.

Sitting uncomfortably on my father's knees, my face averted to avoid the raw smell of gin on his breath, I felt ashamed. More than that, I felt cheated - I was now quite sure that I had wanted to go on that drive into the country with Tom. But I was used to disappointments. My father was always promising me things, and then not coming through with them. He called this 'character-building'.

We drew up opposite the apartment. 'I won't come upstairs,' Tom said. 'Tell Giselle I'm waiting for her.'

My father had difficulty in getting out of the car, and I had to help him. Where once he had been lithe and agile - I remembered him leaping on to the rim of that fountain a few years before - he had suddenly slowed up. His movements had become cautious, and it took him a long time to cross a road; he had recently developed a fear of traffic. Now, taking his hand, I managed to steer him over gently, though, at that moment, I almost hated him.

As we reached the door of our building, I glanced back.

Tom sat, relaxed in the driving seat, watching us coldly. He raised one hand in an indifferent salute, couldn't be bothered to smile. I felt that, like the concierge, who glowered at us as we passed, he was fed up with all the Lees.

But later, when my father had a drunken argument with my mother, about her letting me go out with that 'disreputable fellow', I started to revise that impression in my mind. It had been only my father Tom had been fed up with. Me he was eager to see again. Soon he'd come around – my parents would conveniently both be out – and take me for that drive.

However, I never saw Tom again. The Storeys went back to the States. They didn't come to say goodbye: I even told myself that Giselle had been jealous of me, and that was why – one can make oneself believe anything at thirteen. Six months later, Tom and some woman passenger in his Bugatti were killed in a night accident on a country road in Maine. He had been driving at top speed. The car had gone off the road, through a fence, and caught fire in a field.

The passenger could have been me, I had reflected, and for a long time I had felt romantically sad about Tom whenever I remembered to. But of course, I thought now, that hadn't been 'love'.

'Is it really as bad as that?'

My head jerked up from the unseen page under my eyes, and I saw my employer watching me expressionlessly.

'As bad?' I said. I had no idea what he was talking about.

'My play. I agree it's rather awful, but you've been looking at the same page for at least five minutes – and I've never heard a more heartfelt sigh than the one you just gave.'

'Oh,' I exclaimed. 'Oh no – it wasn't that at all. My mind wandered. I'm sorry.' Really, I thought, I was proving to be the worst secretary imaginable. At this rate, I would soon follow my 'stupid' predecessor into whatever oblivion had swallowed her – had she been fired? I wondered.

He had stood up. He paced across from the table to the door, back again to the table.

'Your mind wandered. Exactly. What you mean is that the play didn't hold your attention.'

'No,' I said quickly.

'Don't sound so anxious. I'm not offended, I assure you. I have the greatest respect for those rare people who tell one the truth.'

I hesitated. How could I describe to him the regions in which my thoughts had been straying? I imagined myself telling him about Tom – what a pointless, childish anecdote it would seem to him. On the other hand, I couldn't tell him that I was enthusiastic about what I had read of this new play. I had too large a share of that respect which he had said he had for the truth. Living with a drinker makes one hate lies.

My father never told them when he was sober. He was accurate – as he was in his work. To write as he did, one must observe faithfully, record exactly. On the other hand, when he was drunk, he became boastful and vague. Drink, he said (when he was drunk), was 'an enhancement of life'. It extended one's range, sharpened one's perceptions. 'I do my best work when I'm drunk,' he would say – although he could never write at all when he had been drinking, something which added to the torment of his hangovers. And he told other lies, quite pointless ones, as if for the sheer joy of it. Did he believe them himself? That was something I had never been sure about.

So I looked silently at Nicholas Forrest as he paced back and forth between table and door.

It was he who spoke, and I felt as if he were talking to himself as much as to me.

'The thing is,' he said, 'when I wrote my first play, *Love à la Carte*, I really enjoyed it. I was young, and I thought that life was a tremendous joke. And there were lots of young people just like me – as well as older people who wanted to feel modern, or to be shocked. So it was a very great success – as was my next play, *Foolish Virgins*. Then I tried something rather different, *The Walnut Tree*, and that was a disaster; it closed after a week. I hated failing, so back to the old formula I went with *Monday's Child* - and that was the most successful of all, though the next one, *Meringue Chantilly*, did almost as well. And now here I am - with *Summer's Lease* boring me to distraction, just as it was boring you.' He looked at me. 'No - please don't make polite disclaimers. Do you know any of my other plays?'

'I've read *Monday's Child*, and seen it - well, half of it.'

'Ah, now you're being truly candid. You walked out at the interval?' He gave his abrupt laugh.

'No, no. I was with my parents. They never used to see a play right through. Honestly.'

'Hmmm. Well - go on. Any others?'

'I started *Meringue Chantilly* last night, but then I went to sleep—'

'Annabel, you're a critic after my own heart. When you don't walk out of my plays, they send you to sleep.'

'No. You don't understand. I was terribly tired. I'd slept so badly on the train.' How appallingly tactless and stupid I felt. Unexpectedly, tears welled up in my eyes, though I tried to force them back. I grabbed for my handkerchief, in my sleeve, and the sudden movement of my arm brushed his manuscript off the table. It was the last straw. I gave a kind of wail as I stooped to start picking up the scattered pages.

Nick said, 'Leave those alone. I'll pick them up in a minute. You're crying.'

I rubbed my hand across my eyes, shook my head, but he said, 'Yes you are. Don't try to deny it. Your eyes are full of tears, and now one of them is rolling down your cheek. This is quite preposterous. Wipe your eyes, while I pick up that paper. No, don't try to help me.'

He squatted down on the floor, and started to sort out the pages. I blinked, found the handkerchief, dried my eyes, swallowed. He was quite right - tears were preposterous. But I was so anxious to make a success of this job.

He said, 'I never imagined that you'd take me so seriously. You must never take me seriously, Annabel. Anyway - and please don't start crying again - I'm quite in agreement with you about my plays.'

'But I thought *Monday's Child*, and what I read of *Meringue Chantilly*, very amusing, very sparkling.'

'Yes, yes. But not *Summer's Lease*. Anyway, I'm not sure that I can be bothered to sparkle and to amuse any more.'

He had sorted out the papers. He stood up and handed them to me. 'Right,' he said. 'I see you've pulled yourself together. Now you'd better struggle on with your work on the first act - whatever you feel about it - while I struggle on with mine on the second.' He looked at his watch. 'Eleven o'clock,' he said. 'I feel very much like a drink. You won't share a half bottle of champagne with me, I suppose?'

'Oh, no thank you,' I said. Why were people always offering me champagne? I asked myself, remembering Tom. 'But could I have a *citron pressé*?'

'By all means. I dare say I'll be able to dispose of the champagne on my own.'

As he pressed the bell, I couldn't help thinking that eleven was a very early hour at which to start drinking. Even my parents had tried to wait until noon - although, admittedly, they had seldom succeeded.

Emil took the order, brought the drinks. After placing my *citron pressé* on my table, he opened the champagne bottle with that hatefully familiar pop.

Soon afterwards, I finished reading the first act of *Summer's Lease*. Determinedly I held my critical faculty in abeyance. I didn't find Nick's handwriting difficult to read. There were only two words that I had to query.

I had never typed a play before. Now, carefully, concentrating to the full, I started. I wanted to do it perfectly, wanted to show Nicholas Forrest that I wasn't the fool he must think me. For I had to admit to myself that this morning, up until now, I had indeed proved myself 'intolerably stupid'.

{5}

Madame Marèchal's husband was at luncheon that day. He had come to take his wife home - they lived in Cannes, and were returning there that afternoon.

He was a fat little businessman, with a big moustache, and strands of hair plastered over his bald crown. I wondered how such a pretty woman could have married him, and at once felt ashamed of myself, of my tendency to be influenced by appearances. I was always trying to remind myself that good looks weren't really important, and yet I knew that they always affected me strongly. Would I, I speculated, have thought the Graf and Gräfin so appalling, if they had been handsome? But to that I could firmly answer '*Yes*'. Nothing could have made me find those two likeable.

There was a lot of talk, that day, of investments. It took place chiefly between Monsieur Marèchal and the Graf. Mr Cressingham, though he listened to every word with an air of absorption, said little. I glanced at Nick. Now he, of course, was extremely handsome, and yet I didn't like him. I watched his eyes moving coldly from one speaker to the other.

Suddenly I was struck by something the Graf was saying. 'Money-grubbing Jewish pigs' - those were his words. 'We know how to deal with them in Germany,' he added, and Monsieur Marèchal nodded in vigorous agreement.

I was horrified. So the Graf *was* a Nazi. I did not know much about Germany, but I had heard rumours that Jews were badly treated there. I had seen pictures of shops with broken windows, and didn't Jewish people have to wear special armbands? Surely someone would argue with the Graf? I looked around the table. As I would have expected, the Gräfin, like Monsieur Marèchal, was nodding in assent to her husband's words. Madame Marèchal wore a remote, dreamy expression - she was probably planning some new outfit, I thought unkindly. Lady Sarah also looked abstracted. Her husband was simply listening - just as he had been before. My eyes rested on Nick. No, he was showing no reaction. His gaze was fixed on his wife, at the other end of the table. I turned to look at Magda, saw that, at that moment, she was giving a vast, extraordinarily uninhibited yawn.

'You see how my wife reacts to political discussions.' Nick's mocking tone interrupted the conversation, and all eyes turned to her. She was covering her mouth with her hand now, the yawn had passed its climax, but for an instant she looked highly embarrassed. Why was Nick sneering at her? Why wasn't *he* arguing with the Graf? But how did I know that he didn't agree with him? I had no idea whether he did or not. Magda gave a little nervous giggle. 'Yes, I'm very stupid,' she said, and took a sip from her glass of Vichy.

'We are boring the ladies,' the Graf said with ponderous gallantry. 'We must not talk of deep subjects like finance and politics in their presence.'

He would be boring whatever he talked about, I thought viciously. I glanced at Nick again. He was in the act of draining a full glass of wine. He put the glass down and one of the footmen immediately refilled it.

The Gräfin was now saying something about how she and her husband would be leaving in a short time - well, *that* was good news.

'We shall be so sorry to go,' she said. 'But you will have our dear Udo to console you.'

'Udo is the son of the Graf and Gräfin,' Magda explained to the rest of the party. Her embarrassment had obviously subsided though, as usual, she was twisting her pendant. 'He is coming to visit us. He and I spent much time together when we were children. We were like sister and little brother.'

'Yes indeed. He is so devoted to you, dear Magda,' the Gräfin said ingratiatingly.

Could Nick really have finished *another* glass of wine? Yes, he must have, for the footman was at his elbow again, pouring. And before luncheon, he had drunk that half bottle of champagne. Yet, as on the previous day, I saw no evidence in his behaviour of the amount he had consumed. He must have a very strong head, I decided. All the same, how much I disapproved of such excessive drinking. In this respect I was indeed the puritan he had described me as that morning.

That night was one of my occasional restless ones. I had fallen asleep in the afternoon, missed tea - which I had learned from Magda was not a compulsory meal - and stayed upstairs reading. (Apparently I was only expected to spend my mornings working, as I started so early.) I had dutifully finished *Meringue Chantilly* - dutifully because, although it was amusing, I felt I had had enough of its author for that day - and had embarked on the novel which I had taken from the library.

Dinner had proved appalling. Magda had not been present, was in bed with what Nick referred to indifferently as 'one of her headaches', leaving it to the Gräfin to describe to us how infrequent but intense migraine had plagued Magda 'since her girlhood'.

Certainly the absence of her gracious, smiling beauty had made the party drabber than it would have been otherwise. The Cressinghams, the von Eisenspachs, an almost totally silent Nick and myself did not compose a sparkling gathering - and dinner, I found to my horror, consisted of seven courses, instead of the five served at luncheon. I was beginning to feel that meals were going to be the most onerous part of my life at the villa. When the Gräfin rose, followed by Lady Sarah and me, to leave the men to drink port, I simply could not face the prospect of coffee on the terrace with the two of them. Murmuring a vague excuse about 'something I have to do', I escaped – I was quite sure *they* would not mind. As I went upstairs I resolved to make it a habit to retire to my room at this time on every evening when I was obliged to dine downstairs.

I read in bed for about an hour, then switched out my light and fell asleep almost at once. But I had a bad dream, a sort of rearrangement of luncheon, except that the Forrests were absent. The Marèchals, the von Eisenspachs, the Cressinghams had developed beaks and claws like vultures, and were tearing at their food with them. All of it devoured, they gathered around me with a kind of flapping movement, although they had no wings. I awoke sweating, and switched on the light. It was two in the morning, and I was wide awake, would be quite unable, I was sure, to go to sleep again.

I was not in a mood for reading. It was very hot, and I was restless. I went out on to the balcony, and thought how much I would like to go for a swim. If I went down to the pool at this hour, no one would see me in my old, tight, out-of-date swimsuit. But a cowardly thought held me back. I did not know where the dog, Karl, spent his nights, could not face the possibility of an encounter with him in house or courtyard.

So I tried to read, but could not concentrate. It seemed an age before the first faint paling of the sky heralded daybreak. At five I rose. Surely the servants would be about soon. I need no longer fear a sudden meeting in the dark with Karl. I decided I would go for a walk – I did not want anyone to see my awful swimsuit.

I washed, dressed. I did not meet anyone in the passages or on the stairs. The hall was rather dim, lit only by the early light coming in through the front door, which was open. I had nearly reached it when I became conscious of voices coming from the terrace. I took a cautious step sideways. Framed by the doorway, two people were standing outside by the balustrade. They were Nicholas Forrest and the little maid whom I had spoken to the day before, the one who had showed me the way to his study.

He was in a loose shirt and white linen pants, and carried a towel over his arm. She, today, was not in her maid's uniform; she was wearing a cotton skirt, a white blouse, a shabby cardigan, and down-at-heel black shoes. A scarf was tied over her head. She carried a worn purse, and a scuffed brown suitcase was on the ground beside her.

She was crying, crying uncontrollably. Great sobs were shaking her body, and I saw that her face was red and swollen. In contrast, he, despite his suntan, had a blanched look. He was frowning. He was talking to her, in French, very rapidly, in a very low voice - I could not distinguish any individual word. But he seemed to be arguing with her, trying to persuade her of something, and, between sobs, she was shrugging, shaking her head; she looked, I thought, utterly bewildered, dazed, lost. At that moment, he put out a hand, rested it on her shoulder. She gave a violent shudder, and jumped back. He frowned more deeply at that, started to talk more vehemently, although not more loudly. She raised her face to look at him. Her expression now seemed not so much dazed as - I searched for a word - hesitant.

He made a gesture obviously indicating that she should wait where she was, and turned. He was coming across the terrace towards the house. I didn't delay - in a second, I was inside the dining-room, behind the door. I heard his footsteps going past in the hall.

How deplorably I was behaving, but what was going on, despite the unpleasant feeling it gave me, was so baffling, so dramatically compelling. I went over to the window, peered out between the slats of one of the shutters. The girl's hand rested on the balustrade. Her head was bowed. She looked so forlorn that I wished I were able to do something to comfort her.

Now I heard Nick's returning footsteps and, in a minute, he was back, standing in front of her on the terrace. He was holding something out to her - and I saw that it was a thick bundle of banknotes. Her fingers crept out towards it. There was an instant when her hand halted, as if she might change her mind, but then she almost snatched the money from him.

As I saw his shoulders relax, I realized how tensely he must have been holding himself. She muttered something - she was stuffing the money into her purse. Then she picked up her old suitcase and set off down the steps from the terrace. He stood watching until long after she had gone through the gate, and disappeared to the left, up the slope. I wondered what expression was on his face.

Suddenly, abruptly, he straightened, shifted the towel which he was still carrying over his arm, and hung it around his neck. It was briskly that he crossed the terrace, ran down the steps, and, outside the gate, turned in the opposite direction from the one the girl had taken - towards the sea. Mr Nicholas Forrest, I presumed, was off for his customary morning swim.

I no longer felt like going for a walk. I returned to the hall, then went upstairs. I could hear sounds of the household coming to life. I passed a maid on the landing. Back in my room, I relived the scene I had witnessed, turned it over in my mind.

The girl had looked so distressed - and I remembered how she had jumped away from the touch of his hand on her shoulder. But she had taken the money; to her, it had probably seemed a small fortune.

Her dowry perhaps? I raised my eyebrows, and gave a little shrug of disgust. Surely there could be only one explanation for what I had seen? He had been 'paying her off'. I doubted whether my opinion of Nicholas Forrest could sink any lower than it was at that moment. But, as far as my job was concerned, I told myself again, such considerations were entirely irrelevant.

That day, and the day after, I followed the same work routine: coffee with Nick at half after seven, a letter or two, then breakfast. Afterwards, I worked on the typing of the first act of *Summer's Lease*, which I completed on the second day.

'Well,' he said on the day after, a Friday, when the letters and breakfast were done, 'I haven't anything more for you to do this morning. And my wife has suggested that you will be able to make yourself useful to her, now that I don't need you all morning. You will find her in her boudoir - the second door on the left, at the top of the stairs. But don't go to her before half past ten; she will not be ready for you.'

I spent the intervening three-quarters of an hour reading in my room, and wondering what it would be like to work for Magda Forrest. On the previous day, when she had appeared at lunch, she had said that she was quite recovered from her migraine, but I had thought that she looked tired. However, when she spoke to me, she was as kind and smiling as ever.

At exactly half after ten, I knocked on her door, and heard her call 'Come in'.

She sat at a gold-and-cream-painted desk - a portrait of herself hanging above it - in a very feminine room. Everything in it was fresh and immaculate, though it was not to my taste at all, with its looped pink curtains, its pink carpet, its satin-upholstered chairs and chaise-longue. Vases of sweet-smelling flowers were everywhere - their scent making me feel almost dizzy. The dog, Karl, was lying at her feet. He looked me over, but did not stir.

'Ah Annabel,' she said, 'so my husband has released you

to help me a little.' As always, she was perfectly groomed; this morning she was wearing a blue linen dress.

I soon realized that she was efficient. Her mind was as tidy as her appearance – '*alles in ordnung*' was her watchword. She knew exactly what she wanted me to do, and explained it clearly.

Apart from entering engagements in her white vellum-bound diary, which had her initials on it in gold – and was companion to an address book of the same format, but bound in blue – my main routine task was dealing with accounts.

She herself first studied them keenly – that morning I was deputed to type letters querying various items in two of them. (I had my own cream-and-gold table, in a corner, and I used a typewriter which, at other times, was kept in a cupboard.) It was surprising to me how, though she was quite unruffled by the vast totals of many of the accounts, she would light with an unfailing eye on errors which might only involve a franc or two. My father and mother, I remembered, had never dreamed of examining bills in detail, just as they had never counted change – I supposed now that they must often have been cheated.

Where nothing was in doubt, I made out the cheques for her to sign, scrupulously filling in the counterfoils in her chequebook – my father had never filled in his counterfoils, which had, I recollected, resulted in many miscalculations. All bills were settled immediately – Magda Forrest was not one of those wealthy people who keep their creditors waiting.

I also had to organize immediate household expenses – servants' wages, and so on, and to write out the daily menus: typed menus, apparently, were vulgar.

'Your handwriting is good and clear,' she said to me approvingly.

'Thank you,' I murmured, thinking that my father, rather than I, deserved her praise. He had insisted on my writing legibly, had always said that illegible handwriting was a discourtesy.

None of the work was difficult, but all of it had to be carried out punctiliously. The time passed quickly. We had just finished for the morning, when she said suddenly, 'And how is my husband's play coming along?'

How strange that she should ask me, I thought, instead of asking him. But then, remembering how he spoke to her, I thought that she might be nervous to. She said, 'My husband is so sensitive about his work. I think that perhaps authors are often like that with their wives - not liking to discuss their writings, you know.'

She was waiting for my answer. I heard myself say, 'Oh, I think it's going very well.'

I usually blush on the rare occasions when I lie - and this occasion was no exception, but she did not seem to notice; she was swinging her apple to and fro on its chain, like a pendulum. She smiled, said, 'I am so glad to hear that, Annabel. You reassure me. Sometimes I have felt anxious that he may be worried about this new play of his, but now I know that is not so.'

I smiled back, but my smile was false. I felt guilty about having lied to her. Why had I done so? What harm would there have been in telling her the truth? Perhaps my long history of loyalty to my father had bred in me a loyalty to all authors in difficulty - even one as unpleasant as Nicholas Forrest.

She rose from her chair and came over to stand beside me. She put her hand, with its rosy nails, on my arm, and stroked it, lightly, briefly. 'I am sure,' she said, 'that we are going to get on very well together, Annabel.' She paused, then added, 'It is pleasant to have a sweet, modest girl like yourself working for us. Such a change from the previous secretary!'

I looked at her questioningly. Was I to hear more of the object of my secret curiosity - my 'incredibly stupid' predecessor?

'Great beauty is not everything,' Magda Forrest said. 'And especially not in a secretary.' She smiled again. 'In fact it can prove quite tiresome.'

So my predecessor had been beautiful. I wondered in what way her beauty could have proved 'tiresome' - and then thought how naïve I was. Surely I could guess - where a man like Nick was concerned?

'She was a great beauty?' I asked, repeating Magda's own words, curious to learn more.

'Oh yes. Elizabeth was very lovely. Hair as black as ebony, skin as white as snow, lips as red as blood - though perhaps *they* were not natural.' She laughed. Perhaps she had a sense of humour after all. 'And green eyes - truly green eyes, which are very rare.' She gave another little laugh. 'Anyway,' she said, 'it was almost a relief when she vanished.'

'*Vanished*?' I said.

'Yes. We had gone out for the day - and when we came back, she had disappeared, taking all her things. Without a word, without leaving a message of any kind - what behaviour! It was, of course - is it necessary for me to say so? - on the day after she had received her wages.'

'But how extraordinary!' I said.

Magda shrugged. 'I presume that she went off with someone, though I have no idea where she met him. Probably on a day out in Antibes, Monte Carlo, Cannes - who knows? Doubtless some rich man is keeping her in an apartment.' She broke off. 'But I should not be talking to a young girl like yourself about such things. At any rate, we are - how do you put it? - *well rid*' - she sounded pleased at her command of the idiom - 'of that Elizabeth.'

'Yes,' I said. 'Yes, I suppose so.'

She was looking at her watch, which was narrow, framed with diamonds. 'Our guests will be expecting me,' she said. 'It is time for me to go downstairs.'

As I tidied in preparation for luncheon - I delayed my

descent until the actual sounding of the gong – my thoughts dwelt on the beautiful, vanished Elizabeth. I visualized her ebony hair, her green eyes. I saw her, mysterious, a faint Mona Lisa smile on her blood-red lips, seated in my place in Nicholas Forrest's study. 'Incredibly stupid'. 'Very lovely'. My reverie was interrupted by the booming of the gong.

It was at luncheon that day that Magda mentioned to the Gräfin that the Roquebrune procession would be taking place at the end of the following week. They had been talking about peasant customs, in which, apparently, the Gräfin took an interest. 'Peasants are such fine people,' she now remarked, 'so different from the workmen in the towns.'

'We could have gone,' Magda said, 'but unfortunately that is the day when we shall be lunching with the Marèchals in Cannes.'

I could not prevent myself glancing at Nick, remembering his suggestion, on the day of my arrival, that we should go to the procession. But though he heard the exchange – I saw his eyebrows flick up, when the Gräfin made her remark about the peasants – he made no comment. He had forgotten his offer – or, more probably, had decided against the idea. He had proposed it, I remembered, before that stupid kiss. Though it would have been interesting to see the procession, I felt relief that I would not be going to it with him.

It was on the following Thursday that Udo came – the Graf and Gräfin's son, and the dear companion of Magda's youth.

We were on the terrace before dinner when he arrived, apologizing for being late. My first reaction was one of astonishment at his good looks – his appearance was so different from that of his parents.

He was tall, blond, even-featured. His eyes were of the same blue as Magda's – not so vivid as Nick's, not so pale as Lady Sarah's. Perhaps his hair was cut a little too short, the way he held himself was a little rigid – but that was the

German style. He gave a small bow, a smile, when Magda introduced him to me. I did not feel that acute awareness of being 'the secretary' which the Graf and the Gräfin invariably aroused in me.

A coolness between him and his host was immediately apparent to me. They shook hands briefly. Udo's smile was stiff. Nick did not smile at all. 'Oh hullo, Udo,' was his only greeting to his new guest.

'And how are you, Nicholas?' Udo enquired.

'Oh, as well as can be expected in the circumstances.' A cryptic answer, I thought, though no one else appeared to find it odd or to feel that 'the circumstances' might be those of Udo's arrival. But surely, I reflected, as Udo excused himself to change for dinner, nothing quite as rude as that could have been intended, even by Nicholas Forrest. All the same, I wondered what could be the cause of the hostility I had felt between them. Perhaps Magda's childhood friend might resent her husband's treatment of her?

Towards the end of the long meal, Magda mentioned the luncheon with the Marèchals next day. 'We shall be seven, shall we not?' she said. 'The Graf and Gräfin, Sarah and Paul, Udo, Nicholas and myself. I must telephone Renée after dinner, and confirm it.'

'No, you will be six,' Nick said. 'I shall not be coming. I told Annabel that I would take her to see the Roquebrune procession.'

I was absolutely astonished - and my heart sank, both at the prospect before me and at this public announcement of it. All eyes were turned on me. I could feel myself blushing. Did I imagine the waves of hostility I felt lapping around me, as if I were stranded on a rock in an unfriendly sea? No. The Graf and Gräfin were definitely scowling, and Lady Sarah's eyebrows had almost disappeared into her hairline. Even Udo's face wore a frowning, puzzled look. Only Paul Cressingham looked supremely indifferent.

Did Magda's lips tighten? I thought that they did, a little, but when she spoke it was in her normal tone. 'Yes, I see. Yes, it will be interesting for Annabel to attend the procession. Nicholas is always so thoughtful,' she continued, with an unusually sharp glance around the table, as if she were daring her guests to disagree. And, sure enough, as if she had issued an actual command, their expressions returned to normal; I felt the waves recede. 'Of course,' she added, 'the Marèchals will be most disappointed. But I shall give them a good explanation.' She smiled.

A good explanation. It was obvious that she felt the real one to be inadequate, and that the Marèchals would not comprehend Nick's last-minute refusal of their invitation on the grounds that he was taking his secretary sight-seeing. Well, I could understand that perfectly.

I felt that I must say something - but to whom? Nick was really the only possible person. As I turned to him, he raised - as usual, I thought - his glass to his lips.

'Oh, please don't bother about taking me to the procession,' I said. 'I'm sure it will be inconvenient. Truly, I had forgotten all about it.'

Magda answered me. 'Nonsense, little Annabel. Do not disturb yourself. It is all arranged now - and my husband never inconveniences himself, I can assure you.'

There was some conflict, I thought, between that statement, and her previous one about Nick's thoughtfulness. I looked at her. She was smiling. Again I wondered whether, after all, she might possess a sense of humour of her own.

'My dear wife knows me too well,' Nick said. He smiled blandly - yes, that was the word - around, at his guests. A polite titter circled the table.

'Next year, we must *all* go to the procession,' Magda pronounced. 'As the Gräfin says, the old customs are so quaint and interesting. But tomorrow we shall be "frivolous"' - she spoke the word as if it were rather daring - 'and lunch in Cannes.' She rose - it was time to leave the gentlemen.

As I did every evening, I said goodnight to the women,

and gladly escaped to my room. That evening I felt particularly thankful for my release.

In my room everything was immaculately tidy. The bed was ready, its coverlet neatly folded on top of the chintz-covered trunk, my nightdress laid out on the turned-back sheet. Certainly, in this house, a secretary's life was a luxurious one. I could distinguish no difference between the service I received and that which would be accorded to a guest.

As always, I went out on to the balcony. There was no moon that night, and the courtyard was dark and still. Resting my elbows on the smooth stone of the baluster, I thought about what had been decided at dinner.

My predominant emotion was nervous dread of a considerable stretch of time spent alone - at leisure, not working - with Nick. Would he be chilly and sarcastic, or - worse - might he make another advance? No, I didn't believe in the second alternative; the first was far more likely. Well, I would just have to put up with it. I would concentrate on the procession, which, after all, was the object of the expedition.

I considered the reactions of the other members of the party. I did not care at all what the Graf and Gräfin, the Cressinghams, or the as yet unknown, though so handsome, Udo felt. But Magda's feelings were another matter. *I shall give them a good explanation. My husband never inconveniences himself.* Had any displeasure underlain those words? If it had, was it directed at Nick alone - or at me as well?

Surely she had realized that it had not been my fault? After all, she had smiled, had reassured me, had told me not to 'disturb' myself. But mightn't she well suspect me of being deceitful? After all, Nick had announced that I knew of his intention to take me to the procession. I remembered what Magda had said the week before: *It is pleasant to have a sweet, modest girl like yourself working for us.* I hoped she had not changed her mind. I recollected her words about my predecessor: *It was almost a relief when she vanished.*

Suddenly I wondered if Nick had taken the beautiful, vanished Elizabeth to the Roquebrune procession. He had said that he had not been to it for some years, but I placed no reliance on his word. I remembered what he had written about her stupidity, but he might have been interested in other things than her brains - I had a sudden distressing vision of that weeping little maid. Anyway, some of my father's most intelligent friends had had wives or girlfriends whom I had considered silly. My mother had not been silly, though - far from it. I wished she had been, instead of . . . but as always my thoughts veered away from the subject.

My eyes were becoming accustomed to the dark. Now I could distinguish the shapes of the trees, the outline of the wall that surrounded the courtyard. The pool glinted - I had still not swum at night, as I would have liked to if only I could have overcome my fear of Karl. Possibly, if my parents had ever owned a dog, I might have been able gradually to conquer my deep-rooted terror. But animals had played no part in their existence. Their restless, irregular way of life had precluded the keeping of a pet - which would inevitably have made unacceptable demands for exercise and attention.

At that moment, two rectangles of light appeared on the flagstones on the right-hand side of the courtyard. They must come, I realized, from Nick's window, and now I saw his shadow cast from one of them. He was standing, as I was, looking into the dark courtyard. I wondered if my shadow, like his, was visible, silhouetted against the lit bedroom behind me.

I went inside, reflecting that he had not spent much time with his guests that evening. Magda, I supposed, was bearing that burden - as she would do next day, on the trip to Cannes. But did she find it a burden? Certainly she gave no indication that she did, nor indeed, on the other hand, that she particularly enjoyed it. She had, of course, known the von Eisenspachs for years, but I could see no close bond between her and the Cressinghams. They were surely her husband's friends, but they did not seem to be very close ones. He never paid them any special attention. I felt no current of warmth flowing from him towards them - though, of course, I had never seen him show warmth towards anyone. I often saw Lady Sarah watching him, but he never reciprocated her long stares. Or did I imagine that she stared at him? Nobody else seemed aware of it. What strange people they all were. I sighed as I started to undress.

I fell asleep quickly, only awoke once, and very briefly, to absolute darkness, absolute silence. The night was so quiet that I could have been alone in the heart of a desert. Then suddenly the peace was shattered by one great, penetrating shout of laughter. Silence fell again. I had started up in bed. Now I lay down again. Had the laugh been a man's or a woman's? I did not know. It had not been weird, creepy, ghostly. Apart from its unexpectedness, I tried to analyse what had been disturbing about it, for something had been. The word came upon me: its *abandon*. That laugh had been utterly abandoned, totally - though so brief - uncontrolled. Who in the villa, I wondered, could possibly have laughed like that? But the problem did not exercise me for more than a minute or two before I fell asleep again.

When I awoke next morning, the sky, for the first time since my arrival at the villa, was cloudy. Might it be going to rain? If it rained, Nick would probably abandon the expedition to Roquebrune. Perhaps, after all, he would go to Cannes with the others. But no, Magda would already have telephoned Madame Marèchal with her 'good explanation' for his absence - I wondered what it had been.

Of course I would be pleased if I did not have to go with him - and yet, not wholly pleased, I found. I realized that my feelings were mixed; childishly, I saw the procession itself as a 'treat' - and my father had deprived me, always at the last minute, of so many of those, that I had a wistful readiness to be disappointed at 'missing something'. Yet surely missing an outing would be more than compensated for by not spending an afternoon with Nicholas Forrest?

As I dressed, I wondered for whom I would be working that morning. Always, first, at half after seven, I went to see what Nick had for me to do. But ever since those first three days, he had dismissed me as soon as we had done his letters and had breakfast, and I had gone to my room until Magda required me at half after ten. Though she always had something for me to do, I had found that I was far from overworked at the villa.

Today, when I entered Nick's study, he was dressed in a light summer suit, and was standing, riffling through some papers in the open filing cabinet.

'I have to go to Monte Carlo unexpectedly,' he said. 'I shan't be needing you this morning.' So we would probably not be attending the procession anyway. But he continued: 'I'll be back by lunchtime. I'll see you then.'

I said, 'It's very cloudy this morning. Do you think it's going to rain?'

Abstractedly, he glanced through the window at the grey sky that showed between the branches of the trees. 'Rain?' he said. 'No, I shouldn't think so.' He returned to his papers, evidently instantly oblivious of my presence, and I left, quietly closing the door behind me.

I met Emil in the hall, and asked him for breakfast on the terrace. I knew that it was too early for any other members of the household to be there. They seldom breakfasted before half after nine.

As I ate my croissant, and a fig, and drank my coffee, I wondered what business had summoned Nick to Monte Carlo – a place I had never been to, though I remembered my parents visiting the casino and grumbling about the money they had lost there. Monte Carlo was one of the towns in which Magda had speculated that the 'vanished'

Elizabeth might be being kept by 'some rich man'. Really, I reflected, her subsequent apology for mentioning such a topic to me had not been necessary. Despite my father's periodic bursts of solicitude for me, I had certainly 'seen life' in the company of my parents and their friends.

Punctually as ever, I arrived in Magda's boudoir. The lean black dog at her feet raised its head as I came in, gave me what I thought of as its usual nasty look, then rested its muzzle on its paws again.

Magda was not her normal perfectly ordered self this morning. She was not dressed - she wore a white chiffon robe with great ruffles from neck to waist. Her maid, a sallow, middle-aged woman, always clad in black, was brushing her hair, which I had not seen loose before. It hung, a glittering golden curtain, to below her waist. Strands flew up under the vigorous brushing - metallic, almost seeming to give off sparks. I could not restrain a gasp at the sight of her - she did indeed look, in Nick's words, like a Rhine maiden. When she saw my expression, she gave a little laugh.

'How you stare, little Annabel. You are shocked that I am so lazy today?'

'Oh no,' I said. 'It's just that you look so beautiful.'

She smiled. 'Ah Marie,' she said, 'we have a flatterer with us.'

The maid, standing behind her, brushing, brushing, said nothing, and her face remained expressionless. I supposed that Magda had expected no reply from her. Certainly it would hardly have been polite for the maid to have agreed with what she had said.

'So you like my long hair, Annabel? I am afraid that it is very old-fashioned nowadays. I have often thought of cutting it off.'

'Oh no, Mrs Forrest. You mustn't do that.'

She smiled again - with unmistakable warmth. No, I

decided, she couldn't be annoyed with me about the expedition to Roquebrune.

She said, 'Somehow I have never been able to bring myself to cut it. And Nicholas says that it would not become me. I could not, of course, go against his wishes.'

I had always thought of German women as submissive. But somehow, in spite of her public deference to her husband, I had not viewed Magda in that light - perhaps because she looked so like a goddess. She seemed somehow different this morning - softer. And she had referred to 'Nicholas'. Always before, when speaking to me, she had said 'my husband'.

'I think that will do for now, Marie.'

'Very well, Madame,' the maid replied, immediately halting the regular movement of her brush. She went through into Magda's bedroom which led off the boudoir. As she opened the door, I glimpsed the great bed, all white, covered with a lace and satin spread. Over it, filmy white festoons hung from a silver coronet. *A bridal bed*, I thought.

Marie came back into the boudoir, closing the door behind her. She picked up a tray, with one of the red-and-gold cups and a silver coffee-pot on it, from Magda's desk. An inexplicable shadow which had crossed my mind, as a cloud crosses the sun, passed, as a cloud passes, and was gone.

'Please run my bath now, Marie,' Magda said. 'The jasmine bath essence.' *She will have her bath with oil of jasmine in the water.* Nick had said that.

Magda was looking at her watch. 'A quarter to eleven! We shall have to make some haste. I am due to go out in an hour.'

'Yes, Madame,' Marie said. Carrying the tray, she left the room by the door into the passage.

Magda sighed. 'She is so sour and gloomy, that French-woman. But she is a good lady's maid, so I must be content.' She put her hand up to her mouth to cover a yawn - a yawn of languor, not of boredom - then stretched like a cat. The sun came out, and poured through the window, lighting her coin-bright hair.

'Oh, I am lazy today,' she said. 'I have not had my swim. I have not had my massage.' With a little shake of her head, she sat upright in her chair. 'But I must be lazy no more. There is so much that I must do. We leave at a quarter to twelve for Cannes. We are stopping for cocktails with friends on the way.' She felt within the ruffles of her robe, brought out the crystal apple, started to finger it. I realized that, until now, she had not touched the jewel – no wonder I had noticed something different about her. Now she was once more the Mrs Forrest I was familiar with. As if in response to her change of mood, the dog at her feet stirred restlessly, stood up, circled, then sat again, resting its nose on her knee.

'Ah Karl, what a pair we are,' she said. 'But soon Emil will take you for your exercise, and there will be no more idleness.' She turned to me.

'Well, Annabel, as you see, I have no time to spare for our work this morning. You, too, are having a lazy day, it seems – or did my husband give you many tasks to do?'

'No,' I said, 'he was in such a hurry before he left.'

'Left?' she said.

'Yes – for Monte Carlo.'

There was a pause. Then it was in her usual calm tone that she said, 'Ah. So he has gone to Monte Carlo?'

I had taken it for granted that she knew. Perhaps he had been in too much of a hurry to tell her. But he had been wearing a suit – something he never did at the villa. Surely she would have noticed that? Then I realized that they could not have seen each other that morning. Evidently they didn't share a room – but I knew that was the case with many rich couples.

'He said he'd been called away unexpectedly,' I told her.

'I see.' But she didn't sound, I thought, as though she 'saw'. 'Did he say when he would be returning?'

'For luncheon.'

'For luncheon,' she repeated. How busy her fingers were, twisting the apple. Then she said. 'So he will be able to take you to the procession still. I am pleased.'

Pushing away the dog, she stood up. 'And now I must really *bestir* myself. *Auf Wiedersehen*, Annabel. Enjoy your afternoon.'

'Thank you,' I said. 'I hope you enjoy your luncheon party.'

'My luncheon party? Ah, yes.' But she sounded preoccupied, did not notice as I left the room.

At a quarter of one I went down to the terrace. There was no one about, not even, as I was thankful to discover, the dog, Karl. The possibility of his company had been one reason why I had not come down earlier.

I relished the absence of the house party, though at the same time I felt some trepidation at the prospect of my solitary lunch with Nick. I wondered what sort of mood he would be in.

I went to lean on the balustrade just where, I thought suddenly, and frowned, that wretched girl had stood. I concentrated on the view. Beyond the garden, with its orderly ranks of roses, beyond the wall and the umbrella pines and eucalyptus trees, the sea was a deep brilliant blue – every trace of cloud had now vanished. The midday hush was broken only by the noisy whirring of cicadas. Long ago, my father had explained to me how cicadas made that sound, but I couldn't remember a word of his explanation now, although at the time I had found it fascinating. He had possessed so many pieces of information on so many different subjects. It was surprising how, considering the rackety company he chiefly kept, he'd managed to acquire them. I decided that he had absorbed them unconsciously, as a sponge absorbs water. Often, in his books, something he'd heard a year or two before would emerge fresh and sudden as spring flowers.

The sun was beating down on my head. I retreated to a chair in the shade. I wondered if Nick were back yet or if he would be late. Perhaps he would be delayed, and I would miss the procession. But I was being childish again. That 'character-building' of my father's had not been very successful.

I was thirsty, wanted a *citron pressé*, and yet could not make the effort to summon a servant. At that moment I heard a car door slam. A minute later footsteps rapidly ascended to the terrace. It was Nick. He was smiling.

'Hullo, Annabel. All alone? How restful! Goodness, I need a drink.'

He went to the front door, called for Emil, who appeared at once. 'Your usual, I suppose?' Nick asked me. I nodded, and he told Emil to bring a *citron pressé* and a champagne cocktail. 'And now, Annabel,' he said, 'I must go and change out of these clothes. I'll only be a moment - I'm dying for that drink.'

I thought I had never seen him so buoyant, so cheerful - and when he reappeared, his mood was unchanged. After our drinks, we went into the dining-room where two places were set at the table under the window.

'I hope you don't mind,' he said. 'I ordered a light meal. In this weather, I find all those courses rather tedious.' He smiled at the alacrity with which I agreed.

I found myself actually enjoying that lunch. We had my favourite iced consommé - last time I had eaten that had been on the Blue Train; it seemed an age ago. Afterwards there was cold *langouste* with salad, and then fruit. I drank Vichy, he champagne - 'To celebrate,' he said.

'Celebrate what?' I asked.

'Oh, I don't know. Something . . . anything. Let's say the Roquebrune procession - or perhaps the absence of my wife's guests. It's really rather splendid not to be sharing a sty with the Graf and Gräfin, though they're departing tomorrow - that's certainly something to celebrate. If only they were taking their appalling son with them, but one can't have everything. And the Cressinghams will manage to hang on a bit longer. They're so thick-skinned that I can't envisage any means of deterring them. Have you noticed that they, too, always eat as if each meal were their last? Though, poor things, they're probably storing up food, like camels, against the hungry winter ahead.'

'Hungry?' I asked, puzzled.

'Well, they haven't a penny between them, though I've heard he has distant expectations. Very distant though – involving the deaths of three or four perfectly healthy people.'

'Goodness,' I exclaimed. 'I thought they were rich.'

He laughed. 'You mustn't judge by appearances, Annabel, especially where the English upper classes are concerned. No, the Cressinghams are anything but rich. But don't feel too sorry for them – they're natural survivors. They'll always find hospitality somewhere. Probably, as has happened before, from some *nouveaux riches*, impressed by Sarah's title. They must watch out, though, or they'll become *déclassé*.'

I smiled, though I thought how merciless he was. 'I can see you think I'm cynical,' he said. 'You probably will be too – when you've seen as much of the world as I have.'

I said, 'I know I'm young, but I've seen quite a lot of the world, I think.'

'How indignant you sound at being called innocent – that shows just how young you are. I'm sure you've seen something of the world – but a different one from the one I'm talking about. Your father's world must have been one of real artists: writers, painters, musicians.'

In the course of this speech, his tone had changed entirely. When he spoke of 'real artists', his voice was almost reverent. Suddenly I almost felt older than he, remembering those drunken evenings when 'real artists' (though there hadn't been many of them, mostly just hangers-on) had become blind, stumbling fools. *I need a drink. I'm dying for that drink.*

Those words of Nick's had jarred on me.

'You're looking too serious. Remember, this is meant to be a holiday.' He glanced at his watch, stood up. 'Must you have coffee? No? Splendid - let's go.'

He ushered me out of the dining-room, through the hall, and on to the terrace, but when we reached the steps, he almost bounded ahead of me, down to the gate. No, I had certainly never seen him so exuberant.

An open two-seater sports car stood outside. 'Edwards has taken the Rolls to Cannes,' he said. 'Today, I'm your chauffeur.'

As we drove off, the movement of the air brought a wonderfully welcome coolness - how lovely it was to drive in an open car. Suddenly I remembered that morning with Tom in Paris. Today, my 'chauffeur' drove fast, but without Tom's recklessness.

Soon after we crossed the Moyenne Corniche, we started to climb a steep winding road. 'I suppose I should tell you something more about the procession,' Nick said. 'I mentioned that it's held to celebrate the village being spared by the plague, didn't I? The people made a vow, that if it was, they'd commemorate it every year. Extraordinarily enough, the plague did pass over Roquebrune. Hardly anyone was killed - and, even more extraordinarily, the villagers have kept their vow. They re-enact scenes - tableaux - of the Way of the Cross and the Crucifixion. The parts they play have been handed down from father to son for generations. Some of the actors you'll see today will be directly descended from the fifteenth-century peasants who made that original vow. The population of these mountain villages changes very little.'

'How extraordinary,' I said, 'to have roots like that. Sometimes I feel I haven't any roots at all. I can hardly remember the States - anyway not enough to miss the country, or feel that it's my home. I have relatives over there, but I haven't seen any of them since I was a small child. When my father died, my mother's family asked me to come and live with them in Georgia. But I didn't want to. I was afraid to take the plunge.'

I felt astonished that I had made such a long speech to him. Would he make some chilling comment? But he said nothing. 'Do you miss England?' I asked him after a moment's hesitation.

'England?' He was steering the car around a steep bend. A thoughtful frown wrinkled his forehead. 'Hardly ever. Perhaps I'll get more sentimental about it as I grow older. Sometimes, during the Sirocco – you've been spared that, so far – I think of muddy lanes. But otherwise it's the boredom I remember. I grew up in a small provincial town in the Midlands. I picture my mother meeting women in felt hats – she wears one herself; one would never guess that she's half French – for morning coffee in the Olde Tudor Tea Room. I see the old copies of *Punch* in my father's waiting room – he was a doctor; he's dead now. I feel the heavy weight of Sunday afternoons after roast beef and apple pudding, and then I hear the church bell tolling to force me to Evensong. Boredom – oh, boredom.'

How coldly he conjured up his home. It was indeed a boring scene he presented – 'muddy lanes' the best thing he could offer! – and yet, thinking of his normal behaviour, I couldn't help reflecting that he had brought his boredom with him to the Villa Aurore. I didn't say so, however. I said, 'Your mother is half French?'

'Yes, I spent a lot of my youth here, with my grandmother. That was when I first came to love France so much.'

'And why your French is so good' – I had noticed its perfect fluency when he spoke to the French servants.

He made no comment on this trite, if amiable observation. We had been climbing between rugged formations of the red-brown rock. Now we made another turn, and suddenly we were in a big, dusty square, floored with bare brown earth, and planted with precisely-spaced rows of pollarded lime trees.

'I sometimes think the French are *too* tidy,' Nick said. 'I like trees planted at random, and they should have great, spreading branches.' He laughed. 'Perhaps I'm more English than I realize.'

The square was deserted. He said, 'There are usually old men here, playing *pétanque* - that's a kind of bowls - but not today.'

A few cars were parked by the ancient wall which surrounded the village. He drew up beside them, came around to open my door.

The cobbled streets of the village were steep and winding, crossed by stone arches. We reached the village church. The space outside it was crowded with people in their Sunday best - the older women invariably clothed in black. Dark-eyed children darted here and there like swallows, or clung to their mothers' skirts. A few tourists were scattered amongst the crowd, immediately identifiable by their cameras and bright holiday clothes. Suddenly I saw a face I recognized - the face of a Frenchman, not a tourist. It was long, with narrow eyes and a crooked nose.

Where had I seen it before? I smelled a mixture of pungency and sweetness. An old woman stood in front of us, holding out neatly tied bunches of lavender and a herb I did not know. I asked Nick what it was. '*Sarriette*,' he replied. 'Sorrel in English. It makes an excellent soup - but you don't want to make soup, do you?' He laughed. 'However, I'll give you some lavender.'

Suddenly I remembered where I had seen that face before. In the courtyard of the villa on my first night. But I had now lost sight of the man in the crowd, and Nick was handing me three of the little bunches of lavender. I sniffed them - and was reminded of the sachets my mother had kept among her clothes. Except when she was becoming ill, when her habits had changed, deteriorated, everything she wore had been fresh and crisp, faintly fragrant with lavender.

The crowd started to move. The route of the procession was from the church to a chapel about half a mile away.

We were pressed among the densely packed people. I found it almost claustrophobic. Nick, being taller than everyone else there, could see over their heads. I could not. I had to peer between their shoulders, stand on tiptoe. And when at last I glimpsed the first tableau – Christ receiving the kiss of Judas – my eye was riveted by something beyond it, in the crowd on the other side: a face. This was not a face I recognized, but it was one of the most beautiful I had ever seen – a pale face, bright-lipped, framed in dark hair. One expects blondes, rather than brunettes, to dazzle. But dazzling was the only word for this girl. In fact, I actually gasped at my first sight of her.

The procession continued on its way. There were four more tableaux: Christ beaten by soldiers while Pilate washed his hands; then, clothed in red, he held a reed. In the next, he fell beneath the weight of the cross. Finally, he hung from it while the holy women watched and wept.

Though I had had no religious upbringing, I found these scenes more impressive than anything I had ever seen on a stage. The actors' absolute belief in their roles was very moving. Yet – just as in the middle of a great piece of music one can find oneself thinking of some quite irrelevant episode – so my eyes kept searching in the crowd opposite for that astonishing face. But, after the first tableau, I did not see it again.

How secret the little stone houses looked, with their shutters. Above them was perched an ancient castle. It was between the third tableau and the fourth that I turned to say something to Nick – and found he was not there. I looked all round, but could see him nowhere. Could he possibly have become bored and deserted me in Roquebrune, without a word? Surely not even he . . . but I couldn't help feeling some alarm. Suddenly things seemed insubstantial. The crooked-nosed man had vanished, and the lovely girl, and now Nick. I forced my panic down. Even if Nick had done the unthinkable, I was only a few miles from the villa. I could get a taxi if necessary. Meanwhile I continued along the route of the procession.

Between the fourth and fifth tableaux, someone brushed against me. I heard Nick's voice. 'You have remarkably soft hair,' he said, but in as detached a tone as if he had been reporting on the weather.

I did not look round, not wanting to have to reply to his comment. I decided to pretend not to have heard it - and not to have noticed his absence. I buried my nose in my bunches of lavender but, a moment later, to my annoyance, I found myself running a hand over my hair. Was it really 'remarkably' soft? I thought it very ordinary, especially when I remembered Magda Forrest's golden Rhine-maiden tresses.

The procession was drawing up outside the chapel when Nick said suddenly, 'I feel restless. Shall we slip away now, and avoid the crush? You've seen everything there is to see. We might go for a drive, I think.'

How changeable he was, I thought, as we retraced our way through the now deserted streets. Our footsteps, loud on the cobbles, raised echoes from the stone walls.

'It would be rather fun to live in one of these little houses,' I said.

'Do you really think so? Indoors, you would feel shut in, and out of doors people would always be watching you and gossiping about you. You would never really feel that you belonged. Even if you stayed for twenty years, your neighbours would still consider you an alien.'

How seriously he seemed to have taken my idle remark. At that moment, a piercing sweetness filled my nostrils, drowning even the strong odour of the lavender I held in my hand.

I paused. 'Oh, what a lovely scent,' I said. 'What is it?'

He wrinkled his nose, then looked up, and gestured to a

bush with white starry flowers which sprayed over the top of a wall.

'Jasmine,' he said. 'You like it, do you? I loathe the smell of jasmine - so sweet, so sickly, so corrupt.'

He increased his pace - to escape from the detested jasmine? He was positively scowling. Really, I thought, he was an impossible person.

But, once we reached the car, he smiled again. 'Now for our drive,' he said. 'We'll go to Nice. I like its faded Edwardian grandeur - so different from the vulgarity of Cannes.'

As we drove down from Roquebrune, he even sang a little jigging tune.

> '*Si tu vas à Nice*
> *En avion, en chemin de fer*
> *Ou à cheval,*
> *Si tu vas à Nice*
> *Tu auras la mer*
> *Et les lampions de Carnaval.*'

The youthfulness of his light tenor voice surprised me. Suddenly I imagined the young man who had thought life fun, who had enjoyed writing *Monday's Child*. I wondered how someone could have changed so much.

'They have a glorious Battle of the Flowers in Nice at the carnival,' he said now, 'but my wife doesn't care for it. She finds it vulgar - all the noise, and people throwing dyed carnations.'

After that, he drove in silence. I was happy not to talk - just to look at the scenery and to feel the breeze on my face, in my hair. *Remarkably soft hair* - how ridiculous I was being to think about that again. I supposed it was because I'd never heard him pay anyone a compliment before - though it hadn't really been a compliment, just an observation, cool and detached. Suddenly I thought of Magda's jasmine bath essence. I wondered why he didn't tell her that he disliked the scent so much.

'We'll have tea somewhere,' he said, as we came down from the Corniche into Nice. 'But not, if you don't mind, at the Negresco. We'd be certain to bump into boring acquaintances - and anyway I no longer relish luxurious hotels.'

'You used to like them?'

'When I was a young man, fresh from that provincial town I told you about, they had a certain glamour for me. But that evaporated long ago.'

We had passed the harbour, and were driving along the sea front, with its beaches and palm trees. He turned off to the right. 'We'll have tea here, in the Place Masséna,' he said, as we came into a vast square where there were great palm trees, and red arcaded buildings. He parked the car, and we sat down at a table under the arcade in front of a café.

He ordered tea. When the waiter brought it, and I was pouring it out, he said, 'I don't usually have tea. But today I'm pandering to your prejudices - I notice how you frown and turn up your nose whenever I have a drink.'

'Oh!' I exclaimed.

'Don't deny it. But try to keep your disapproval to yourself in future. I find it rather monotonous.'

How I detested him at that moment. Why had he brought me here, if all he wanted to do was to be unpleasant? His next words came as a complete surprise to me.

'You must find life at the villa very boring, I imagine. It's hardly a whirl of gaiety. I think we've been remiss. We must invite some young people to meet you.'

I could just imagine them: the gilded offspring of Riviera visitors. Blasé, beautifully dressed, bored to distraction at the task of making conversation to 'the secretary'.

'Oh no,' I said.

'What a cry from the heart! And such a strange one. Don't

you like your contemporaries, then?'

'I've never really known any of them,' I said. 'I'm used to older people.'

'That may be why you're so unnaturally serious. I see you at meals, observing us with those large grey eyes, and I often wonder what's going on in your mind. Sometimes I suspect that you look on us as strange specimens in a private zoo.'

'Oh no,' I said - again.

'You feel bound to deny it - but I don't believe you. I think it's a most reasonable response. How do you see the Graf and Gräfin? Pigs are too obvious a comparison, perhaps. A pair of wallowing hippos, do you think? The Cressinghams, of course, can only be horses. Udo is more difficult - I can't think of any animal that's so wooden. And what about me? No answer! I was trying to entertain you, but evidently not succeeding. Come, we must go home, to face the delights of the evening.'

He paid the bill. As we got into the car, he said, 'You must learn one of the essential social graces, Annabel - to smile, even when you're not amused. Now, smile at me. Come on - I insist. If you can't manage any other way, you must say "cheese", as people do before they're photographed.'

Suddenly I realized that he possessed charm: that dangerously deceptive quality. For, annoyed with him though I felt, I couldn't help smiling. 'Cheese,' I said, and then, cross with myself for succumbing, 'cheese, cheese, *cheese*,' in an aggressive crescendo.

He laughed. 'That's better.' He started the car. The journey back to the villa passed quickly. The sun was setting; the colour was fading from the sea. I felt tired.

He drew up by the iron gate, leant quickly across me to open the door. 'Out you get,' he said. 'I'll take the car round to the garage.'

As I got out, my bunches of lavender in my hand, I said rather stiffly, 'Thank you so much for a very pleasant afternoon.'

'Cheese,' he said, and drove off.

The terrace was empty. They had probably not yet returned from Cannes. 'Vulgar' Cannes, as Nick had called it - yet he enjoyed the Carnival at Nice which Magda, apparently, in her turn, thought vulgar.

When I reached my room I felt exhausted. I wondered why. I hadn't really spent a very active day. I lay down and fell asleep, waking just in time to bath and change for dinner.

'We had tea at the Negresco on the way home,' Magda said. I avoided looking at Nick. Neither of us mentioned our tea in Place Masséna.

That evening, I was seated between Udo and Mr Cressingham, neither of whom was a sparkling conversationalist. Udo smiled frequently but said little. His profile was wonderful, but he was rather stiff. I could not help remembering Nick's unkind remark - 'I can't think of any animal that's so wooden'.

It was almost a relief to turn to Mr Cressingham. I asked him about Cannes, made comments on the Roquebrune procession - I was determined, that evening, not to be caught 'observing' with my 'large grey eyes'. *Large grey eyes . . . remarkably soft hair.* I glanced at Nick - his glass was at his lips as usual. Mr Cressingham was talking about fishing. (How had we got on to that?) He was really quite a pleasant man, I thought, under that 'British reserve' which my father had been accustomed to deride. My father hadn't cared much for the English, perhaps because of his Irish blood. I wondered what he had thought of Nick, who had found *him* so charming.

I had slept so deeply before dinner that when I went up to my room I wasn't at all tired. It was stiflingly hot, even out on my balcony. The leaves of the fruit trees were absolutely still: not a quiver, not a rustle. I imagined how it would be to drive down into Nice, with the movement of the car setting up a coolness, and a necklace of lights circling the Baie des Anges. I tried to envisage a companion. The handsome Udo? Perhaps, on his own, he might be more relaxed, but I was doubtful.

I went inside and tried to read, but I couldn't concentrate. I felt extraordinarily restless, and wondered why. Perhaps it was the heat. After about half an hour, I went out on to the balcony again. Between the silent trees, the swimming pool glinted coolly - the only coolness in that airless night.

Why shouldn't I slip down for a swim? No one would see me. The Forrests and their guests would still be on the terrace. Karl would still be lying at Magda's feet.

Anyway, I thought, I'd chance it. I thought of sliding into the water, floating, looking up at the stars. It was irresistible.

I put on my awful swimsuit. Over it I wore one of my cotton dresses. I didn't meet anyone on the way. In the passage behind the stairs, Nick's door was closed. I opened the door into the courtyard.

Two rectangles of light on the flagstones indicated that Nick was in his room. He was probably working. Perhaps his play was going well that night - I hoped so. I wouldn't disturb him. I walked on tiptoe, but, as I passed the window, I glanced in.

He had taken off his dinner jacket, but otherwise was fully clothed. Lady Sarah, on the other hand, was completely naked - her clothes discarded in a heap on the ground. He lay on his back, on the divan, eyes closed. She was twined all around him like a restless vine, nuzzling him, stroking him, pressing avid little kisses on his neck.

PART TWO

{6}

The wind came up in the middle of the night. It did not wake me – for I was not asleep.

It came first as a shiver, rippling through the leaves, making them rustle as though they were tissue paper. Silence fell. Then, not a shiver but a shudder shook the trees. Under the tumult of the leaves, I heard the branches groan. In the stillness that followed, a lemon fell, with a thud, to the flagstones.

Now it was as if the wind – which twice had shaken the bars of its cage – were set free. It moaned, it sighed, it battered. Somewhere in the house, a shutter banged.

My first sense was of a vague relief. I had been so hot, tossing and turning in my bed. I felt that the wind would bring coolness, might hold a promise of rain. I swung my feet over, on to the floor, and sat on the edge of my bed for a moment, feeling dazed. I had a headache: not a solid substantial pain, but one that flickered like lightning behind my eyes.

The shutter banged again, and a dog barked. I stood up, went over to the window. The window and the shutters rattled, but they were firmly hooked to the wall. I stepped on to the balcony – shrank back, as a hot blast struck me in the face, caught at my hair, my nightdress. I fought my way out, clung to the balustrade. The courtyard was a whirl of leaves and dust. The dust rose, and stuck to my hot cheeks. It dried my lips – I licked them, and felt the gritty film of it on my tongue.

This was no harbinger of rain, emissary of coolness. This was the Sirocco, hostile visitor from Africa, with its implacable *souffle de feu*: its breath of fire.

I turned and – the wind behind me now – was almost pushed back into my room. I unhooked one side of the window and, using all my strength, managed to force it shut, and to push down the bolt that fastened it to the floor. It was easier to close the other side, and twist the catch. Now the noise of the tormented trees diminished, but the wind blasted against the glass. I wished I had thought of closing the outer shutters, but I was not prepared to wrestle with the windows again in order to repair my error.

I sat down on my bed, switched on the bedside light. The glow which came from its rose-coloured shade made me feel safer, although it seemed to intensify the heat which now, with the windows closed, was almost unbearable. Trickles of perspiration stung my eyes – they already ached from the tears I had shed earlier.

—

My eyes had taken in the picture of Nick and Lady Sarah before my mind did. I even wondered, for an instant, what on earth was happening. Then I turned blindly back the way I had come. Yet, shocked though I was, I took care to be absolutely quiet. Softly I turned the handle of the door into the house. Silently I closed it behind me. I crept along the passage to the hall. There I abandoned caution. I ran to the stairs, and up them. I blundered along the passages.

At last, panting for breath, I was in my room. But I felt stifled there. I went out on to the balcony. Down in the courtyard, the rectangles of light from Nick's window, bright and sharply defined – how *could* he have left the shutters open? – suddenly blurred and wavered as tears filled my eyes.

What I had seen had jarred on me so violently. That long lean body, entwining his – her lips on his neck and her hands all over him. She naked and he clothed. Suddenly I remembered a picture of Manet's, *Le déjeuner sur l'herbe.* Two completely dressed men having a picnic with two girls, one naked, the other in a transparent chemise. My father had thought it funny, but something about it had repelled me: the way it made the women look subservient, like women in a harem. But, of course, there wasn't anything subservient about Lady Sarah, so hard, so cold, so supercilious.

How *could* he - that was what I couldn't understand - after the things he had said about the Cressinghams that very day, comparing them to horses, mocking their sponging habits? And then there was the way he always seemed almost to ignore Lady Sarah. I supposed all that had been a calculated deception? Or was he really indifferent to her? For him, probably, any woman would do; how disgusting!

I stared down at those yellow rectangles which, as my tears dried up, regained their former clear outlines. Why on earth should I care what he did?

I didn't of course - in any personal way, but it had been a shock. After all I had seen real people, not a picture like the Manet. And it was depressing to find the man I worked for more and more despicable every day.

Now my thoughts turned to Magda. I saw her, in one of her white dresses, with her anxious fingers plucking at her necklace. I remembered the radiant smile she had given me that morning and her hand stroking my arm. Poor Rhine maiden - going to a bath scented with the jasmine that her husband loathed.

That was typical of him - not to tell her that he detested her scent. He never showed her any consideration - look at the way he had refused at the last minute to lunch with the Marèchals. Why?

In order to take me to the procession? I really found *that* hard to believe. It was then that I recollected the expression on Magda's face when I told her that he had gone to Monte Carlo. An extraordinary flash of intuition lit my mind. *The beautiful, vanished Elizabeth.*

It was not 'some rich man' who was keeping Elizabeth in 'one of those places'. It was Nick - and Magda knew. Had her discovery of the *affaire* led to Elizabeth's sudden departure, or had Nick simply found it more convenient to establish her elsewhere?

The beautiful, vanished Elizabeth. And now, before my eyes, appeared the face of that extraordinarily lovely girl whom I had glimpsed in the crowd at Roquebrune. I had not noticed the colour of her eyes, but I remembered Magda's words. *Hair as black as ebony . . . lips as red as blood.*

That had been she. Not content with visiting her in the morning at Monte Carlo, he had made an assignation with her at Roquebrune in the afternoon - that was why he had disappeared during the procession. How mad about her he must be to want a second meeting in one day. But he couldn't be, really - for there was Lady Sarah.

At that moment the two yellow rectangles in the courtyard disappeared. Nick had turned out his light - or Lady Sarah had. Again there were tears in my eyes. Why? For poor Magda. I said the words aloud, giving them added weight, added meaning.

'Poor Magda.'

Now, as the Sirocco attacked the window, and I sat on the bed with my tired eyes and fitful headache, I was conscious of dread: a dread that was precisely focused - on seven-thirty the next morning. Next morning? I looked at my watch. The time was twenty after one, so what I meant was today. Anyway, in just over six hours, I must apppear in Nicholas Forrest's study, ready for work.

I stood up, and went over to the wardrobe mirror. Even in the dim light from the rose-shaded bedside lamp, I could see how pale my face was, especially in contrast with my reddened eyes. I must do something about how I looked before I met that cold glance which always seemed to notice so much.

The nightdress I was wearing felt hot and sticky. I found a fresh one - beautifully washed and crisply ironed, as all my clothes were nowadays. Then I went into the bathroom, and drew a tepid bath.

I lay in it for a long time, frequently splashing my face with water - lay in it until the tips of my fingers started to crinkle and, despite the weather, there were goosebumps on my arms. Then I dried myself, put on my clean nightdress and went back to my room. There, after remaking my crumpled bed, I took two aspirin and drank some mineral water, of which, each evening, there was a fresh, cold bottle on my bedside table. I lay down, and willed myself to sleep.

When I awoke, at six, it was to the rattle and soughing of the night before. An unaccustomed light came through the window. I got up, for a moment, to look out. The sun had risen, but its rays were a curious yellowish grey, hazy and yet harsh, filtered through whirling particles of dust. I certainly felt no inclination to open the window, and returned to bed. In spite of my early morning bath and change, I was hot and damp again.

It was precisely at seven that I rose. I washed and dressed. I saw in the mirror that I was still pale, and my eyes were still slightly pinkish. I powdered my face carefully, and used my Tangee natural lipstick. I had never possessed rouge, but I wished I had some now. I debated rubbing a little lipstick into my cheeks, but thought it might stand out, look strange. What I wanted was to look just as usual. Anyway, thank goodness, my headache had gone, I thought as I went downstairs.

Briskly I knocked on Nick's door. There was no answer. I waited, then knocked again. Apart from the wind, battering against the courtyard door, there was silence.

Could he and Lady Sarah possibly be in there still? But I dismissed that idea at once. This was not a household where the conventions would be flouted so flagrantly. He must be out, having his swim. But, in this weather? I knocked once more.

No answer. I put my fingers on the door handle, hesitated, then turned it. The room was empty. Irresistibly my glance was drawn towards the divan. Its cover was smooth, the red cushions propped as usual against the whitewashed wall.

I supposed a maid must do the room each morning, while he was swimming. A voice behind me made me start. It was one of the maids - a girl I hadn't seen before, perhaps a replacement for the one who had left. (I wondered how *her* departure had been explained to Magda.)

'Monsieur is gone - gone away,' she said in English.

'Gone?'

'Yes, away in the big car - about an hour ago. With the chauffeur and the luggage.'

'Oh,' I said, and then, 'thank you.' I closed the door of the study, stood in the passage for a moment, wondering what I should do next. I decided to go to the library, choose a new book, and read until it was time for me to go to Magda's boudoir.

What could be the reason for Nick's sudden departure? Anyway, I had been spared an embarrassing confrontation with him.

In the library I wondered what to read. Not, I decided, a novel. That was what *all young girls* would choose. Something serious and difficult. I scanned the shelves. *An Outline of Philosophy* - how about that? Not what anyone would expect a 'young girl' or 'the secretary' to choose. I took it from the bookcase and opened it, skimmed the pages. Such long paragraphs crammed with abstractions: nothing about people, about love, about life - or what I meant by life. I put it back, moved on, came upon the row of books by my father.

I had them, of course, upstairs, in manuscript, in that tin trunk of his which, since his death, I had not found the courage to open. How I dreaded confronting all the relics of my parents' life. But I knew I must, for a variety of reasons, do so soon. However, this morning - that bad night behind me, the horrible Sirocco beating against the windows - was not the moment, I felt with a sense of guilty relief. I pulled my favourite of the novels from the shelf, sat down with it in a large leather armchair.

It was the last book he had published - how well I remembered all the agonies that had gone into its composition. It had taken him five years to write, in version after version, struggling on, despite the constant pressure from his creditors, the admonishing letters from his agent and publisher, to both of whom he was heavily in debt. I remembered, too, the vows of sobriety and the lapses - the descents into three- or four-day drinking bouts, and the weary crawl up from them. And always the interruptions, the pressing, immediate need to write short stories, more short stories. Good though some of them were, I often felt that I hated his short stories.

But now, once I started reading, I forgot all that. Just as I had hoped, I became completely lost in his world. When I looked at my watch, I saw, with a start of astonishment, that the time was a quarter after ten. I became conscious once more of the Sirocco which I had been deaf to, and I realized that I had even forgotten to have breakfast.

Now, in a few minutes, it would be time for me to go to Magda. After the scene I had witnessed, I felt almost as embarrassed at the prospect of seeing her as I had felt earlier about seeing him. *Poor Magda.*

No one, however, could have looked less 'poor' than Magda did that morning. When I went into her boudoir, she was already sitting at her desk, her pen in her hand, making a list. Her hair was fastened in its imperturbable coil. She was wearing a shirt-dress of natural silk. Karl and she looked up together.

'Good morning, Annabel,' she said. 'You slept well?' She did not wait for an answer. 'This dreadful Sirocco!' she exclaimed. 'But I am sure that the best way to deal with it is to ignore it. We must not allow Nature to become our master.'

It was cooler in this room than elsewhere – an electric fan whirred on the table. But I felt that, even without the fan, Magda would have looked cool in her creamy silk. I could not imagine her dishevelled or perspiring. I could hardly even visualize her as she had been on the previous morning – in her white, ruffled robe with her hair loose.

'So you found my husband "flown" today?' she said. I could tell that 'flown' pleased her. I always found the pride with which she delivered an English idiom rather touching.

I nodded. 'Yes, Mrs Forrest.'

'He only told me this morning that he had decided to go away for a week or so – he will visit my Papa in Germany, I think. Anyway, he said he wished for a change of scene. These writers are such restless people. The artistic temperament – is not that so?'

'Yes,' I said, though I wasn't sure if I agreed or not.

'For me,' Magda said briskly, 'it is in one way – opportune. You and I will be busy, Annabel, for do you know what I am planning?'

'No,' was, of course, all I could reply.

'I am planning a party. For the moment, that shall be a secret between us. Yes?'

'Oh yes, if you want,' I said.

'We shall go through my address book and decide on the guests. And I must consider when to hold it. Perhaps at the end of this month or the very beginning of September. I plan that it shall be a white party. Everyone shall come in white. Do you not agree that will be pretty?'

'Very pretty,' I said, but I could not help thinking that I did not possess a white evening dress. However, probably I would not be expected to be present, and so that would not matter.

'I love white,' she went on. 'That is why I wear it so much. Do you think that I am getting too old to wear white,

Annabel? Really, it is more the colour for a *Mädchen*, I suppose.'

'You look beautiful in it,' I said sincerely, and added, 'just like the Snow Queen.'

She was twisting her jewel. Now she smiled radiantly at me. 'Ah, you flatter me again, little Annabel. The Snow Queen! So you know those charming stories of Hans Andersen. The poor student in the garret, the storks on the roof – ah, they remind me of my dear homeland. We Germans are very fond of fairy tales. I think that, in England, they have no fairy tales. They do not dream as we Germans do. Are there American fairy tales, Annabel?'

I searched my mind. I knew that there were Indian legends, and a maid who had worked for us when I was very small had frightened me with stories of 'spooks'. But no, I couldn't remember any fairy stories except Grimms' and Hans Andersen's. Hans Andersen's had fascinated but somehow chilled me. I shook my head.

I started that morning typing names which she selected from her address book. But we had only reached the letter 'C' when she stood up.

'I must go downstairs now, Annabel. The Graf and Gräfin leave this morning, and I must say my farewells to them. Here are some accounts which came in yesterday. Please check over all the items and the totals.'

'Of course,' I said, although I knew that she would go over them again herself when I had done so. 'Say goodbye to the Graf and Gräfin for me,' I added, thinking it only polite to do so, despite my aversion to them.

She looked surprised. 'What is that?' she said, and then, 'Oh yes. Why, thank you.' Suddenly I felt tediously conscious of 'my position'. Perhaps she thought it pushy, 'not done', for a secretary to send a message to her employers' guests. And yet I had my meals with them. Really such shades of social distinction were beyond my comprehension – too bad, I thought with a touch of irritation. After all, I was an American. In the States, people were more democratic than these Europeans - or so I'd always heard.

Magda was moving towards the door, and suddenly I became conscious of Karl, curled under her desk, asleep. Her hand was turning the white porcelain doorknob, patterned, like the fingerplate, with pink rosebuds, when I exclaimed, 'Mrs Forrest!'

She turned, her eyebrows raised at the urgency of my tone. 'Yes?'

'I'm sorry, but,' I stammered, 'the - the - the dog.'

'The dog?'

'I'm sorry,' I said again, though more calmly. 'Could you . . . take him with you?'

I saw understanding dawn on her face. Then she gave a tiny frown. 'Really, Annabel,' she said, 'this is quite ridiculous. See - the poor little *Hündchen* is sleeping. Should he wake and wish to go out, you have only to open the door. Karl would never harm anyone, unless they were attacking me.' She shrugged with a trace of impatience.

It would have been absurd to apologize again. I did not do so, but the word '*Please*' was wrung from me.

She spoke gently: 'In this life, we must learn to conquer our fears - especially when they are foolish ones, little Annabel. That is how we learn to discipline ourselves, and to be strong. Strength is the noblest of all qualities.'

For a moment, after this lecture - I was so anxious that, at the time, I was quite unable to absorb its message - I thought that she was going to proceed on her way, leaving me with Karl. I do not know what I would have done if she had - possibly, to my eternal shame, rushed after her. But then she shrugged again, more tolerantly.

'Karl,' she said clearly, though hardly raising her voice. At once the dog was awake, alert. It bounded to her. She looked at her watch, frowned, shook her head at me - but smiled. Then, Karl at her heels, she left the room, closing the door behind her with a little click.

Alone – my recent tension relaxed – I gave a sigh which turned into an enormous yawn. I glanced around the room, so pink, so feminine, yawned again. But I must return to my work, must concentrate fully on my simple task – simple tasks can lull one into making careless errors. I did not want to make mistakes for Magda – she was so efficient, so well organized.

Now I thought over what she had said to me: *Strength is the noblest of all qualities.* Was that true? I wanted to be brave in life, but I'd never thought of being 'noble'. The word only summoned up history for me: the Field of the Cloth of Gold, King Arthur and his Knights of the Round Table.

Well, I certainly hadn't been brave this morning – about that awful Karl. *Strength is the noblest of all qualities.* I could see why Magda would admire it so much. It was an attribute, I reflected, that she must need constantly, married, as she was, to a man like Nicholas Forrest. I picked up the little pile of accounts she had given me and started to check through them.

At luncheon that day, a leaf had been removed from the table by the window, for now we were only five. Magda had Paul Cressingham on her right, and Udo on her left. Lady Sarah was next to Udo, and I to Mr Cressingham.

In two days' time, it suddenly appeared, we would be only three. It was towards the end of the meal that Lady Sarah made her announcement. 'Paul and I have been thinking that we really ought to make a move. You must be getting tired of us – we've been here for such ages.'

'No indeed, my dear Sarah,' Magda put in. 'I am glad for you to stay as long as you wish. And so is Nicholas of course. It is a shame that he has been called away so suddenly, but he would be sad not to find you here on his return.'

'Sweet of you, Magda,' Lady Sarah said. As she was seated directly opposite me, I could hardly help 'observing' her, noticing how, as she spoke, her heavy lids were lowered over her protuberant eyes. How blasé her drawl was, making the word 'sweet' sound faintly mocking as it emerged from her pouting lips. A sudden vision of her, as I had seen her the night before, made me look away.

'But you see,' she went on, 'just this morning we had an invitation from the Macdonalds – you know, the whisky ones – to go for a cruise on their yacht. They leave from Monte in two days – for the Greek islands, which does sound rather divine. Of course, old Hector's a bit of a rough diamond, and *she* never speaks, but they've asked some quite amusing people.'

'We shall miss you, Sarah,' said Magda. If she had known what I knew, I thought, she could never have managed to sound so sincere. 'But certainly the Greek islands sound most interesting: all those archaeological excavations.'

'Mmm,' Lady Sarah said – I couldn't imagine her being interested in archaeology – 'and this dreadful old Sirocco is rather depressing.'

'Though that seldom continues for more than two or three days,' Magda said, and the weather became the general topic of conversation – always a dull one, I thought, and, as usual, I welcomed the moment when Magda rose from her chair.

But upstairs in my room, that afternoon, a sense of acute claustrophobia assailed me. I did not feel like reading. I had no work to do. *You could open the trunk*, a voice in my head told me. That was when I decided to brave the Sirocco and go for a walk. I tied a scarf over my head, and set out at once.

I took the only route I knew – the one I had taken with Nick on my first afternoon. At least I knew there were no houses on it from which snarling dogs might emerge. In the olive grove, the trees gave some protection from the wind. I lingered there, trying to sort out my feelings about my new life.

I had never imagined that I would live in such luxurious

circumstances – surely I could have no complaints on *that* score? Perhaps the furnishings of the villa were rather oppressively ornate, and the meals, of course, lasted far too long. But I mustn't be so 'picky' – I must remind myself of that poky room in London, the tasteless boarding-house food which most of the residents doused with bottled sauce, the stale smell of the dining-room, the grumpy waitress, the table-napkins in their wooden rings, stained and dingy like the tablecloths because they, also, were only changed once a week. When I found the Villa Aurore too rich, too opulent, I must think of *that*.

I was sure that I could cope with the job itself well enough. Now, the preparations for this party of Magda's would probably keep me busy, but so far my work had been much lighter than I had anticipated. Perhaps Nick, on his return, would bring some more of his play. *On his return* – at the prospect, my mind twitched as a tooth does when one eats something icy cold.

So much for the surroundings, for the job itself. Now I thought about the people amongst whom I found myself. The Graf and Gräfin had left, the Cressinghams would soon follow them; of Udo I had formed no opinion. Magda was kind – I hoped she didn't despise me after the episode with Karl that morning – and Nick was . . . abominable.

I emerged from the olive grove into the rough open country beyond which lay the mountains. The hot, dusty wind hurled itself at me. Through the dust, I could hardly discern Roquebrune, perched above me on its spur. Cobbled streets, scents of sorrel, of the lavender I had put with my handkerchiefs, of jasmine; a beautiful face glimpsed, then lost in the crowd. *Hair as black as ebony . . . lips as red as blood.* If he had *her*, why should he want Lady Sarah or – my mind faltered – that wretched peasant girl?

Lady Sarah – from what she had said at luncheon, it sounded as if Nick had been uncannily accurate about the Cressinghams finding a *nouveau riche* refuge. Perhaps she'd really made her plans earlier, and had told him. I wondered whether Paul Cressingham guessed at their *affaire* and, if he did, whether it upset him. And Magda? At luncheon I had assumed her ignorance, but perhaps she had just been putting on a show.

Suddenly I regretted my parents' world; *they* had always expressed their feelings. And yet, in the long run, that hadn't helped them.

If Magda did know, she was probably secretly glad of the Cressinghams' departure. I wondered whether other visitors would be replacing them at the villa. But it was one of my tasks to record, in her vellum-bound engagement book, the invitations she gave and received, and I had seen no mention of any new house-guests.

Now, ahead, I noted the outcrop of rock which I had climbed with Nick. I turned abruptly - the wind and dust were really unendurable. I would go back. And besides, I thought, how stupid I was being, stewing over all this stuff about the inhabitants of the villa, sniffing at it, stirring it around like some old witch with her cauldron. *Eye of newt and toe of frog . . . Make the gruel thick and slab.* After all, I was an employee, not a member of the household. In a way it was a pity that the Forrests had decided I should eat with them. It would have been better and much less tedious if I had taken my meals alone, like a Victorian governess: an austere, solitary figure, exactly distanced between the family and the domestic staff.

Well, it was too late for that now. But I must detach myself, must pay less attention to the Forrests' life. I must *be my own person.* And I mustn't idle away the free time which this (excellent) job afforded me: time which I could use as I chose.

As I chose. For me, that was the heart of the matter. I was burdened by a weight of guilt, and I knew exactly what was causing it. I knew that the time had come for me to open my father's trunk and go through its contents.

Until now, I had always had the excuse that I was too busy. In London, after a day at the cold but stuffy business college, I had been so tired that I would go to bed and fall asleep immediately after my meagre supper – and I had felt that my long weekend walks were essential for my health, to exercise my body and, still more, to relax my mind. For I was still dazed after my father's death: not only by grief but by horror. The terrors and hallucinations of *delirium tremens* are not pleasant to witness.

A short settling-in period at the villa had been permissible too, but now I could postpone no longer the opening of the trunk. If I did so, I would be as bad as the Cressinghams, hanging around in one house till they received an invitation from someone else. Worse – for 'staying with friends' was apparently their livelihood. I would not have cared for it myself but, if they could find willing hosts, why should I criticize them? I had no grounds for self-righteousness.

But why should an old tin trunk – my father's name and his dead parents' Philadelphia address, in black paint, still partly visible between old torn labels recording his journeyings – hold such terrors for me? It was irrational. Particularly as I had two good practical reasons for 'tackling the trunk' as I put it to myself.

I must sort through my father's manuscripts, check that they were all complete and had all been returned to him by his publisher. For I was well aware that the time might soon arrive when my mother's treatment could necessitate my selling them. Contrary to what I had told Nick, royalties from my father's books were almost non-existent. I had my salary, my 'little hoard' – and the manuscripts. There was an old friend of my father's in New York – a well-known critic – who I was sure would advise me about them.

My second reason was my conviction that, sooner or later, my father's literary reputation would be firmly and permanently re-established. There had been hints of it in some of the more perceptive of his obituaries, although the majority had shallowly epitomized him as the 'nostalgic chronicler of the Gay Twenties'. And hadn't Nick who, whatever his character, was not a fool, referred to my father as 'one of the finest novelists of our time'? Anyway, when his true worth came to be recognized, there were sure to be applicants for the role of biographer. When that happened, I would want everything in good order: the cuttings, the letters, the photographs. Besides, I would allow no one, however well qualified, well-intentioned, to delve into aspects of my parents' lives which were unknown to me.

So I must make my own personal expedition into the past. I must myself try to make sense of, come to terms with whatever I discovered on that journey. That, of course, was what I really dreaded about 'tackling the trunk'.

{7}

Dramatic and startling – I suppose many people would consider the events that occurred at the end of the next ten days in such a light. But, from my point of view, that was far from being the case. For me, that whole span of time was rich in incident, permeated with emotion.

It was on Saturday that I made my resolution and put it into action. Sunday was a day when I had no secretarial tasks to perform. But from Monday, when the Cressinghams left – and, incidentally, the Sirocco ended – I had an amount of time to myself which I had not anticipated. There were small routine tasks for Magda, but these never took longer than an hour or so. She said absolutely nothing more on the subject of the white party: I decided that she must have abandoned the idea. After the Cressinghams' departure, she and Udo were hardly ever at the villa.

Often she was gone, leaving me my brief instructions, only a few minutes after I reached her boudoir – off with Udo in his Mercedes. I had no idea of the objects of their expeditions: I supposed that they visited friends. Often they took Karl with them; otherwise the dog was left with Emil – never, thank heaven, with me.

Magda held two dinner parties at the villa – neither of which I had to attend. One, for the German ambassador, who was on a visit to the South, from Paris, involved her in tremendous discussions with Emil, but made no work for me, except the preparation of a particularly thoroughly deliberated seating-plan – how Magda brooded on the arrangement of sixteen people! – and the copying out of a particularly lengthy, complicated and lavish menu. The other dinner was a smaller affair – for only twelve. I knew nothing of the guests at either, except that the Marèchals attended the first one – Monsieur Marèchal, I had gathered at that luncheon when he and the Graf had talked so much together, and he had been so appreciative of the Graf's disgusting remark, was engaged in many business transactions with Germany.

During that period of Nick's absence, I should think that, in all, I had three meals with Magda and Udo – they tended to break into rapid chatter in German, but would usually recall my ignorance of the language and apologize pleasantly. For the rest of the time, I was on my own.

On that first Saturday afternoon, when I had removed the chintz cover from the trunk, had unfastened its metal hasps, and pulled back its lid, it was with dismay that I gazed at the chaos within. I felt a wild impulse to slam the lid down, and replace the cover, but it was an impulse which I managed to resist.

I had not imagined that anyone, even my father, would have kept their most cherished – their only – personal mementoes in such disorder. The smell of old paper – musty, sweetish, reminiscent of attics, curiously depressing – was overpowering. The trunk was packed with paper of all kinds, not stacked or bundled, but seemingly scattered at random, occasionally stirred, forcefully pressed down – for the level seemed to have risen considerably since I had lifted the lid. A theatre programme fluttered on to the carpet. I picked it up – *The Ziegfeld Follies*, 1921.

I had thought that the most recent material would be at the top, but obviously such was not the case. My father, searching for something, had most likely pulled the entire contents on to the floor, then shovelled it back again. I hoped that the manuscripts, at least, were in some kind of order, perhaps stacked at the bottom.

I decided to start sorting the papers into piles: photographs in one, cuttings in another, all the letters together. A fourth pile I headed, in my mind, 'Miscellaneous' - evidently I was learning the art of organization from Magda. In this I would put anything that didn't belong elsewhere - that theatre programme, for instance, and here was the cover of my father's first (and worst) novel, *No Dawn, No Dusk*, the book which had enabled him, like Byron, to 'wake up one morning and find himself famous'. How dated the illustration looked: a girl wearing a bandeau, doing the Charleston with a young man in tails, a new moon overhead.

I picked up a photograph, 'New York, 1919' pencilled below it. It had been taken soon after my parents' marriage, I imagined - they had married that year, on the proceeds of *No Dawn, No Dusk* - he in a dark overcoat with velvet facings, she in a short fur coat with huge shiny buttons and a belt. No neck showed above her fur's high shawl collar; no forehead was visible beneath her pulled-down hat with its scalloped trim - yet her face, edged by fair curls, looked lovely. Both of them, in fact, had an almost scrubbed, shining beauty, something dangerously flawless about it - a challenge to jealous gods? I hadn't realized that either of them had been quite so blond.

Now I saw, lying directly under where the first one had been, another photograph. As I held this one in my hand, I felt as if it had been planted in that exact spot by some cruel moralist.

'Antibes, 1931' - there were the three of us on the *plage*: Delaney, Vanna and eleven-year-old Annabel. How plain I looked, squinting into the sun, with my pudding-bowl haircut. All our swimsuits were identically camisole-topped, although my mother's had a belt and a brief skirt. Hers was black, mine was white, my father's was horizontally striped.

Holding the two photographs, side by side, I noticed how, in the second, the hair of both my parents had darkened to an indeterminate brown - this was the colour I remembered. His was very short, almost *en brosse* - too short, for it drew too much attention to his face: its pouched and shadowed eyes, the vertical line between his brows, the puckers around his mouth, and the soft fold under his chin. And my mother's ear-length bob, swept back in a wave from a right-hand parting, gave her a strangely masculine appearance. Her face seemed to have almost doubled in width since the previous picture, and it had an uneven look, as if its two sides did not belong together - her narrowed, desperate eyes could not have 'belonged' anywhere at all.

Oh yes, I could recognize my parents very well in the second picture, but hardly find a trace of them, as I had known them, in the first: there, they seemed like mythical creatures.

I shook my head, put the two photographs, face down, on the floor. If I were to study every item in the trunk in such detail, allow each to start me on such a train of melancholy thought, *alles* would never be *in ordnung.* I summoned Magda's efficient spirit. First I would classify, in the way I had planned. Only after that would I allow myself to contemplate at greater leisure.

It was on Sunday evening that I completed the first part of my task. All the cuttings were in order, the miscellaneous items together, the photographs arranged chronologically, the letters in a tall pile. And my father had, after all, preserved what was most important: the manuscripts were all at the bottom of the trunk, each fastened with string. The four novels were there, and the two published collections of stories - evidently he had not thought his 'potboilers' worth keeping. But there were also two further manuscripts which I had not expected to find.

One was his. I had never imagined that, in his last two years, he had written so much of a fifth novel. Oh he had *said* that, in between short stories, he was working on another book, but by then I had grown cynical: I had not really believed him. I had thought that perhaps he might have scribbled some notes, sketched the outlines of one or two projected characters, even made the chart on which he always plotted the action of a novel. But here were more than three hundred pages, closely written and scored over with innumerable corrections. I blamed myself for my lack of faith.

The other manuscript was even more unexpected: it was a completed novel of my mother's - completed I knew because, on the last page, in her thin spiky handwriting, she had carefully printed the words: 'The End'.

I had been aware that, while my father was writing his fourth novel, she had spent almost a year, writing furiously, at a table in her bedroom - if ever I went in there, when she was so engaged, she would look up with an angry expression, asking, 'And what do *you* want?' But this attempt at rivalry had ended as abruptly as it had begun, had shortly been followed, in 1935, by her second breakdown - far graver than the previous one in 1930. Although, when I looked at that 'Antibes, 1931' photograph, what had happened to her face made me feel the first collapse had been serious enough. After the 1935 breakdown, she had spent nearly a year in the Zurich clinic, returning home 'recovered' in the Spring of 1936. But then only four months passed before that third journey to Switzerland from which she had never returned.

I felt embarrassed at the idea of reading my mother's novel. I was quite sure that it would be appalling. I would read my father's first, I decided, and then have a look at hers, which, no doubt, would be sheer nonsense, a product of her developing madness, and totally unreadable. Then, both books behind me, I would read all those letters: from friends, from my father's agent, from his publisher. Now that I had started on the work which I had been so dreading, my fears had evaporated. I had become engrossed, and was eager to proceed.

A week had passed. It was the following Sunday - and, after

dinner, I had taken my little chintz armchair out on to the balcony. I wanted to be quiet. I wanted to think.

I had eaten one of my rare meals with Magda and Udo. That evening they had spoken in German more than usual – to my relief, as I was in an almost trance-like state of abstraction. It was not fatigue, although I did feel tired. It was the result of the shattering emotional impact of what I had discovered during the past week.

That afternoon, I had replaced the contents of the trunk. All was in perfect order. I had closed the lid, fastened the metal hasps, even put on the chintz cover. There was no visible evidence that anything at all had happened. But now, what was in the trunk was also in my mind – and it was certainly not neatly stacked and bundled there. Sitting on the balcony in my armchair, I tried to feel calm, to absorb some of the peace of the dark trees in the quiet courtyard. But it was no use. Three things possessed me: they were two books and a letter.

Reading my father's fifth novel, his last manuscript, had been a joy to me – a compulsive one. Each page pulled me on – I resented the interruptions of meals, and even of my minimal tasks for Magda, which seemed pointless and trivial in comparison to what awaited me in my room.

The book was set in Philadelphia – where he had grown up – at the beginning of the century. I couldn't help wondering if it were about his dead parents, of whom he had hardly ever spoken – I had always had the impression that he rejected them.

It was the story of a man who failed at everything he undertook, and of his wife who took refuge in delusions of grandeur, in an obsession with her family's past prominence, until she became as much an object of mockery as her husband. Their son, sensitive and isolated, suffered, yet the author did not give him all his sympathy. His compassion encompassed them all: the boy, the shabby tippling father, the woman whose feathered hats and trailing skirts were as ludicrous as her pretensions. In a sense, the story was told from a god's view - but not a cruel god's: this was a god of understanding and mercy.

The man became ill; the mother retreated ever farther into fantasy; the son, in his teens, was desperate to escape, but trapped by ignorance and pity. There the story broke off, yet, though the book was unfinished, I found it more moving than any recent novel I could think of. In addition to his new understanding, my father had retained all his old ability to evoke the detail of life: sleigh rides on frosty winter nights, summer evenings on shady porches, a child lying awake anticipating a magical birthday which would turn out to be a bitter disappointment.

Surely someone would want to publish this extraordinary piece of work - should I write, I wondered, to my father's old friend, the critic, or to his agent? I decided to put off that decision until I had completed my work on the trunk.

All the same, it had been with a sigh, a self-consciously rueful shake of the head, that I took up my mother's manuscript. Before beginning it, I reflected that this was a task I felt no enthusiasm for. It was with very different feelings that I finished it.

I realized that I had never known her. How stupid I had been. I had always thought her so hard and so remorseless. Oh, I had made excuses for her, on the grounds of her illness, but now I saw that my sympathy - and that was probably too strong a word - had all been on the surface. My true sympathy had always lain with my father, however much I deplored his drinking, and detested the unreliability, the impossible behaviour it had frequently been responsible for. My mother's illness I had seen, essentially, as *his* burden - not hers: as something that had made *him* unhappy, driving him deeper into alcoholism, intensifying his financial anxieties. This picture had been confirmed for me by his fourth novel, which had described – in circumstances different, though not *so* different, from those of my parents – a man whose wife drags him down and drains him dry. How often, in my mind, I had thought: *Why doesn't she pull herself together?* How often, in my heart, I had felt her to be a vampire, drinking his blood.

Reading her novel – the most thinly disguised of autobiographies – I saw the other side of the picture: a girl from a sheltered Southern background, falling suddenly in love, flung into the whirlwind of New York life with a successful New York actor (for my mother had made my father an actor in a pathetic attempt at camouflage). This girl never feels she is a person in her own right. She tries to lean on her husband, but he can give her no stability, drinks more and more heavily – is otherwise only concerned with his work. The couple live more and more extravagantly. As a result, he has to act in cheap, flashy plays which are not worthy of him. She feels responsible – that she ought to be able to manage the household, the family budget, and to cure her husband of his drinking. But she cannot: she has no centre; she is a glass which will crack when a certain note is struck. Overcome with guilt, she becomes incurably mad, is permanently committed to an asylum.

The ending of the book, of course, had been the one part of it which had not been 'true to life'. For twice, in reality, my mother had been restored to a state in which she had been able to come home from the clinic. It had been during the first of these periods – lasting nearly five years – that she had written her book.

I cried while reading it. I cried – for a long time – when I had finished it. There was no one to whom I could turn for comfort, but perhaps, I thought, it was right that I should have to face my grief on my own. *She* was the only person I really wanted to see. I longed to go to her, to embrace her, to tell her that I understood. But it was no use thinking of that.

When I had visited her after my father's death, before I went to London, she had not recognized me, had screamed for a nurse to 'take that awful girl away'.

Apart from her book's emotional effect on me, there had been something else: I had found it good. Though her spelling was appalling and her punctuation almost non-existent, my mother's style was delicate and fresh. I had lived her heroine's experiences, even to the point of accompanying her on her journey into madness.

My mother, of course, did not possess my father's magic powers. Where he was Prospero, a great enchanter, she was an elf, an Ariel. But surely an Ariel's book was worthy of some attention? I wondered if my father had read it and, if so, what he had thought of it. He had never mentioned it to me. Probably, I decided, having written it, having expressed all that she had felt, my mother had simply stuffed it away in the bottom of the trunk - though that didn't seem quite in character. But, leaving that aspect aside, I would have expected that writing the book would have helped her. However, only a few months later, she had been back in the clinic.

It was with a real sense of anticlimax, of responding to the 'call of duty', that, after finishing those books, I had approached the pile of letters. And very dull, to me, many of them were: discussions of terms and contracts, responses - almost always eventually favourable - to the requests for loans with which my father deluged his agent and his publisher. Others were more interesting - letters from old friends, reminiscing about past times or commenting on my father's work.

There were only about twenty letters left for me to read when, opening a torn envelope printed with the name and address of my father's publisher, and expecting yet another financial rigmarole, I came upon the following:

Friday, 13 May 1935

My dear Delaney,

I was most distressed to hear from you how upset you are about Vanna's novel. When I wrote to you about it, I had no idea that you were not aware that she had sent it to me. As you know, I found it attractive and touching. While I never conceived of it as a great commercial success, I thought that enough people might appreciate its special charm and sincerity to make it worth publishing - after I had given an editor a free hand with the spelling, punctuation, occasional grammatical errors, etc!

However, when you now tell me that, as you put it, you feel that she has 'cannibalized' the material that you are using in your own book, and that you cannot endure that this 'amateur effort' should see the light of day, and 'sneak' into publication, 'clinging to the coat-tail' of your reputation (not quite fair - for if I had published the book, it would have been on its own merits), I see that I shall have to reconsider. I need not tell you that you are one of the 'stars' of our not undistinguished list, and that I would not want anything to interfere with your 'work in progress'. Accordingly, I am writing to Vanna to tell her that I do not feel the book is suitable for publication. I shall not suggest - as I imagine that you would not be pleased if I did so - that she should send it elsewhere.

I trust that this misunderstanding is completely sorted out.

My best regards,
Hal

Now, sitting on the balcony, I went over that letter in my head, as I had been doing ever since I first read it. It still had its original power to shock me. How could my father have done such a thing? Surely he must have learned, from her first breakdown, from her book itself - it was evident, from his publisher's letter, that he had read the book - how feeble my mother's hold on reality was? Surely he must have recognized what she was trying to achieve by sending her manuscript to a publisher - some solid link between herself and the world?

He must have known those things - he who was so perceptive. But it had made no difference, and he had acted ruthlessly. It had been only a few weeks after his manoeuvre, in June 1935, that my mother, after managing to cling to sanity for five years, had been obliged to return to Zurich. Now I could guess what had precipitated that: the rejection of her manuscript. And now my thoughts travelled farther.

It had been in October of that same year that my father had sent his own book, completed at last, to the States. What had my mother thought of *his* book? Why had I never wondered about *that* before? For, in it, he had 'cannibalized' her far more devastatingly - as *the destroyer* - than she had him.

When had she seen his novel? He had never showed anyone his manuscripts - and in Zurich, anyway, she would have been in no state to read. She had returned home in April 1936. His book had been published in August. That was the month in which she had made her final journey to the clinic.

A sort of shudder convulsed my mind at this appalling discovery. I had reached the 'solution', the last stage of my journey of detection. *My father had arranged for the rejection of my mother's manuscript. That had forced her back to the clinic. She had come home, read his book, returned to Zurich, where she still remained.*

There she suffered now - mentally always, and recently from a physical complaint: an intensely irritating skin disease. Dr Zeiss had written to me that they had attempted to relieve it by wrapping her in soaked bandages, but this had been unsuccessful, and painkillers brought her little relief. Hence a new treatment - a course of costly injections.

Each week, as soon as I received them, I sent my wages to the clinic, keeping a minimal sum for personal expenses which were few - stockings were my bane; I felt I could not wear obviously darned ones at the villa. But I would have to find more money, if the expensive injections continued to be necessary.

Sighing, I stood up, pushing back my armchair, resting my hands on the baluster. Since I had come to sit on the balcony, a large strange-coloured moon had risen above the trees - as if, I thought, someone had picked an orange from one of them, and flung it into the sky, where it had swollen to this great, shimmering golden ball.

It was at that moment that I heard the sound.

It was a scraping, which was swiftly succeeded by a hammering. There was a pause, and then the scraping started again.

It was coming from downstairs, from somewhere on the right of the house. It was with a shock that, looking down, I saw that the light in Nick's room was on. But he was not expected until Monday evening - tomorrow - as Magda had announced at dinner, saying that she had received a telephone call from him just before the meal.

What could be happening? Could one of the servants be engaged in some domestic task? I looked at my watch. No. Surely not at a quarter of eleven on a Sunday evening, in this well-regulated house?

The hammering started again: loud, persistent. Had someone broken into the villa? Surely not with Karl about? But perhaps Magda and Udo had gone out after dinner, taking Karl with them, or they and the dog might be on the terrace - possibly the sound wasn't audible there.

There was silence again. When it had lasted for about half a minute, I thought that I ought probably to forget the whole thing. But no, there was the scratchy scraping again.

How awful it would be if someone were rifling my employer's study - and I heard it, did nothing, went to bed. Perhaps someone was stealing his manuscripts, but that was a ridiculous idea - I must have manuscripts on the brain after my recent experiences! However, wasn't it my duty to investigate? And didn't I feel suddenly, despite my nervousness at the prospect, a little twitch of relief at the thought of escaping from the closed world of my own problems, from the room where I had been confronting them so obsessively?

The hammering was back: little sharp blows with a metallic echo. What I would do, I decided, was go downstairs - Karl *couldn't* be on the loose, would have been bound to be roused to barking by that hammering - and see if Magda were at the front of the house. If so, and if the sound were inaudible there, then I'd tell her about it. Yes, that was the answer.

I went into the passage, switched on the light - ever since I had arrived at the villa I had been the only person occupying this corridor. But the lights on the landing were on, and so were those on the stairs and down in the hall. All was silent - perhaps one could hear the scraping only from the courtyard side? But that hammering? I crossed the hall. The front door was closed. I opened it a crack, but the terrace was unlit, so I shut it again.

As I returned across the hall, the scraping was renewed, and it actually sounded louder here. I had no idea what to do. Magda and Udo must have gone out. With Karl? Or perhaps, at night, Karl stayed in the back yard where the garages and servants' quarters were.

That was another thing. Surely *all* the servants couldn't have gone to bed? They certainly wouldn't have done so if Magda and Udo were out; someone - Emil probably - would have waited to be on call, at their return. The kitchens - into which I'd never penetrated - lay beyond a green baize door at the end of the passage where Nick's room was. But say I opened that door - and Karl bounded out?

Wasn't that a worse prospect than braving Nick's room? Evidently it was, for it was the second course that I decided on.

Under the staircase was a small cloakroom where raincoats hung on hooks, and walking-sticks and umbrellas stood in a great Japanese porcelain jar. I slipped in there, and chose a substantial ash stick – I didn't intend to face a possible burglar with no means of defence at all. Though if there were a burglar, I'd immediately run – calling out loudly – for the green baize door.

The stick – its handle clutched firmly in my hand – gave me courage, which was just as well, for, when I stood in the passage outside Nick's door, the hammering started up in the room – very loudly indeed. Now or never! Shifting the stick to my left hand, I seized the door handle, twisted it, flung the door open – and gazed in astonishment at what I saw.

Udo, with a hammer, was attacking the lock of the filing cabinet between the windows. Magda stood beside him, her right hand holding a chisel, her left – as always – fingering her crystal apple. At that moment, two things happened – the top drawer of the cabinet slid open with a crash, just missing Udo, who leaped aside, and Magda's silver chain snapped: the apple rolled across the floor and landed at my feet. Automatically, amazed though I was, I stooped and picked it up. A deep growling made me straighten abruptly, and take a step back. Karl, over by the divan, was standing facing me, teeth bared. The growling became louder. I felt that the dog was about to spring.

'Down, Karl,' Magda called sharply. Reluctantly, or so I felt, the dog subsided, its growl dying away.

Udo had spun around, was looking at me with an expression of astonishment on his face. Suddenly I felt extraordinarily silly. I glanced at Magda. There was a frown on her forehead, and her lips had tightened. She extended her hand, palm cupped, towards me. For a moment I was puzzled, until I realized that she was waiting for me to return her apple. I went over, and gave it to her; her hand closed on it.

I looked up, met the considering gaze of her blue eyes: crystalline, I thought suddenly, as her apple, and, at the moment, as frosty as its diamond leaves. She gave me a long, assessing stare.

'Well, Annabel?' she said at last.

'I-I-I'm sorry, Mrs Forrest.' I was stammering. My heart was thudding - Karl was responsible for that. 'I heard the noise, from my room, and - and I thought it might be a burglar. I looked for you,' I added, 'but I couldn't find you.'

'I see.' Her glance encompassed the stick still clutched in my hand. Again I felt ridiculous. An absurd memory of having played a shepherd in a Nativity play when I was five - I had held a crook - flashed across my mind. 'And you armed yourself I see,' she said.

Suddenly she was smiling. 'Foolish little Annabel,' she said, and shook her head. 'You were brave - was she not, Udo?' she asked, turning to him. My glance followed hers. His face had lost its startled look, was quite blank, but, as she spoke, his normal, rather stiff smile appeared on it. He murmured, 'Yes. Yes, most brave.'

Magda turned back to me. 'But you were very, very foolish.' She shook her head again. 'Did you think that you could have defended yourself against a criminal with that stick?'

'I would have called for the servants.'

'*Afterwards*?' she queried gently. 'That is what you should have done in the first place, silly girl. Though, as it turns out, we can feel relieved to have avoided all the disturbance *that* would have caused.'

I agreed - but surely she must see that I had had to do something? Now, for the first time since I had burst into the room, I wondered what she and Udo were doing there. Why had they been breaking open the cabinet, late at night?

Magda gave a little laugh. 'How surprised you must have been to find us here – but better than those robbers, *hein*?'

I nodded, smiled uncertainly.

'I had a telephone call,' Magda said. 'There are some business papers, which are kept in here, which I had to look up urgently. It was not possible, on a Sunday night, to get a locksmith to open the cabinet – I shall, of course, send for one tomorrow, to repair it.' She laughed again. 'I do not know why I bother you with all these details, but, after being so brave, you deserve some explanation. Brave little Annabel – like the little boy who marches into the dark forest to catch the big bad wolf!'

I felt more foolish than ever. 'Yes, it was silly of me, I suppose. I should have realized . . .' Though I didn't know quite what I should have realized, I reflected.

'Yes,' she said. 'Well, there is no harm done. Except that I must have my necklace mended. Off you go now, to your bed. And sleep well. Do not dream of burglars and big bad wolves.'

I smiled. 'No,' I said. 'I won't. I'm sorry about your necklace – and about disturbing you.'

'Oh, it is nothing. I have other silver chains. And my nerves are very strong.' Smiling, she gave me a nod of dismissal. I turned to go, but she called me back.

'Oh, Annabel.'

I turned. 'Yes, Mrs Forrest?'

'There will be no need for you to mention this to my husband – I am sure you would not want him to see you in such a foolish light. I will not tell him about you and your big stick when I explain to him about the papers tomorrow night. It was a pity I could not wait for his return with the key, but the matter was so urgent. Anyway, you need not worry.'

'Oh,' I said. 'Oh, thank you.'

'Very well. So you will not feel you have to confess to him?' She paused.

'No,' I said.

'Very well. Good night then, little Annabel.'

'Good night, Fraulein,' said Udo.

'Good night.'

8

I did not dream of burglars or of big bad wolves, but other nightmares reared in my sleep that night. My father and mother were playing a game of tennis. Or, rather, he was playing it, serving ball after ball at her. She had to duck from side to side, to prevent herself being hit, and eventually she curled up small, on the court, with her head between her knees. Now Magda Forrest, in a long white dress, was walking down an endless avenue of lime trees. 'It reminds me of *Unter den Linden*,' she said to me, smiling. But suddenly she stamped her foot. 'The trees must be pollarded,' she said. 'Where is the pollarder?'

I could see him. He was coming along behind us, down the avenue, dodging between the trees. He wore a black cloak, with a hood, and carried an axe. I tried to point him out to her, but she would not listen. She was talking about the menu for a dinner party. 'We shall have larks to begin with,' she said, 'larks in aspic.' 'Oh, not larks,' I pleaded. 'They're so small, and they sing so beautifully.' 'Sing?' she said. She started to unwind her hair. 'I will sing Brünnhilde for you,' she announced. 'Brünnhilde is one of my finest roles.'

Suddenly the pollarder was upon us. His head was bowed; he was swinging his axe to and fro. I wanted to run away, but that would not have been polite to Magda, who had started to sing. She sang just one note. It started quietly, almost like humming, and then grew until it boomed and reverberated. If it became any louder, I knew that I would be deaf for life. Slowly the pollarder began to raise his head.

I was awake – sweating, fearful but, even now that the dream was behind me, thankful that I had not seen his face.

As I got up, washed, dressed, I kept thinking about the episode in Nick's room. Business papers? How extraordinary to have had to look for them at that time of night, to have had to break open the filing cabinet to get at them. On a Sunday, too. But of course I knew nothing about the business affairs of the rich. They probably took financial decisions, required vital information, regardless of the day of the week or the time. But it was odd that the papers should have been in Nick's cabinet. Or perhaps it had been Nick himself who had required the information? But no, for Magda had spoken of explaining to him what had happened. That had been when she had said that she would not tell him about me and my 'big stick'. How strange that she should imagine that I would be so worried about that, about what light he saw me in – though, of course, she didn't know what a low opinion of him I had, so low that I didn't care what he thought of me. Unless it led to my losing my job – but not even he would dismiss a secretary for trying to prevent a burglary, however clumsily.

Perhaps it was all part of that German deference to men that I'd speculated about before. She felt nervous of him – that would provide another explanation for what she'd said. Possibly she didn't intend to tell him at all about breaking open the cabinet. She might well feel that, even though she'd been obliged to find the papers, he would resent her and Udo – especially Udo! – ransacking his private domain. That would fit in with her declared intention of getting a locksmith to mend the cabinet before Nick's return tonight.

Poor Magda – what a lot of fuss! It still seemed peculiar, but I felt able to dismiss it from my mind. I did so almost with regret – for it had distracted me from other matters so much more disturbing. But I would postpone consideration of those until after my morning session in Magda's boudoir.

She was at her desk, fresh and lovely in a white blouse and a dark blue skirt – and yes, she had found another silver chain, for, as usual, her crystal apple dangled from her throat.

She positively 'twinkled' at me – that was the word that came to my mind. 'Well, Annabel,' she said merrily, 'and how are you after your night's adventures?'

I smiled back. 'Oh I'm quite all right,' I said. 'This morning I could hardly believe it had happened.'

She laughed. 'Don't apologize.' (I hadn't, had I?) 'We will say not one word more about it! Now, here is an invitation I would like you to enter in my diary – and here is an account for which I would like you to make out a cheque. There is also a letter I wish to dictate to you. Let us deal with that first.'

The letter was to a dressmaker in Paris, about a model dress which she had decided that she wanted copied in a different colour. When I had typed it, and completed my other little tasks to her satisfaction, she told me that she had nothing further for me to do. I was about to leave the room, when she said to me, 'What do you do with all your free time, little Annabel?'

'Oh,' I said, 'I read a lot.'

'Ah yes, the reading. But it is not good for you to stay shut up in your room all the time. That is not healthful. You should go outside more, take more exercise. You are a little pale, I think.'

'I do go for walks,' I said defensively – although, during the past week, I had not stirred from the house, absorbed as I had been by my researches into the contents of the trunk. But she could not know that – she had been out with Udo for so much of the time. 'I might go for a walk this morning,' I went on, 'if you're quite sure there's nothing else you want me to do.'

'No, there is nothing. Go and get a little colour into your cheeks. Remember, my husband will be back tonight. We cannot have him thinking that you have been starved and neglected in his absence.' She laughed.

I joined in, reflecting that there was certainly no danger of my starving at the villa – if anyone were to land in such a predicament, surely it would be Magda herself? I could not imagine how she survived. Perhaps she ate when she went out visiting.

She was giving me a solicitous look now. 'I feel very well,' I assured her, 'but I'll go out for a walk, I promise.'

'That is good. I go out again today – how much I have been going out lately. However, after my husband returns, I shall be once more the proper *Hausfrau*.'

I could not quite see beautiful, elegant Magda in this role, and she herself made a little grimace. As I left, I was speculating about that sense of humour of hers.

It was half an hour later that I set off, following my usual route – how unadventurous I was! – up the dusty path beside the wall of the villa and the courtyard. I had almost reached the gate into the olive grove when something made me turn.

Across the open yard where the garages and servants' quarters were, Karl bounded straight at me – aiming himself at me like a bullet.

Instantly, spontaneously, I screamed at the top of my voice. The dog did not halt for an instant. But, at that moment, Marie, Magda's maid, emerged from the garage block, carrying what looked like a bundle of washing. Startled by my scream, she turned her head. She dropped her bundle . . . and I saw the astonishment on her face as she took in the scene. She called out, shrilly, to someone. The dog was almost on me. There was slime at the corners of its mouth. Its teeth were bared. *I don't want to die* – so that was to be my last thought! A shout brought the animal skidding to a halt.

Karl stared at me. I stared at him. He growled, deep in his throat. Then he turned and, tail between his legs – *baulked*, I thought – slunk back the way he had come, towards Emil.

It was Emil who had shouted. Now he and Marie were running to me. Marie outdistanced him. Her eyes were wide. She stumbled, righted herself. She was panting when she reached me. She gripped my arm. 'Mademoiselle is all right?'

Emil, too, had reached me now. Karl was at his heels, and I shrank away. There was sweat on Emil's forehead and his bald crown. 'Fraulein,' he exclaimed. 'But how can this have happened? I do not understand.' He shouted in German at Karl, who cringed in response.

'Mademoiselle!' Marie was saying. Her eyes were anxious.

I was being half carried through a back door into the courtyard by Marie and Emil. My limp arms were around their necks. I tried to stand upright. 'What . . .?' I said.

'Mademoiselle fainted.'

'Fainted? I've never fainted in my life.'

It was the first time I had seen Marie smile. It improved her. She said, 'Well, you did so then.'

Magda was hurrying toward us, between the citrus trees. 'Annabel! But what has happened?' Her eyes were full of concern. I had not imagined that a skin as white as hers could turn so much paler.

Emil started to talk in rapid German. Marie joined in, in French. I closed my eyes. When I opened them again, I was in the salon, lying on a great gilded sofa with brocade upholstery. Magda sat down beside me, took my hand. At that moment, Emil appeared with two glasses on a salver, which he put on a small table next to me, before leaving.

Magda picked up one of the glasses. It had brown liquid in it. She held it out to me. 'Brandy,' she said. 'Come, Annabel.'

I shook my head.

'But I insist,' she said. 'It is medicine. It will revive you.'

When I still refused, she frowned. Quickly I raised the other glass, a tumbler of water, and drank from it thirstily. She herself took a sip of the brandy.

'I am shocked,' she said. 'I cannot tell you how horrified I am. Never before in his life has Karl done such a thing. I think that we must have him destroyed.'

'Oh no,' I said weakly. 'You're very fond of him, aren't you?' I found it hard to understand, though, how anyone could be 'fond' of that terrifying brute.

'I have had him since he was a tiny puppy, you know. Yes, I am fond of him. Though I am angry with him now – so angry. You will be pleased to hear that Emil is giving him a good beating.'

But I wasn't pleased. Beating the dog didn't seem to solve anything. I said, 'I wonder why Karl has taken such a dislike to me.'

'I cannot understand it,' Magda replied. 'Something to do with last night, perhaps, when you came bursting into my husband's room? Dogs are nervous creatures – they are easily upset by people who do unexpected things. And then, of course, there is the fact that you fear him. That makes him uneasy. With dogs, one must be calm and strong.'

Strong, I thought. There was that word of hers again. I sighed at the idea of being 'calm and strong' with Karl.

'You can be sure that I will devote much thought to the whole question,' Magda said. 'When my husband returns, I shall discuss it with him fully. Whatever happens, I shall make quite certain that Karl never comes near you.'

Well, I thought, that suited *me*. Magda looked at her watch. She said, 'And what would you like to do now, Annabel? Rest in here for a time, perhaps?'

But I longed for the refuge of my own room. I said, 'You're going out aren't you? Please don't let me keep you. Perhaps Marie could take me upstairs? I'd go on my own, but I feel a bit weak.'

'But of course you must not go alone. You would like Marie – that old sourface?' She smiled.

I said, 'She saved my life.'

Magda stood up, went over to the fireplace. She pressed

the bell-push. 'Saved your life?' she said. 'Oh, I do not think . . .'

She left the sentence unfinished. I felt that she did not want to face up to the fact that, if I had not been rescued, Karl would have killed me. She was staring down into the empty, gleaming grate. She said, 'I am so glad that Emil was there to call Karl back.'

At that moment, Emil appeared in the doorway. I gave a little grimace at the idea of him beating the dog. But then, thinking of what Magda had just said, I realized how much I owed him. How disgraceful it was that I should be so influenced by appearances, that I should feel so repelled by squat, jowly Emil with his pallid, sweaty forehead. I thanked him now, with all the warmth I could summon, for what he had done.

He said that it was nothing. 'No, it was good,' Magda interposed. Then she asked him to summon Marie, who arrived a minute or two later.

'Now Annabel,' Magda said, 'it is most important that you should rest. You must lie down and sleep. I will have your luncheon sent up to you.'

I thanked her, feeling a ridiculous impulse to apologize to her for having been a nuisance - I suppressed it firmly. Certainly, what had happened had not been my fault. I felt terribly tired. Going up the stairs, I leant on Marie's arm. When I was lying down - Marie made me undress, get between the sheets, not just rest on the bed as I had intended - she put a hand on my forehead.

'No, mademoiselle is not feverish,' she said. 'I would not have been surprised if you had been. That Karl - *quelle horreur*! But we will not talk of it. I go now to fetch you some drops that will make you sleep.'

Marie's 'drops' were certainly effective. A short time after taking them, I feel into a deep sleep, quite untroubled by dreams. I awoke when one of the maids brought my lunch, but the minute she had gone was asleep again, waking over an hour later when the girl came to collect my tray. Looking at the meal, cold and congealed, she shook her head and asked if she could bring me something else. I refused. I wasn't hungry - all I wanted was more sleep.

It was late in the afternoon that I finally awakened, feeling calm, refreshed, restored. I wondered whether Nicholas Forrest had returned yet. I was not looking forward to seeing him, but the busy period of his absence had made the prospect less disgusting, less embarrassing than it had been. Anyway, I was determined not to malinger in my room on his account. When, at about six, Magda sent Marie to enquire how I was feeling, I said that I was very well, and that I would come down to dinner.

Nick was not back. I ate alone with Magda and Udo, who enquired most solicitously after my health, and expressed his dismay at what had happened. 'I cannot understand it - little Karl!' he said. He seemed to have the same strange picture of the dog as Magda - I remembered the occasion when she had referred to 'the poor little *Hündchen*'. Well, I had certainly been justified in not wanting to be left alone with the animal. Yet, from Magda and Emil, and now from Udo, I gained the impression that Karl had never reacted to anyone else in the way he had to me. Udo's handsome face looked so puzzled, his concern was so vigorously expressed that I wondered if that woodenness Nick had been so scathing about was merely due to shyness. Certainly, Udo seemed fully at ease only with Magda, the friend of his childhood . . . and she with him, I thought suddenly.

It was as we were eating dessert that Magda had said, with a sigh, 'I suppose that my husband will arrive back in the middle of the night.' But it was only about an hour after I had gone to my room - which I did, as usual, directly after dinner - that I heard footsteps in the courtyard: regular steps, pacing to and fro. Quietly I slipped on to the balcony. Down below, hands in his pockets, head bowed, was Nick.

I retreated – I didn't want him to look up and see me – but I heard his pacing for another five minutes or more.

It was about half an hour later that there was a tap at my door. 'Come in,' I called. It was one of the maids. She said, 'Monsieur Forrest wonders if you are still up and, if you are, whether you can come and see him.'

'Oh,' I exclaimed. Then I said, 'Yes, of course. I'll come down.'

'I will tell him,' she said as she departed.

Wondering what the reason for this unexpected summons could be, I glanced at myself in the mirror. I was wearing my blue evening dress. As I had anticipated, I had become heartily tired of it – and its pink alternative – during my stay at the villa. I wished I possessed a third, but that was quite out of the question, financially. I sighed with relief that Magda had abandoned her white party.

I powdered my nose, put on lipstick, combed my hair. I was delaying the moment when I must face him – but I must do so no longer. An efficient secretary should respond promptly to a summons from her employer.

I supposed he would be in his study – the maid hadn't said. I was right. He was sitting at his table with a tray in front of him. On it were red wine, toast and a plate of soup. He put down his soup spoon, raised his glass of wine to his lips as I came in.

'Good evening,' I said – for I always avoided calling him by his first name, and he had told me not to use his surname. I was glad it had never occurred to his wife to ask me to call her 'Magda'.

'Good evening, Annabel.' He smiled. 'Please sit down.' He gestured to my usual chair – which, indeed, apart from his own, was the only one in that austere room. As I went over to it, I glanced at the filing cabinet. It looked as it had always done – presumably the locksmith had come from Nice and accomplished his mission. I sat down. Nick broke a piece of toast, and buttered it.

'I asked you to come down this evening because I've something important to tell you,' he said. He ate his fragment of toast, raised his glass to his lips again.

Immediately I felt alarmed. What could he possibly have to tell me that was important except that I had lost my job? I was wondering desperately what I would do about my mother when he spoke - and that made his words particularly surprising.

'On my way back from Germany,' he said, 'I called at the Zeiss clinic in Zurich. I did not - was not permitted to - see your mother, but I had a long talk with Dr Zeiss.'

I heard myself draw in my breath, expel it in a long sigh - 'Oh!' To have direct news of my mother, after all I had been feeling about her during the past days! 'How is she?' I asked.

Now, with my eyes fixed on Nick's face, I saw that he looked exhausted. There were shadows under his eyes. The lines from nose to mouth seemed even deeper than usual. As he put down his glass, I thought that his hand shook a little.

'The doctor is not sure how the injections they are giving her for her skin disease are working. It is too soon for him to say anything definite about that. What does seem certain, though, is that there is an improvement in her mental state.'

I said nothing, but my expression must have told him how excited I felt. 'Yes,' he went on, 'I thought you'd want to know at once. Dr Zeiss says that she's experiencing increasing periods of lucidity, as he puts it - periods when her delusions seem far less marked. And she's even beginning to speak of the past - something which, until just recently, she utterly refused to do. The other day, Dr Zeiss said, she spoke of you.'

'Oh, do you think—'

He anticipated me. 'I asked the doctor if he thought you might visit her, but he was convinced that isn't advisable yet. However, perhaps in the not too distant future . . .'

'How kind of you,' I said. 'How kind of you to go there. How kind of you to bring me this news.'

He raised his hand. 'Please don't thank me. I wanted to do it.' He poured more wine into his glass, took a sip. Then, holding the glass, moving it in a circle, staring into it, he said, 'I had a long talk with Dr Zeiss. When I told him you work for me, he spoke very freely. He told me about the financial problems you've been facing, about the expense of the injections, about how you send him everything you earn except a shilling or two.'

'Oh,' I exclaimed, 'he shouldn't have—'

'Don't interrupt. I think he was perfectly justified. I also think it's quite absurd that you should be so bedevilled by anxiety, should have to scrimp and calculate, and worry over every penny. To put it briefly, I told the doctor I'd make myself responsible for your mother's treatment. Oh, you can send a little money if you wish – there may be extra comforts you'd like her to have from time to time. Flowers, for instance. Dr Zeiss told me that she's very fond of flowers – as a matter of fact, I had some delivered to her before I left Zurich. But, Annabel, the basic responsibility's mine now. I've made an advance payment, covering the next three months' treatment.'

'I can't let you,' I said.

'Let me? I'm afraid you've no choice. It's a *fait accompli.* And please set your mind at rest, if you're worried because you feel you're under some kind of personal obligation to me. You aren't at all. I'm not doing this for you – after all, I hardly know you. I'm doing it as a tribute, a tribute I'm proud to make, to the memory of your father – a very great writer, a delightful man.'

Gratitude, astonishment at such kindness from someone I thought so badly of, embarrassment, an overwhelming relief from my constant anxiety about how I would be able to afford the clinic's fees: all these mingled in an emotional turmoil I felt unable to cope with.

I burst into tears.

He stood up. 'Please don't cry,' he said. 'Please don't.' I

tried to stop, but couldn't manage it. He went on, in a lighter tone, 'I can't bear women crying. I never know what to do, except kiss them. And I know you wouldn't like that. Really I seem to have the most unfortunate effect on you. Why, the very first time you came to this room, I reduced you to tears. And now I've done it again, when I thought you'd be pleased.'

My tears had stopped during this speech. That reference to kissing had done the trick, I decided.

'Oh, I *am* pleased,' I said. 'I mean, I don't think you ought to do it, but, as it's for my father - and my mother, too, of course - I'm terribly grateful. It was such a surprise - that's why I cried. It was - too much. I can't tell you how kind I think it is.'

He smiled. 'Then don't,' he said. He sat down again, filled up his glass. 'Please never mention the subject again - the financial part, I mean. Of course I'd like news of how your mother's getting on, and when Dr Zeiss thinks you'll be able to see her.'

I stood up now - to thank him once more, to say goodnight. I longed to be upstairs in my room where I would have a chance to sort out my feelings.

'Oh do sit down again, for a little. I'm quite exhausted this evening - I've had a strenuous day. But stay for a few minutes while I have a last glass of wine - my soup's cold now, and anyway I'm not hungry. Another glass of wine will help me to sleep. Even when I'm tired, there are times when I find sleeping difficult, especially if I've been travelling. I don't like drinking alone, though - I can't persuade you to join me, can I?'

I had sat down again, had been listening bemused to his flow of conversation, which I guessed was designed to distract me from my earlier emotional reaction. Now I shook my head.

'I knew you wouldn't, of course,' he said. 'But you're improving. You shook your head, but you didn't frown as you usually do.' He drank some wine. 'Who knows, perhaps, in time, you'll accept me as I am.'

I spoke hastily. 'Was your trip a success?'

He hesitated. Then he said, 'Yes, I suppose it could be counted as one. And you, Annabel? How have you been occupying yourself in my absence? Has my wife been keeping your nose to the grindstone?'

I was going to say that she'd been out most of the time, but realized in time how tactless that would sound. I said, 'Yes, she's given me work, but I've had quite a lot of time to myself.'

'Do you enjoy that? How do you spend it?'

I hesitated. Then I said, 'Oh, I went through an old trunk of my father's papers.'

'Hmmm,' he said. 'That could be depressing. Was it?'

'It was - mixed.' I paused, then added, 'I found a manuscript of his I didn't know about.'

'An early one?'

'No, his last book.'

'A novel?' His face had lit up. His voice was enthusiastic.

'Yes. It isn't finished, but it's long - more than three hundred pages - and wonderfully good, I thought.'

'How splendid. That's really tremendous. Will you let me have a look at it?'

'I'd like you to,' I said.

'I look forward to that immensely. So, in fact, you've spent a very worthwhile time. Essentially, everything has gone smoothly?'

'Oh yes,' I said. Suddenly the episode of the filing cabinet came into my mind. I thought what a funny story I could make of it. He was so relaxed that I was sure he would be amused. But I had told Magda I wouldn't mention it - and I didn't know her reason for asking me not to. If I'd been sure that it was only to stop me looking silly, I would have gone ahead. 'The dog gave me rather a shock,' I said, instead.

'The dog?' he asked.

Why had I taken it for granted that Magda would have told him what had happened as soon as he arrived? They had probably had many other things to talk about. (Would she have told him how she and Udo had been obliged to break open the filing cabinet?)

'Well?' he said impatiently.

'Oh, it was nothing really – or at least it was, but it turned out all right. I was walking, and Karl came after me – he was going to attack me – but Emil called him off. I was rather frightened, though, at the time.'

'I can imagine. I detest that brute. Dobermanns are my pet aversion, they and Alsatians – which you Americans call German Shepherds, I believe. Most unfair to shepherds, if not to Germans. Anyway, I loathe both those Teutonic breeds. However, my wife's extraordinarily attached to Karl.'

I was in complete agreement with him about the dogs, but his face now wore that hard, cold expression I disliked so much, but which, this evening, I realized, I had almost forgotten. And I felt he shouldn't sneer about 'Teutonic breeds' when he was married to a German.

'But you weren't hurt?' he was asking me.

'No, no,' I assured him. I could see no point in telling him how narrow my escape had been or – certainly not! – about how I'd fainted. Fainting and tears – what a false picture of me *they* created. This time it was decisively that I stood up.

'I really must go now,' I said. 'Thank you so much for everything you've done for me – for my parents.'

'That subject is banned – remember? Good night, Annabel. By the way, I shan't need you tomorrow. I'm so exhausted that I'll sleep late, for once. When was this business with Karl, by the way?'

'Oh, this morning,' I said, making my tone as casual as possible.

'This morning! You must still be feeling shocked. If I'd known, I wouldn't have asked you to come down here tonight. But I thought you'd want to hear at once about your mother.'

'Oh, of course I did. And I feel fine. I rested all afternoon. Mrs Forrest was very kind.'

'I'm glad to hear it,' he said, and I turned to leave, but again he detained me. 'I gather things have improved out of all recognition while I've been away.'

'Improved?' I said.

'Yes. Not only have the dreadful Graf and Gräfin left, but also the Cressinghams. I hadn't dreamed that a blessed release from them would come quite so soon. That mare will champ and neigh next to me at dinner no longer!'

'No. Well, goodnight,' I said. *Hypocrite*, I thought.

'Good night,' he said. 'Sleep well.'

However, my long afternoon rest combined with the evening's events to prevent sleep coming for some time. As I lay in bed, I puzzled over Nicholas Forrest.

What extraordinary generosity he had shown - what thoughtfulness. For it wasn't just a question of money. There was the trouble he had taken, going to the clinic and talking to Dr Zeiss. Could his call at the clinic have been his only reason for visiting Zurich? Surely not - but even so . . . And everything he'd done was so totally out of keeping with the picture I'd formed of him: a cold, sarcastic man who amused himself with women without caring for them at all.

Yet that was true, too. The evidence was overwhelming. Certainly he spoke with coldness and sarcasm to his wife - and *of* her, as he did of other people. As for the women - well! There was my personal experience, the casual, indifferent 'pass' he had made on the day of my arrival. Then there was the evidence of my eyes: Lady Sarah. Ugh - but how, in the circumstances, could he talk about her as he had this evening, describe her as a 'mare' champing and neighing? A little smile twitched my lips - but really, it was disgusting. And as for that weeping peasant girl - that was beyond anything. That stuck in my gullet - and what possible explanation for it could there be except the obvious one?

Lastly, there was Elizabeth. And about her, of course, I had no concrete evidence at all. I did not know that he was having an *affaire* with her. I didn't even know that she was the girl I'd seen at Roquebrune. And yet I felt convinced of both things.

On the other hand, of course, there was what he had done in Zurich – and how nice he had been to me tonight, though of course, there I'd been influenced by that dangerous, deceptive 'charm', the quality he shared with my father. But I could not possibly dismiss what he had done for my mother as 'charming'. The whole point of charm, I had always believed, was that it made effort unnecessary. And Nick's kindness had certainly involved effort.

Grateful and relieved though I was, I had a sudden feeling of annoyance at having to modify the firmly black outline of my previous sketch of him, having to add a touch or two of fine shading. Well, he had done what he had done for my father – he had said so. Perhaps his only good quality was a real reverence for literature and for fine writers – the reverence I'd always noticed when he spoke of my father. Yes, that was probably the explanation. But oh – *joy*! I gave a great sigh at the thought that I need no longer worry so much about my mother, that she was better, that she had even spoken of me. Wonderful! And then there were the practical things – I felt myself becoming drowsy. I would not have to break into my little hoard. I would not have to try to sell my father's manuscripts. I couldn't afford a new evening dress, but I could buy stockings, some face cream, new underwear – my own was darned, and how I'd always hated sewing. The prosaic quality of this last thought made me give a little laugh. I was probably still smiling as I fell asleep.

{9}

I must have been unconsciously as well as consciously aware that I did not have to work for Nick next morning, for I awakened very late, at nine - and stayed in bed for another half hour. I was hungry when I got up, and ate a larger breakfast than usual on the terrace before going to Magda's boudoir.

I noticed at once, with relief, that Karl was not there - that was kind of her. She was sitting at her desk as usual - but it seemed far more crowded with papers than it normally was. As soon as we had exchanged good-mornings, she said, 'So, you had a talk with my husband last night?'

There was a question in her tone. Did she know why he had sent for me or that he had? Could she have thought I had sought him out? Might she be thinking about the filing cabinet?

I said, 'He brought me some news of my mother.'

'Your mother?' She sounded astonished. So he had told her nothing about it.

'Yes. He very kindly called at the clinic where she stays in Switzerland.'

'Clinic? Switzerland? She has the tuberculosis? How terrible!' She studied me keenly. 'And you, you have no symptoms? You do not cough or feel feverish?'

'Oh, no, I'm quite well,' I assured her hastily. But I did not correct her impression that my mother was in a sanatorium. I did not want to go into the whole subject of her mental illness. It seemed so much easier to leave things as they were.

She said, 'Perhaps, all the same, we should get a doctor to examine you.'

Deliberately, I lied. 'Oh, I had a complete examination in London, at a big hospital. There's nothing wrong with me at all.' I felt guilty about lying to her when she was showing such concern for me.

'Oh well then,' she said, 'all is well.' She paused. When she spoke again, her tone was different, brisk.

'Today we must prepare the invitations for the party,' she said. 'We shall send them off tomorrow. We must do things very quickly. Why, it is in less than three weeks' time! On Friday, the second of September, to be exact. See, here are the cards. And I myself completed the list of guests last night - I could not sleep. I would like you to write the guests' names at the tops of the cards, in the left-hand corner. Probably you already know that, but it is best to have things quite clear - and these engraved cards are expensive!' She smiled briefly. 'I have put the correct titles by the names on the list. Afterwards I will give you the envelopes to address. *Alles in ordnung*, you know.'

I settled down to my task - giving no indication of the surprise I felt. I had thought she had given up the idea of the party completely - and now here it was, and to be held in a very short time, too. Unpredictable Magda - I had never thought of her as *that* before. It made her more interesting - but there would be a lot to do.

The list was long - there were certainly more than a hundred names on it. Carefully I started to copy them on to the 'engraved' cards - rich people never just had things printed; that was 'common'.

Mr and Mrs Nicholas Forrest
at home
Friday 2nd September

R.S.V.P.
Villa Aurore
Cap-Martin

10 pm - Dancing
Ladies are requested to wear white

Mr and Mrs Nicholas Forrest at home. As I copied names on to cards, I turned those words over in my mind. *Mr and Mrs Nicholas Forrest at home.* There was something ironical about the phrase, I thought with detachment. It would have been hard to imagine two people who were less 'at home' together than Mr and Mrs Nicholas Forrest.

I wondered what Mr Nicholas Forrest felt about this dance. I remembered the distaste with which he always spoke about a dinner party or, indeed, a mere household gathering. Presumably he had acquiesced reluctantly, after making a battery of sarcastic comments. Poor Magda. I supposed that occasions like this provided a distraction for her from their life together.

I glanced at her. She was writing a letter, quite absorbed, her fountain pen moving rapidly over the page. And yet, all the time, she twisted her crystal apple round and round between the thumb and two first fingers of her left hand. I wondered when she had started the habit - and why? Its obsessive nervousness was so out of keeping with everything else about her.

When I looked up again, some time after, she was fastening her letter in its envelope, moistening the gum on the flap with a little sponge. She had insisted, when I started working for her, that I should follow the same practice. Licking the flap, as I normally did, was, she said, 'most unhygienic'.

This operation completed, she stood up. 'You have enough to do until luncheon?' she asked me, moving towards the door with her letter in her hand.

'Oh no, I don't think so,' I said. 'I've nearly finished writing the names on the cards.'

She gave me her address book, and told me to start addressing envelopes for the invitations. 'Perhaps you will finish doing that this afternoon,' she said. 'We must get the invitations off. But do not fasten them up - I would like just to check them first.'

Typical Magda! I thought. I was in an irreverent, light-hearted mood. But I felt energetic, too. I had addressed more than half the envelopes by the time the gong sounded.

The Marèchals were at luncheon that day, and also an English couple – of the same class as the Cressinghams, but much older. He, with his barking voice and reddish complexion, seemed to me almost a caricature, a Colonel Blimp. His wife was as lean and horsy as Lady Sarah – Nick, I thought, was sitting once more beside a champing mare – but, with her cropped hair and shapeless clothes, one that had obviously long abandoned any pretensions to attractiveness.

It was during the entrée – a *blanquette de veau* – that Magda made her announcement. She spoke brightly, after taking a larger sip than usual from her glass of Vichy: 'I have a surprise for you. We are giving a party.'

'A party! But what tremendous fun!' Madame Marèchal exclaimed with animation.

'A party!' Now it was Nick who spoke. '*We* are having a party? Why, how perfectly fascinating. Do tell me, my dear Magda, what kind of party it's to be, and when we're holding it.'

So the party was a 'surprise' even to Nick. I had imagined that Magda would have discussed it with *him*.

She smiled now. 'Nicholas, you must show more enthusiasm. Ah, these authors – they are so morose, so solitary, always bent over their books. But it is good for them to be diverted occasionally. All work and no play, as the English saying goes.' I couldn't help feeling that her animation sounded forced, almost desperate as she prattled on – it wasn't really her style.

'I'm well aware that I'm dull, my dear Magda, even if not a boy. You don't have to convince me of that – but you haven't answered my questions.' There was that tone of his I hated – cold, sarcastic, killjoy.

'It is to be a white party, a dance. Everything will be

white. I have told the guests to wear it. The decorations will be white – and the wine. The food too – as far as possible. And it will be soon – a fortnight on Friday, on the second of September!' Releasing her necklace, childishly she clapped her hands – I felt the strain behind the artless gesture.

'White!' Nick said. 'We are all to wear white? No, Magda, it is too late for me to masquerade as a virgin.'

The Englishman gave a little bark of laughter.

Magda looked momentarily puzzled, then laughed also. 'Ah Nicholas, you are joking I see.' She glanced around the table. 'He is always so amusing, my husband. Of course I did not mean that the gentlemen would wear white. They will wear their usual evening clothes. Only the men in the orchestra – they perhaps will wear white. But it was the ladies I was speaking of.'

'Ah,' Nick said, 'you relieve me. Or would, if it were relevant. But in my case it isn't. You see, I'm not affected. I'll be away on the second.'

Now there was only dismay on Magda's face. 'Away? But you cannot be away! Where are you going?'

'If you'd consulted me,' he answered, 'I would have told you. I find that changes of scene make my work go better. I intend to motor through Italy and Austria, and visit Germany again. I'll stay there, with your father, for a few days. I leave on the thirty-first of August.'

'But it is only last night that you returned from your last trip,' Magda exclaimed. 'Of course, dear Papa is pleased to see you at any time. But surely it will be quite easy for you to put off your journey for a few days.'

'No,' Nick said. 'It would not be easy. I've already told various friends, whom I intend to see *en route.* I've made several engagements. No Magda, it's for you to change your plan. I shan't be away very long – ten days at the most. You must postpone your party till I come back.'

'But already the Season is ending. Many English people have already left for the grouse-hunting–'

'Grouse-*shooting*, Mrs Forrest,' the Englishman interjected seriously. 'One hunts foxes, but one shoots grouse.'

She hardly glanced at him. 'Grouse-shooting then,' she said impatiently. 'The grouse-shooters have gone, and many others will be following them. There will be no one left on the Riviera by the middle of September.'

'*No one*?' Nick said. 'It always amuses me so much when people say "There's *no one* in Paris. There's *no one* in London". I wonder how the omnibuses manage to keep running.' Now he sounded amiable - deceptively so, I thought.

'You know quite well what I mean,' Magda said. Her voice had risen. She was flushed - something I'd never seen before. It didn't suit her - the colour had come up in uneven patches, almost like a rash, on her face and neck. 'Besides,' she said, 'it is impossible to change the date now. Why, the invitations have already been sent out. They were posted this morning - were they not, Annabel?'

I have seldom felt more taken aback. Everyone's eyes were fixed on me. I hated telling lies - and this would be the second today. But what alternative had I? I jerked my chin up, gazed past Udo's head, opposite me, at a dark landscape on the wall.

'Yes, Mrs Forrest,' I said clearly.

I turned to look at her. She gave me a brief smile, nodded her head. 'You see, Nicholas,' she said, 'it is quite impossible to cancel now.'

'Then I'm afraid,' he said, 'that you'll have to hold your party without a host.'

She simply stared at him. All the colour faded from her face and neck. She was pale again. Now the silence that fell upon the table was more oppressive than anything that had gone before. I sensed that everyone felt it. The Englishwoman picked up her glass, and it clinked against her plate. We all started.

Magda spoke again. This time it was in a different tone

entirely: soft, gentle, wheedling. 'Ah, Nicholas, please. I beg you to change your mind. Why, if you don't' – now her voice was small and pleading, like a little girl's – 'I shall write to my Papa. He would be so angry if he heard that you were going to spoil my party that I am quite sure he would not want to have you to stay.' She gave a little laugh, as if what she had said had been a joke. And yet, anyway to me, it had not sounded like one.

There was another silence, but it was much shorter. This time, it was Nick who broke it. 'Well, my dear Magda,' he said, 'since your invitations have gone out, I suppose I must surrender gracefully. It would be a bit boorish of me, wouldn't it, to leave you to cope with everything on your own? So – I won't leave till the third of September.'

I cannot say that an actual sigh of relief ran around the table, but certainly the atmosphere was as if one had. Emil and a footman materialized to remove the entrée plates, though I noticed that no one had finished the *blanquette*, now grown quite cold.

I was thinking – thinking that I did not, for a moment, believe a word of what Nick had just said. I was sure it had not been because of the despatched invitations that he had surrendered 'gracefully' – as he had so inaccurately put it. No, it had been because of Magda's threat – for it had been a threat, though such a gentle one – to write to her father. First, why should it have influenced him so deeply? And secondly I hadn't thought him the type of man to yield to a threat.

But he was speaking to me, from the end of the table. 'So, Annabel, you've been slaving away, sending out invitations? You didn't tell me how busy my wife had been keeping you with preparations for her party, in my absence.'

I had to look at him – it would have seemed so strange if I hadn't. His blue eyes were fixed on me. 'Yes,' I said. 'Yes, I have been busy.'

'And are you looking forward to this occasion which has

been keeping you so busy?' How I wished he'd leave me in peace. But yet another question followed: 'Are you fond of dancing?'

I glanced at Magda. Did she intend that I should be present at the party, as a guest? But her serene expression told me nothing.

'Oh,' I faltered, 'I'm sure there'll be plenty I can do behind the scenes . . . and no, I haven't ever done much dancing.'

This was true in one sense, though not in another. I had never been to a dance. But my father had believed that knowing how to dance was an essential part of a girl's education. I had been to ballroom dancing lessons in Paris, as well as to those awful ballet classes my mother insisted on. And later, in my teens, my father himself had taught me. He kept in touch with the latest dances – it was part of his fascination with every detail of contemporary life. I remembered circling the salon of our Paris apartment – carpet rolled back – with him, remembered the tinny sound of Ellington and Cole Porter on the Victrola which it was my task to wind up after each record. My father had been a good dancer when he was sober. Unfortunately, he was usually drunk when he felt the impulse to give me a lesson.

'Behind the scenes!' On Nick went – how I wished he'd *shut up*. 'What nonsense. If anyone ought to attend this party, Annabel, it's you. You're the age for dancing. As for the rest of us, it will be a sad case of mutton dressed as lamb.'

The expressions on the faces of his guests – especially Madame Marèchal – were hardly happy, but no one said anything.

'And white,' he continued remorselessly, 'is, of course, an ideal colour for you, Annabel. Otherwise, Magda, I'm not sure you've been very kind to choose it. Think of some of the raddled old dowagers who'll come tottering along in snowy satin.'

'Annabel looks well in white, I am sure,' Magda said. 'But

about the rest you are quite wrong, Nicholas. White is becoming to all women.'

Hadn't she once asked me if I thought she was too old to wear white? I smiled politely now, but actually I dreaded the prospect of the dance. However, at the back of my mind was the knowledge that like Cinderella, I had nothing to wear. And, unlike Cinderella, I possessed no fairy godmother. My lack of a white dress, or so I hoped, might well provide a perfect last-minute excuse for avoiding the occasion.

I would never have guessed how much effort could go into giving a party until I became involved in Magda Forrest's dance.

There was the food. Although a firm of caterers from Nice had been hired to supplement the staff of the villa, Magda herself still spent hours planning and discussing every detail of what would be served for supper, and suggesting appropriate dishes. The white theme of the party presented some problems. Compromises had to be made over both food and drink. I could see why, especially when, at luncheon one day, Nick unkindly suggested that the buffet would look like an array of corpses and that no one over the age of twenty could reasonably be asked to drink a White Lady. Magda frowned and said, 'Sometimes, Nicholas, I do not quite appreciate your humour.' More often than she realized, I couldn't help thinking. But that was just as well. If I had been she, I would have found his sarcasm unendurable. Anyway, adjustments were made to the catering.

Then there were the decorations – the banks and trailing masses of white flowers needed a considerable amount of organization, especially at that time of year, the end of summer. In addition to professional local growers, a Paris florist was called in. For that night only, white curtains were being made for the enormous windows of the ballroom –

and, yes, the members of the band, which was coming from Paris, were to wear white outfits which Magda specified in detail.

Replies to the invitations poured in – despite the departure of the 'grouse-hunters' and others, they were mainly acceptances I noticed as I listed them. Lists, lists, lists – a list for everything, and everything on its list. We checked them constantly, though it often seemed to me that Magda hardly needed them. She appeared to have every detail engraved on her mind. Her memory was prodigious. Her capacity for organization was awe-inspiring.

More astonishing to me even than the work involved was the cost. I couldn't help feeling rather shocked by it. Pictures I had seen, of dole queues, of children waiting outside soup kitchens, of men standing, with a hunched look, on street corners, kept appearing in my mind. I supposed that all the things Magda was ordering gave employment to people. Yet when she demanded three hundred pots of camellias – 'they must be in full flower' – I couldn't help feeling a pang. All this, just for one evening of pleasure.

Two days after Nick's return, he had asked me to show him my father's manuscript and I had brought it to him. Next day he had expressed an enthusiasm as great as mine had been, and had told me that he had stayed awake most of the night reading it. Of course it must be published, he said, and I agreed. I must type it, I told him, before sending it to my father's agent. I did not mention my mother's manuscript to Nick. It was so personal; it touched such wincing nerves in me.

Otherwise I saw little of him at this time. I still presented myself in his study each morning. Nowadays, he was usually frowning over the newspaper, which he would drop, with a sigh – whether of relief or exasperation I did not know – as I came in. He would dictate a letter or two to me. I did not know if his play were progressing – I saw not a line of it.

My sessions with him were so brief that I no longer breakfasted with him. I can remember only one occasion on which our exchanges were other than formal.

That morning he had dictated a letter in connection with a November revival, in New York, of *Meringue Chantilly*. It was to be an important Broadway production, starring a legendary married couple of the American stage. The producer, who believed that theatre audiences were longing to be distracted from their troubles – 'ready for something light and frothy', as he put it – hoped that Nick might come over for the last rehearsals and the opening.

His reply was that this would be quite impossible – he was far too busy working on his new play. I wondered why, when he seemed so eager to escape from the villa, he did not seize on the pretext of a trip to the States. However, that was no concern of mine. When he had read his own typed letter through, he glanced again at the producer's.

'So the poor dears want to be distracted,' he suddenly burst out. 'They need their little minds taken off their little troubles. There they sit, safe and sound, across the Atlantic, while Europe waits for its death agonies. Well, damn the lot of them.'

Some hidden spring of patriotism welled up in me. I felt furious. I said, 'I don't really understand what you're talking about. Death agonies, and so on. But I can't see why it's any worse for Americans to watch your plays than it is for you to write them.'

I had never before seen him look astonished. He put the producer's letter down on his table, and stared at me.

'You know,' he said, 'I've never actually seen anyone's eyes flash before. I thought it only happened in books – but yours flashed then. Remarkable – I'd never have guessed that such a fierce temper lurked behind that demure exterior.'

Really I had been very rude. Hesitantly – not with great conviction – I murmured, 'I'm sorry.'

'No, Annabel, it's I who should apologize. You hit the nail on the head. It was myself, the author of such nonsense, I was angry with, and I took it out on your unfortunate compatriots. By the way, when I spoke, I'd quite forgotten that you're an American.'

His voice was so kind, and his words sounded so genuine. *Charm*, I told myself.

'Let's forget all about it – though I shan't easily forget those flashing eyes.' He signed the letter I had typed – almost with a flourish. Then he said, 'By the way, there's something I've been meaning to ask you. This preposterous gathering of my wife's – the white wake as I call it to myself – do you have a dress for it?'

'A dress?' I said, playing for time.

'Yes, Annabel, a dress.' He was putting the letter in its envelope – he always did that himself. 'One of those things women wear, you know. And, in this case, a thing that is long and white.' He licked the flap of the envelope, pressed it down. 'Well,' he said, 'I'm waiting for an answer.'

There was only one I could give. 'No.'

'I see. Do you intend to buy one?'

'I don't think so.' I realized I couldn't leave it at that. It sounded so bald. Anyway, he would be sure to ask another of his questions.

In spite of his help, I really couldn't afford a new evening dress yet. I had bought stockings, underwear, a cardigan, handkerchiefs – all things I really needed. I said haltingly, 'I don't think I can – should – spend . . . so much.'

He raised his hand. 'You don't have to explain to me. That's all I wanted to know. Well, Annabel, I don't think there's anything more I need you for today.'

Leaving the room I wondered what had been the reason for his question. I found out next day, from Magda.

'Ah Annabel,' she said, 'before we start our work – there is something I have been wondering about. What are you going to wear for the dance? I have the impression that you do not own a white evening dress. Am I correct?' She smiled at me encouragingly.

I nodded. 'Yes, Mrs Forrest,' I said.

'Well, we must do something about that, must we not? Of course you do not want to buy a dress just for this one occasion – that would be foolish. I have thought of another solution. Marie, my maid, is an excellent needlewoman. She shall make something for you. We will choose the material tomorrow – you shall come to Nice with me. The dress, of course, will be my gift to you.'

'Oh Mrs Forrest, but I couldn't . . .'

'Yes, Annabel. It is my wish – and, indeed, my pleasure.'

What could I say? 'Thank you so much. It's very kind of you.'

She made a small dismissive gesture. 'And now we must settle to our business, *hein*?'

Kind of her it was, I thought afterwards – and how tactfully she had arranged it. Marie making the dress for me was somehow less embarrassing than Magda buying it in a store or taking me to a dressmaker.

Magda had been kind. Magda had been considerate. And yet I felt certain that the suggestion had originated elsewhere. Nick's questions the day before could not have been coincidental. How thoughtful of him – there was that unlikely word again. All the same, I could have wished he had not shown the quality on this occasion. My excuse had been snatched from me. A fairy godmother – and godfather – were forcing a reluctant Cinderella to attend the ball.

Regrets were useless. Magda was as good as her word. Next afternoon, Edwards at the wheel, we motored into Nice. A large draper's, on Avenue de la Victoire, was our destination. Here Magda was greeted effusively, and soon the counter was covered with bolts of material of every kind: all that they had in common was their whiteness.

My role was hardly more than that of a spectator. Her choice for me – inevitably, I suppose – was girlish. Tulle, flounced and gathered over taffeta, was to be my lot – what could I do, in the circumstances, but submit?

Before we left Nice, she told Edwards to stop at another store, a shoe shop this time. Here she bought me a pair of white satin shoes, beautifully made. I liked them, though their spiky heels were higher than any I'd worn before.

I had my first fitting next day. Ever since the episode with Karl, I had felt strongly prejudiced in Marie's favour – but, in spite of her kindness on that day, she had since always responded to my greetings in the polite but deadpan way that was, I supposed, what made Magda call her 'sour-faced'.

She was as inexpressive as ever when she came to my room with her tape measure and pincushion. I found the silence in which she carried out her task oppressive.

'Mrs Forrest is very kind,' I ventured. This was greeted with a nod, though with no vestige of a smile.

I plunged on. 'And it is very kind of you to spend so much of your time on me. I'm afraid there's an awful lot of work in all these flounces. I would have been quite happy with something simpler.'

Did I detect a slight softening of her features? 'The dress will be very appropriate, very *jeune fille*,' she said, 'and Mademoiselle is slim enough to wear the style.' Her glance assessed me. 'I shall no doubt find time to set Mademoiselle's hair on the evening of the dance.'

'Oh,' I said, 'I'm sure you'll be too busy with Mrs Forrest.'

'No,' she said. 'I can find the time. Madame Forrest always wears her hair the same. I could arrange it with my eyes shut – should that be necessary, of course.' Yes, she was faintly smiling.

'It's very kind of you,' I said again.

Marie shrugged, her smile widening. 'It will make a nice change for me to look after a young lady. Always, in all my situations, I have to try to make the old ladies look young.'

I made no comment, though I couldn't feel that what she

had said was fair to beautiful Magda.

It took three more fittings before Marie's exacting standards were satisfied. Frowning she knelt, from time to time leaning back to study the results of her labours. Under her skilful fingers, the dress took shape. Soft, romantic, with its flounced skirt and gathered bodice, it was the kind of garment I had never imagined possessing, the sort of dream I had never indulged in.

Despite all the work involved in the organization of the party, despite the fittings with Marie, I still had a considerable amount of time to myself in the fortnight before the dance. There were several free afternoons and, once or twice, Magda and Udo went out for the whole day together. Nick did the same, more often, and never in their company. He would set off, sometimes alone, sometimes with Edwards. I would hear, coming from the area behind the courtyard, the inimitable deep growl his powerful car made as it started.

I should have spent my leisure hours in typing out my father's manuscript – and yet I did not do so. Something held me back. I realized that, ever since I had read that letter from his publisher which had made me reassess his relationship to my mother, had made me aware of his ruthlessness, I had felt a resentment towards him.

Of course there had been many occasions in his lifetime when I had felt dissatisfied with him – I remembered my frustrated expedition with Tom Storey. His rages, his drinking, his broken promises had aroused flashes of anger, passing shame, momentary if bitter disappointment. Yet – genius, wise instructor in the ways of the world, charmer of the birds from the trees – he had, in some sense, always remained my idol. And now? Now I felt a sort of revulsion – no other word – for him, and the revulsion extended to his manuscript.

While my mother suffered alone in the clinic, and I endured with him the horrors of his last two years, he had, incredibly, managed to create that book. And to me, the book's very goodness made its creation, in those circumstances, horrifying - turned my father into something inhuman. A monster.

That was why I could not bring myself to start work on the manuscript, though I longed - really I did - for the world to acknowledge its merits. I needed a little time to come to terms with what I had discovered when I tackled the trunk. Yes, 'tackled' had certainly proved to be the right word! But that didn't stop me feeling guilty about the delay.

As a result of all this, in my free hours I was restless, felt almost a captive in the villa. I must break away or, to put it in more down-to-earth terms, I must get out more. Here I was, in one of the most beautiful places in the world, and I never moved from the house.

I could afford now to go on one or two modest expeditions - I found out about the local bus-service. My first trip was to Antibes.

I realized that I had no recollection of where my parents' villa or that of the Sprotts had been. Anyway I wasn't in the mood for pilgrimages. Instead, I explored the old town, strolled along the narrow promenade by the sea front, wandered among dusty Roman inscriptions and plaster casts in the Château Grimaldi. I ended the afternoon with coffee in a great tree-lined square crowded with little restaurants.

The outing had relaxed me. When the opportunity for another arose, I wondered where to go. Cannes? Monte Carlo? Neither of them appealed to me. Then I had the idea of revisiting little Roquebrune, looking at the castle, making my way along those narrow winding streets when they were not crowded with people.

Everyone was out that day. I told Emil I would not want luncheon. When I had done the work Magda had left me, I went to catch the bus. When I arrived, I found a café where I ate bread and cheese and drank a *citron pressé.* Then I went up a narrow street and climbed the long stone stairway that wound up from the village to the castle. By the time I reached it, I was panting. The steps had seemed interminable, and the day was very hot.

How small and few the rooms were in which those feudal lords had lived. They had required less space than we had in our Paris apartment. We had had a bathroom – they had found a dungeon more useful.

From the third-floor terrace of the castle, I looked down on the red roofs of the village, each of which seemed to be set at a different angle. In the distance were Cap-Martin and the sea, its blue brilliance hazed by the heat. I tried to distinguish the Villa Aurore, but was unable to do so.

Descending the stairway was far more pleasant than climbing it had been – and much quicker. Soon I was back in the twisting streets of the village, with their stone arches. I was just emerging from one of these when, in the street ahead, a door opened – the door of one of those little houses which Nick had said I would find so claustrophobic.

I could hardly believe it when, at that moment, he himself emerged from the house. How extraordinary – I took a step back, though he was not looking in my direction. And now my eyes were riveted on the person who followed him. It was the beautiful girl of the procession, with her black hair and crimson lips, the girl who, I was certain, was Elizabeth. For a ray of sunlight lit her face, and I saw the green glint of her eyes. As Magda Forrest had said, *truly green eyes are very rare.*

So Roquebrune was their place of assignation – but now they had turned, were facing the house. The chauffeur, Edwards, was helping a stooped old man, formally dressed in a dark suit, over the threshold. Nick stepped forward, and now the old man took his arm, leant on it, smiling, and saying something to him.

They all stood together for a moment. A fifth person appeared in the doorway, but did not follow the others into the street. He merely raised a hand in an abrupt salutation, before stepping back into the house and closing the door. But

I had time to recognize the crooked nose and the narrow eyes of the man whom I had seen by moonlight in the courtyard of the villa, and glimpsed by day on my last visit to Roquebrune.

The other four set off in the direction of the square – the direction in which I myself was going, but now I hung back, sheltering behind the arch. Fortunately my bus was not due to leave for another half hour.

Nick and Edwards must have arrived at Roquebrune after I had, I decided, or I would have seen the car, which must be parked in the square. Had 'Elizabeth' and the old man come with them or met them in Roquebrune? What could they all be doing there? I watched them moving slowly down the street – almost like a miniature procession; the old man leaning heavily on Nick's arm, Elizabeth and Edwards following behind. Once more I had that sense of a conspiracy that I had felt, looking down into the courtyard on my first night – a sense that had been heightened by the brief appearance of the man who was now back inside that small stone house.

Nick and Elizabeth – the presence of the others made *their* relationship a less obvious one than I had thought at first. It was all a complete mystery, I had decided when, after about ten minutes, I set off again, feeling sure that I had given them enough time to reach the square. In fact, there was only one thing I felt certain of – that I would not raise the subject with Nick, or mention it to anyone else at all. This was a secret. It was not my secret. And yet, although no one had enjoined me to silence, it was a secret which I felt obliged to keep.

{10}

Now the last few days before the dance were upon us, and my leisure was at an end. I was always busy. I had no time to brood. Each night, as soon as I got into bed, I fell into a deep sleep.

It was the second of September. How particularly hard Magda and I worked that day. There were a thousand details to be checked. When, finally, I went to my room, I felt completely exhausted. Pretty though my dress was, the sight of it, hanging freshly pressed on the outside of the wardrobe door, produced a sinking sensation in me. And even now I couldn't relax. I must take a bath and wash my hair – which Marie would be coming to set in a few minutes.

I watched the swift, deft movements of her fingers in the dressing-table mirror, wondering what the results would be. She fastened up the hair that usually hung about my shoulders in innumerable little pin curls, smoothing it tightly over my crown. When she had finished, I was at last able to lie down to rest, a towel protecting my pillow. I fell asleep at once, awakening on Marie's return. Two hours had passed, but I felt as if it had been only a few minutes.

She carried a small bag. 'A special *maquillage*,' she said. 'No, do not look anxious, Mademoiselle. I know exactly what is suitable.'

She smoothed a flesh-tinted cream into my face and neck, then dusted them with a matching powder. 'Now – a *soupçon* of rouge,' she declared.

'Oh, do you really think so?' I asked doubtfully, but she

ignored me – and when she had applied it, the effect was only a faint, becoming blush.

Next she produced a coral lipstick – I saw that it suited me far better than my almost invisible Tangee. Then she put drops into my eyes, and lightly ran over my eyebrows with a brown pencil. 'Mademoiselle has naturally fine brows,' she said. 'There is no need to pluck them as most ladies must.'

At last it was time for her to unpin my hair and brush it out. She looked, I noticed, as though she were enjoying herself. 'Close your eyes now,' she said. 'I do not want you to see until all is done.' Obediently I shut my eyes, feeling like a blind person, as her fingers, her brush, moved through my hair.

'Keep your eyes closed, Mademoiselle, and stand up.' Marie was firmly in command. It was rather fun having a ladies' maid, just this once, I thought. She helped me out of my dressing-gown and into my dress, put my feet into my shoes – how high the heels felt.

'You have the jewels at all, Mademoiselle?'

'Hardly anything,' I said. 'But they're in the little leather box in the dressing-table.' I wondered what she would think of my modest treasures: a coral bracelet, a small turquoise brooch, a seed-pearl necklace which had belonged to my father's mother.

'The pearls,' I heard her say decisively, and felt her fastening them around my neck.

She smoothed the flounces over my hips, took my hand and led me across the room. 'Now, Mademoiselle,' she said, 'you may open your eyes.'

I was facing the wardrobe mirror. I stared at my reflection – I really looked transformed. The tulle was like a white cloud from which I emerged startlingly, vividly. My hair, shining and smooth on top, clustered in soft curls around my neck. The tiny pearls made my skin glow. I looked much taller than usual in my high heels, and my coral lips made my teeth look very white. My eyes had an unaccustomed sparkle – the effect of the drops, I supposed.

'Oh Marie!' I flung my arms around her neck.

'Mademoiselle!' she exclaimed, but she was positively beaming as I released her.

'Thank you so very much,' I said. 'I don't feel nearly as frightened as I did. I'd never have believed anyone could make me look so nice.'

'Mademoiselle is too modest,' Marie said. 'My task was by no means a difficult one.'

A sudden gaiety had taken possession of me. I circled in front of the mirror. The flounces of my skirt rippled, giving a glimpse of my white satin toes.

Marie giggled – an extraordinary sound coming from her. Then she said, 'I must be gone. There are still one or two things that I have to do for Madame. Enjoy yourself – why should you not do so? There will be many women of a certain age who will look at Mademoiselle tonight and sigh.'

That was nonsense, of course, I thought, as she left the room. All the same, I couldn't help feeling that I looked – pretty. My cheeks flushed, my eyes sparkling – I saw absolutely no resemblance between myself and that 'little mouse' my mother had always disparaged. (Oh when would I manage to forgive her that?)

Perhaps I really would 'have fun' tonight. I tried to visualize myself dancing – circling in the ballroom, as I had circled before the mirror – with some young man. The handsome Udo, perhaps? But no, he really was too 'wooden'. The features of my prospective partner remained obstinately blank, and I could imagine no words to put into his mouth – or mine.

How I wished I didn't have to attend the dinner party which was to precede the dance. There were to be twenty people at it, and the prospect of that stiff formal gathering, all that rich food – the vast 'supper' that would follow later would surely be superfluous? – almost killed my tentative hopes of enjoyment. All too soon the moment came when I must go downstairs and meet the dinner guests. But as I went along the passages I was pleasingly conscious of the rustle of my dress as I moved, and of the scent of *Quelques Fleurs* – a birthday present from my father the previous year – which, at the last moment I had dabbed on my wrists and behind my ears.

I reached the top of the stairs, involuntarily smoothed my hair, and then carefully started down, very conscious of my thin spike heels. The marble banister was cool under my fingers. I was half way down when Nick came out of the library.

I almost hoped he wouldn't see me – though, at the same time, I couldn't help wondering what he would think of my transformed appearance. Anyway, he glanced up immediately – almost as if he had been expecting to see me.

I had paused. Now I continued my descent of the staircase – how long it seemed. He had crossed the hall and stood by the bottom step, face very brown, eyes very blue above the expanse of his white waistcoat, stiff white shirt, white tie.

'Good evening,' I said.

'Good evening, Annabel. All the women are in white tonight, but you're the only flower I've seen. A snowdrop? No, that's too much of a cliché. A camellia? Too artificial. There's a line of Whitman's . . . yes, I know. *When lilacs last in the dooryard bloom'd.* That's just what you remind me of, though, when I come to think of it, I haven't the faintest idea what a dooryard is. Anyway, let me take you into the salon now. You may meet carnivores in there – but I can promise that they won't devour you.'

The only flower I've seen. There was something about those words which made me feel suddenly and extraordinarily happy. That charm of his! Of course he didn't mean a word of it. Hadn't he said himself, 'You must never take me seriously.' All the same, it was a relief not to have to brave the gathering in the salon alone.

The moment we were in there, I felt how stupid I'd been to have taken so much pleasure in my own appearance. *You're the only flower I've seen.* But how these women glittered. What jewels they wore. How brilliant their complexions were. They all seemed much taller than I was, in spite of my high heels, and they all stood so straight. I noticed one red-headed beauty, her extreme slimness flaunted in sculptured, backless white satin, fastened at the throat with a great diamond cluster. But it was Magda whose appearance dominated the scene.

She had cheated – for her white dress was really silver: clinging *lamé*, cut in a deep vee, her apple nestling in the *décolletage.* And the sparkle of her dress was more than matched by the heavy diamond bracelets which weighted her wrists, the diamond fillet which crowned her hair. Frosted, starry, the Snow Queen indeed – I gazed at her with real awe.

'Cheese,' Nick murmured in my ear. Yes, of course, I must smile. Now he was introducing me to people who looked me up and down. Udo, very handsome in his evening clothes, gave me a sudden surprised stare as if I were someone he hadn't met before.

They were drinking cocktails or sherry – all except Magda, whose abstention made me feel less isolated when I refused a drink. I edged over to stand near her by the fireplace.

She looked at me, smiling. 'Yes,' she said, 'our dress is a success.' She turned to a woman with a lorgnette, who stood on her other side. 'My maid is a fair seamstress, wouldn't you agree?' she asked. 'She has done well with this dress which she has made for our dear little secretary.'

At that moment there was a sudden lull in the conversation, and Magda's voice rang out so clearly that I couldn't help feeling embarrassed. Suddenly everyone seemed to be surveying the 'dear little secretary'. A man behind me – Nick, I thought – drew in his breath with a little hiss. Then, to my relief, people all started to talk again.

At dinner I was seated between Udo and a middle-aged Frenchman, stout and wearing many decorations on his coat. I wondered what they were for. Perhaps for feats of valour at the table, I thought unkindly, for he ate and drank with a dedication which made more than a few grunted remarks out of the question for him.

Udo was more talkative than I usually found him, and several times complimented me on my appearance, though not very romantically. 'Miss looks most pretty tonight,' was the sort of thing he said – not 'You're the only flower I've seen.' Udo, I noticed, was drinking more wine than usual.

When Magda rose, and the rest of us women followed, I found myself regretting that I wouldn't be able to escape upstairs in my usual way. The elation I had felt earlier had evaporated during that long dinner. Now, in the salon, Magda was busy with her duties as hostess, and none of the other women bothered to speak to me – they were all talking of people and occasions I knew nothing about.

The men joined us – Nick looking sombre, I thought, as though his session over the port had been anything but entertaining – and, soon after, the guests started to arrive for the dance. Later there was a general move to the ballroom. Against the background of the specially ordered white curtains, and with white flowers banked in front of them, the band, in their white outfits, started to play. I couldn't help smiling – something about the scene suddenly struck me as absurd.

I was sitting by the wall, next to two women – rather corresponding to Nick's description of 'raddled old dowagers' – who were engrossed in conversation, heads close together.

The room smelt powerfully of flowers and expensive perfume. People were moving on to the floor, which the maids had treated with French chalk that morning.

No one asked me for the first two dances. Then, to my surprise, the elderly Englishman who had been at luncheon on the day Magda had made her announcement about the party, approached me and suggested 'taking a turn around the floor'. On, what a splendid man he was, and how could I have thought him a Colonel Blimp! He didn't dance at all well – we shuffled through a foxtrot – but what bliss it was not to be sitting by the wall.

However, I was back in my chair for the next dance, a quickstep. I occupied myself watching the dancers. Nick was partnering Madame Marèchal, chic in figured brocade – he nodding while she kept up a flow of animated chatter. Magda moved regally past, well distant from her partner, a distinguished-looking man with thick grey hair. I stopped myself tapping on the floor with my foot, in time to the music. I was glad when the quickstep ended, and there were more people crowding around the walls.

But, all too soon, the music began again – another foxtrot. 'Well, Annabel,' a voice said. I looked up – I had been studying the parquet floor – and Nick was standing in front of me.

'Come and dance,' he said, and I could not prevent myself from springing up with what must have been undignified alacrity.

I stared at the material of his white waistcoat. He certainly danced much better than my last partner had.

'How light you are, and what a cool little hand,' he said. His own hand, holding mine, was warm and dry. How extraordinarily near to each other we were physically. It seemed almost illegal, immoral – but what ridiculous words to think of in connection with perfectly ordinary dancing. I said, 'Mrs Forrest is looking very beautiful tonight.'

'What? Oh, my wife. Yes, she looks her best when she's dressed for big parties. Diamonds suit her – they're meant to suit everyone. Do you long for diamonds, Annabel?'

'No, not really,' I said, considering the question. 'Oh, of course they look splendid, but somehow I don't feel they're quite right for me.'

'Hmmm. I think I agree. There's something hard and chilly – almost barbarous – about them. I always think of them as polished stones – which, of course, is exactly what they are.' He laughed. 'I think you're a girl for pearls. They're quite another matter – they have a softness, a sheen. I like that little Victorian necklace you're wearing. And how much nicer it is to think of jewels being found in shells, by fishermen, than hacked out of the depths of the earth by underpaid miners. Are you enjoying yourself this evening?'

I was enjoying this foxtrot, enjoying it very much. He danced so beautifully. 'Oh yes,' I said.

'I'm glad of that. It makes me feel this absurd, extravagant party has served some purpose. It isn't the kind of thing I'm very fond of, myself. Oh well, it will all be over in a few hours. Early in the morning, Edwards and I will be heading towards my wife's beloved *Vaterland*.'

The tone in which he uttered that last word was so contemptuous that I said, 'I'm surprised you go there if you dislike it so much.'

'Are you indeed, you impertinent girl?' Fractionally, his hand tightened on my wrist. 'Obviously you aren't taking *the call of duty* into account, Annabel. Surely you don't expect me to neglect my dear father-in-law – one of Germany's richest industrialists?'

Could *money* be the motive for his visits to Germany? That was something I would never have guessed. Surely there were no financial problems at the Villa Aurore – I glanced around the opulent ballroom. Quite apart from his wife's wealth, his own plays must have earned - must still be earning - enormous sums. Presumably he was just eager to keep in Magda's father's good books. If that were so, he shouldn't refer to him so scornfully.

The music stopped. How short that dance had been. As he took me back to my chair, he said, 'Thank you, Annabel. We must dance again - very soon I hope. But alas I'm committed for the next one.'

Alas? Back in my chair, I saw him rapidly approach the redhead in clinging satin whom I had noticed in the salon before dinner. Suddenly I felt flushed and hot. The music - another foxtrot, but a slow one this time - jarred on my ears, and I decided that the band was playing far too loudly. Surely I could slip away to the terrace for a few minutes, away from the noise, the crowd, the general misery of the occasion. For - yes, I felt miserable. I had been right. This sort of party - like diamonds - was not for me.

The windows of the ballroom were open - the filmy white curtains hung still in the windless night. But I did not want to make myself conspicuous by leaving that way.

I glanced around. Everyone who was not dancing seemed to be talking and laughing. I got up, and went through the door into the salon, where a small group was gathered around the fireplace. They did not look up as I passed them on my way to the hall. In the dining-room, opposite, I saw that, miraculously quickly, tables, covered with white damask cloths had been set for supper. I slipped out through the open front door on to the terrace.

There was no one there - it was too early perhaps for the strolling couples I had expected to see. How peaceful it was; the only light came from inside the house, except for some substance that flamed in two urns at the top of the steps. Apparently this mysterious stuff burned for hours. It had been specially ordered from a shop in Rome - I had typed the letter myself.

I strolled along by the balustrade, looked through the filmy curtains into the bright ballroom, feeling that I wore a cloak of invisibility. There was Nick - the red-haired siren was resting her cheek on his lapel. I paced back along the terrace to the other end, which was deep in shadow. I would stay there for a few minutes before, I supposed, I would have to return to the party.

I leant my elbows on the balustrade, gazed into the dimness of the garden. Light from the fire in the urns flickered on the marble steps.

The night was starry, scented, balmy. It was exactly, I supposed, one of those nights my father had described in his novels: nights of tangos and champagne - and sudden, unpredictable disasters. Only the surface of his people's lives was glossy and romantic. The deep pitfalls underlying their existence were a world away from the gossamer webs in which Nicholas Forrest's characters became entangled. At that moment, a hand came down on my arm.

So lost in my thoughts was I that I started violently. I heard a low laugh as I veered round - and was confronted, so closely that, involuntarily, I drew back, by the tall figure of Udo.

He was looking down at me, smiling. He had a cigar in his hand. Now he inhaled, blew the smoke out over the garden. The smell made me wrinkle my nose.

I felt that he loomed over me, standing so close. I would have liked to retreat, but my back was against the balustrade. I realized that I was frightened - how silly, I told myself, but the smile on his face seemed strange. The band had stopped playing, and, of course, if I called out, someone would hear. But the idea of calling out - what would I call? 'Help!' - was silly too. How humiliated and foolish I would feel if a lot of people came rushing to the scene.

I took a grip on myself. 'Oh, hello,' I said. 'I was just getting some air. It's so hot inside.'

'And I startled you from your dreams,' he said. 'What were you dreaming of, little Miss? Do you know, until tonight I hardly noticed you. You were just the little foreign Miss who sat at meals like a mouse.'

At this most unpopular comparison I was able to summon up a frown.

'Do not look angry. It spoils your pretty face. For tonight, I realized that you are very pretty. I had not seen that before.'

In any other situation I would have laughed at this two-edged 'compliment'. But it was so shadowy in the corner where we were standing. His teeth gleamed. His face had a fixed look, as if the smile on it might crack. He took another puff at his cigar, then dropped it on the terrace floor, and stamped on it. He took a step towards me - there was just enough space for him to do so. I glanced wildly from left to right. But he was almost touching me. The balustrade was hard against my back.

'I think I must go inside now,' I said. There was a tremor in my voice, and I hoped he didn't hear it. I did my utmost to sound casual. 'I'm engaged for the next dance.'

'Engaged with whom? Our handsome host, perhaps? But you were dancing with him just a short time ago, and I do not think that even he would dance with the secretary again so soon. No, Miss, I don't think you are engaged. I think you are trying to get away from me. Like a little rabbit, in the harvest time, you look here, you look there, but you can't escape. All the grass is being cut, and soon there will be nowhere for the little rabbit to hide.'

First mice, now rabbits. And really it was all so corny - but his hands grasped my arms, his mouth, smelling of tobacco and brandy, came towards my face. I jerked my head aside, and his kiss landed on the edge of my jaw.

'You struggle. That is stupid, Miss. Miss is lucky that such a strong, handsome man should want her. Do not struggle, do not struggle.' His voice was a hypnotic drone. 'All I want to do now is kiss you a little. Later, when you ask me, I will come to your room.'

With a sudden movement of his left hand, he seized my chin. He wound his right arm around me, clutched mine from behind, and pulled me against him. I was completely immobilized, but I felt my whole body shrink and clench – I wished I could shrivel up until I disappeared. His mouth was pushing, pressing against mine. I gritted my teeth against the entry of his cold, wet, fleshy tongue. I could not bite it – the only form of attack I could think of – because he was gripping my chin so tightly. He drew away.

'You see, little rabbit, little Miss' – again, the fixed smile, the droning voice – 'there's no point in struggling. *Der Jäger*, the hunter, has caught the rabbit now. Be obedient, little rabbit – or *der Jäger* may hurt you.'

His fingers dug into my upper arm so hard that I could feel them against the bone. But, as he spoke, his head drawn back, over his shoulder I saw Nick.

He was standing outside the front door staring at us. Surely he would do something. Surely I could force some sort of cry from my mouth. But at that moment, he turned and went back into the house.

The hateful mouth came down again. My mind was running in circles. *Like a little rabbit, in the harvest time.* But I wasn't a rabbit. I must *think.*

I forced my body – it was an effort – to go limp. He gave a little grunt of triumph. I raised my right foot, brought down the spike heel with my full strength, and felt the satisfying give of his thin evening pump as I stamped.

He gave a yelp of pain and, as he did so, relaxed his hold on me. With one great shove, I got free, veered past him, headed for the front door.

Thank heaven there was no one in the hall when I rushed inside. I stood still for a moment. I was sure he wouldn't dare to renew his attack inside the house. Anyway – I hoped – he would still be in too much pain.

I wiped my mouth with the back of my hand – ugh! – and then smoothed my hair. Looking down I saw that the marks of his fingers – red, distinct – were imprinted on my arm. I would have dreadful bruises next day. I would have to wear a dress with sleeves to the elbow, and put something around my arms – I had a printed chiffon scarf – in the evening. What about now, though? The printed chiffon would look odd with my white tulle.

But all the time, as these trivial thoughts crossed my mind, what I was really thinking about was the look that had been on Nick's face before he turned and went back into the house – a look of the most extreme disgust. He had believed me to be a willing partner in Udo's embrace – to him it must have looked like an embrace, not like a wrestler's hold.

If only I could explain to him . . . But how could I do so – and why should he be interested? I could imagine that cold, bored look of his as he listened to my stumbling words. Anyway, he would be busy with his guests – probably, at this moment, he was dancing with the redhead again, her cheek resting on his lapel. And why should I want to explain to him? What business was it of his?

I crossed the hall, with the fingers of my left hand spread over the marks on my arm in case I should meet anyone. The same group was still clustered around the fireplace in the salon. The sound of a waltz came from the ballroom now. In the dining-room, the silver and crystal on the supper tables glittered. Down the centre of each table were arrangements of white flowers.

As I started up the stairs, leaning on the banister, I knew I couldn't go back to the party. It wasn't just because of the marks on my arm. I couldn't face the thought of dancing and making conversation, or of perhaps just sitting by the wall. Nick wouldn't ask me to dance again *now.*

Probably no one would notice my absence. Magda might – but I didn't have any work to do at the dance itself, and if she mentioned it next day I would tell her I had developed a terrible headache.

When I reached my room, I thought of Udo – 'I will come to your room' – and locked my door. Udo – what a horrible person there was behind that handsome, wooden façade. How right Nick was to dislike him . . .

The band stopped playing at about half past three. Until then the music had wafted up to my room in tantalizing snatches: tantalizing not because I wanted to be downstairs – far from it – but because my ears involuntarily strained to identify the tunes. *You're the Top*, *There Goes My Dream*, *Night and Day*, *Valencia*, *A Room with a View*: they made a restless, nagging accompaniment to my thoughts.

When I first went to bed, I did drop off to sleep, in spite of my rest before dinner. It had been such an exhausting day.

'*In all of my dreams it seems I hear your voice when it calls to me – Valencia*!' I started awake, sat up, looked at my watch – I had left the bedside light on, as well as locking the door. Only half an hour had passed. Why had I woken? Had it been a dream that had given me this sharp sense that I had to be somewhere, to meet someone, to explain something?

Suddenly, vividly before my eyes was the expression on Nick's face when he had seen me with Udo. No wonder he had looked disgusted – Udo was disgusting. *Like a little rabbit, in the harvest time.* Yes, the words were corny, but they had frightened me, too. I looked at my arm – the marks of his fingers were already darkening into purple bruises.

Surely he would apologize in the morning? He had probably been drunk – he had smelled of brandy, and I remembered how much wine he had drunk at dinner. But, say he didn't apologize, and say he made another attack on me?

Perhaps I ought to speak to Magda about what had

happened? And yet I didn't want to. What was it she had said when the Gräfin had first spoken of Udo's forthcoming visit to the villa? 'We were like sister and little brother.' How could one say something like this about a 'little brother'?

No, Udo wouldn't attack me again – in fact he probably wouldn't have the slightest desire to. It was only because I had been looking unusually nice at the dance that I had come to his attention. Hadn't he said himself that he had hardly noticed me before? I had briefly aroused in him the instinct of the hunter. But that stamp of my high heel would surely have put a stop to that. Exit *der Jäger*! And, incidentally, how much I hoped that he would soon follow his awful parents' example, and depart. Yet, and especially last time Nick had been away, Magda seemed so fond of his company.

How could she like him? Surely, over the years, the horrible aspect of him that had emerged tonight, must have been in evidence occasionally. Could he always have concealed it from her? Could she be so stupid as never to have sensed it? Of course, I'd never thought her tremendously bright, but wouldn't she have reacted emotionally to Udo's nastiness, being a good person herself. Kind, generous, concerned – though she hadn't been very sensitive this evening when she had referred to Marie's work for the 'little secretary'. But I was being too sensitive.

Suddenly, back into my mind came the scene of her and Udo breaking open Nick's filing cabinet, the episode she had asked me not to mention – *why*? Not to prevent me looking a fool – I simply didn't believe that. I had always considered it possible that she wasn't going to tell Nick what she'd done – how urgently she must have summoned the locksmith from Nice. Could it have been just because he might have been irritated? Would that really have worried her? I remembered how she had battled with him – and won – over the whim of last night's party.

Why should her business papers have been in his filing cabinet? *Perhaps she had been looking for something else entirely.* Evidence for a divorce? I supposed that was a possibility. What others were there? I saw again that inexplicable group at Roquebrune: the old man leaning on Nick's arm, Elizabeth, Edwards, the man from the courtyard. Could Magda's investigations have anything to do with *that*?

Questions – nothing but questions. And now here was another one. Should I have told Nick about the episode of the filing cabinet? He had been so kind to me – kinder really, in what he had done about my mother, than anyone else had ever been. Why should his *affaires* with women be my concern? It was the one with the little maid I couldn't stand – but there *could* be some other explanation for what I'd seen. Anyway, it didn't detract from his kindness. Might I have harmed him in some way by not telling him about the filing cabinet?

The cars started to leave soon after the band stopped playing. It was nearly five before the last of them departed, and silence fell. My thoughts had wound in ever narrowing circles, and now I had reached the centre.

I must tell Nick about the filing cabinet. My conscience wouldn't be clear until I did. Of course, I would ask him not to tell Magda that I had. And if she had told him already, if her reason for asking me not to mention it were, in fact, the one she had given me, it would be just too bad. I could bear to look a fool. He wouldn't fire me – I felt certain of that.

And, of course, when I told him about the cabinet, I could explain what had happened with Udo. I didn't want to tell Magda about it – but oh how much I wanted to tell Nick. I couldn't bear him to go away thinking badly of me. Why? I just couldn't. I hadn't time to work out why now.

For he had said that he and Edwards would be leaving early this morning. What did he mean by early? Surely not before six? He'd have to bath and change. He'd probably want a short rest after the dance, wouldn't he? I didn't know. I had better get up at once, and go to look for him. Where did he sleep? I had no idea. I couldn't go wandering around upstairs looking for his bedroom. Was it possible that he slept on the divan in his study? I'd look there anyway. If he wasn't in the study, I would go round to the garages and wait by his car. Might Karl be there, in that yard? I wouldn't think about that till I'd tried the study.

Quickly I dressed and combed my hair. How pale I looked – very different from the girl who had twirled in front of this same mirror a few hours before. I unlocked my door, went quickly along the corridors and down to the quiet hall – the servants must have cleaned up already. I reached his door – and it was open. Yes he had rested on the divan – the cover was rumpled, and the two red cushions were at one end, dented by a head. I must go to the yard. But – *Karl*! I gritted my teeth and clenched my fists.

At that moment, from behind the courtyard, I heard an unmistakeable sound: that deep growl Nick's car made as it started. I would catch him at the front of the house. I ran down the passage to the hall. When I reached the front door, it was locked. I had to struggle with a bolt and a chain. The door open, I headed for the steps. As I reached the top of them, the car flashed past – Edwards at the wheel, and Nick beside him.

I stood there. The sound of the car died away. Slowly I turned, and went back into the house. I locked the front door. As I passed the dining-room, I saw that everything had been cleared away. The room was its sombre self again.

I crossed the hall and, slowly, wearily, started to climb the stairs. Never in my life, I realized, had I felt more depressed, been conscious of such a leaden weight pressing on my spirits. Surely the filing cabinet episode couldn't have been *that* important? And, after all, it had happened nearly three weeks ago. I could explain to Nick about Udo when he came back.

But I wanted to explain to him *now*. I couldn't bear to wait a week, ten days. *Now*! I stopped dead at the top of the stairs. My hand tightened on the banister. It was at that moment that I knew I was in love with Nicholas Forrest.

PART THREE

{11}

I took my hand off the banister. Like an automaton, I moved along the familiar route to my bedroom. There, I closed the shutters to keep out the bright daylight, opened their wooden slats to let in air. I undressed, put on my nightdress, got into bed. 'I love him,' I murmured aloud, and fell asleep.

I felt as if I were being dragged from hibernation when I was awakened at nine by Marie who, bringing me a cup of coffee, came to say that Magda would not be requiring my services that morning.

'Madame did not get to bed until five o'clock. She will sleep late,' Marie informed me, herself stifling a yawn.

'You're tired too,' I said, trying to pull myself out of the drowsiness which cocooned me. 'Didn't you sleep?'

'Well, perhaps for an hour, after I had helped Madame to undress. And you, Mademoiselle, did you enjoy the party?'

'Yes,' I said, 'except that I got a headache. After that, I went to bed quite early.'

'Ah, Mademoiselle, what a pity. Why did you not come to me? I have some most excellent medicine for the migraine. But it has gone this morning - your headache?'

I assured her that it had, and thanked her again for everything she had done for me the night before. But when, smiling, she had departed, I couldn't help reflecting how wasted her efforts had been.

You're the only flower I've seen. For a moment a wild happiness took hold of me as I heard Nick speaking those words, saw him standing at the bottom of the stairs. 'I love him.' My last words before I fell asleep were on my lips again

– when reality, a dark wave, engulfed my dream world, instantly extinguishing my irrational little flame of joy.

'Love him' indeed! What on earth did I mean by it? 'Love' a man whom, apart from his odd streak of kindness, I altogether deplored. 'Love' a man who, in *that* respect, was hardly aware of my existence. I did not delude myself. That kiss he had given me had had two causes: first, he had cynically imagined that I was deliberately provoking it, and secondly – *face it, Annabel* – he made advances to every woman he came across. Anyway, he was married.

I believed in marriage. Whatever agonies my parents had been through, the idea of their being married to anyone but each other had been – was still – unthinkable. Marriage, as far as I was concerned, was a serious commitment. And Nick, even if he treated her badly, even if they were not happy together, was married to Magda.

Magda!

This morning, in my mind, her name rang cold, left a curious echo, the ghostly clang of a bell sunk under water, fathoms down. Magda! It had never possessed this chilling resonance for me before, as if, overnight, I – or she – had undergone some mysterious process of transformation – a true 'sea change'. I shivered.

Really, what on earth was the matter with me this morning? I must pull myself together, regain my sense of proportion. I took a gulp of coffee. It had become tepid. I made a grimace as I replaced the cup in its saucer.

Magda had not altered. It was I who had done so – and not through some mysterious transformation, some romantic 'sea change'. I made myself recognize the true reasons.

The first was Udo's behaviour the night before. The bad light in which – quite reasonably! – I now saw him had cast its reflection on her as his friend, as his accomplice – no, that was too emotive; companion would be better – in the opening of the filing cabinet.

The second was my love – my unreasonable infatuation –

for Nicholas Forrest. Gripped by this feeling as I was - how hard, I promised, I would try to free myself - I had aimed to justify it by depreciating his wife. I had surrounded her with a dark aura which did not emanate from her at all - because I wanted to justify what I felt for him. Yes, it was too obvious - all too crude.

Now I looked back on my projected visit to Nick early that morning - and viewed it very differently. For almost three weeks I had felt no need to tell him about the filing cabinet. Admittedly my changed attitude had been partly caused by Udo. But it had been Magda who had wanted the cabinet opened, and I had no reason for suspecting her. As for explaining to Nick what had really happened on the terrace, that was pure self-indulgence. I had been dictated to by my love - my infatuation. And that was something I was going to crush, stifle, strangle, stamp on - as I had stamped on Udo's foot. I couldn't help feeling a flicker of satisfaction at that memory, though probably, today, he would be feeling repentant, horrified at what he had done. And perhaps he wasn't quite as appalling as I had thought? I, of all people, should know how drink could transform someone. Anyway, crush, stifle, strangle, stamp - that was my programme. *Alles in ordnung*! It was with a feeling almost of complacency that I allowed myself to drift back to sleep.

I went on to the terrace shortly before luncheon - in a dress which covered the ugly bruises on my arm. Magda, Udo and the Marèchals, who had stayed the night, were all there. The Marèchals were drinking vermouth. Udo was gulping morosely from a stein of beer. Even Magda, who usually drank only at meals, was sipping a Vichy.

Monsieur Marèchal stood up at my approach - but not Udo! *He* totally ignored my presence, tilting back his mug, which Emil, hovering as usual in the background, at once refilled. I was immediately and totally aware that there was absolutely no question of Udo apologizing for the night before.

No one mentioned my early departure from the dance – evidently not even Magda had noticed it. She asked me if I had enjoyed myself, just as if I had been present all evening.

I abandoned my 'headache' alibi on the spot – an unnecessary lie. But, answering her question with 'Yes, very much, Mrs Forrest,' I reflected that that was just as untruthful. Though I had enjoyed the dance with Nick. And 'You're the only flower I've seen'. But I mustn't let myself dwell on that. *Crush, stifle, strangle, stamp*!

We went into luncheon. It was with a most uncharitable relish that I noticed that Udo was walking with a definite limp.

Monsieur Marèchal noticed it too. 'You have hurt your foot, Herr von Eisenspach?' he asked.

'I slipped on the stairs this morning. But it is nothing – a small sprain.'

'What the English call "the morning after the night before" perhaps?' Monsieur Marèchal laughed heartily. Udo, I saw, had difficulty in summoning up a thin smile.

There was a certain languor in the atmosphere at luncheon. Even pretty Madame Marèchal was looking a little worn, and there were pouches under her husband's eyes. Glancing at Udo, I observed a nerve twitching at the corner of his mouth, and his normally fresh complexion had a sallow tinge. Only Magda looked – as ever – radiant. Of course, she had slept all morning, but it was remarkable that, after all her work for the party and such a late night, she should appear as fresh and serene as if she had just returned from a long peaceful holiday at a mountain spa.

Most of the conversation at luncheon was between Magda and Madame Marèchal – in Nick's absence, I had noticed, Magda was always more talkative. They spoke chiefly of how the other women at the dance had looked. Dresses, hairstyles and, above all, jewellery, were subjected to exhaustive analysis.

Was it unfeminine of me, I wondered, not to be interested, not to want to know which Paris couturier had made this one's dress, not to care that that one had been wearing her second-best diamonds? Perhaps the fact that I knew little or nothing about the people they were discussing made the conversation duller than it would have been otherwise . . . but not, I couldn't help thinking, very *much* duller. And when, from time to time, the topic shifted to scandal ('Laura' had spent the whole evening with 'Reggie' – what had 'Charlotte' felt about that?), I did not find it notably more interesting.

Yes, I was sure of it – this was, in spirit if not in fact, the longest of all the long meals I had eaten at the villa. I tried to conjure up the smell of that London boarding-house dining-room, the sight of a wedge of gristly shepherd's pie, flanked by a wad of slimy cabbage, dumped in front of me by the cross waitress. But the charm failed to work. At the boarding-house, I thought wistfully, I could at least have read a book while I ate.

Suddenly I was conscious of the empty place at the head of the table, between Madame Marèchal and myself. I imagined how Nick would have responded to the conversation, or – wearing that remote look of his – not responded to it. I pictured how his eyes would have moved from one speaker to the other, as if, having nothing else to do, he were watching a boring game of tennis. I saw how he would have raised his glass of wine to his lips, and drained it with a quick, impatient gesture.

I started. A footman was standing by my elbow, offering me a rich praline dessert, decorated with swirls of whipped cream. I helped myself to a modest spoonful. 'Rather a mistake, I thought, those *pleats* of Angela's,' Madame Marèchal was saying. 'The last thing she should do is draw attention to her hips.'

The Marèchals were leaving after tea. Magda and Udo were to accompany them, for the evening; they were all to dine in a restaurant. How I rejoiced at the luxurious prospect of solitude: a tray in my room, Jane Austen's *Emma* to read again.

But, somehow, Mr Woodhouse's hypochondria, Miss Bates's prattle, even the complications resulting from Emma's impetuosity failed to hold me. *You're the only flower I've seen.* Nick's voice, his face, kept coming between me and what I was reading. Firmly as I resolved to crush, stifle, and so forth, I would find I had turned two or three pages without taking in a word.

Apart from the haunting presence of Nick – ghost that I was determined to exorcize – the episode of the filing cabinet kept recurring. Udo. Udo and Magda. Again, in my mind, her name struck that inexplicable eerie chord.

How hard I tried to focus my attention on the daily doings of the inhabitants of Highbury. It all seemed unreal to me – and yet it was all so realistic. 'I really do not think she cares for anything but *boiled* pork; when we dress the leg it will be another thing.' Which was 'life': that, or Nick, Udo – Magda?

I abandoned my attempt to read, and went to bed, but my preoccupations followed me there. It took every ounce of will-power I possessed to keep Nick at bay, not to repeat to myself that sentence about 'the only flower'. So the filing-cabinet wormed its way in. *Why hadn't I told him?* I did not sleep well that night.

There was not a great deal for me to do for Magda next morning: some accounts to settle, two invitations to answer – that was all. Soon, I reflected, the bills for the party would start coming in. Well, that should keep me busy!

Occasionally, I glanced up from my work at her. Just as daybreak dissipates night terrors, so her appearance – cool, lovely – banished my doubts and anxieties. I repeated her name in my mind. It raised no echo, stirred no trace of alarm.

She was strangely inactive this morning, I noticed – not occupied, as she usually was, reading personal letters or writing them, jotting down ideas for future menus, summoning Marie to issue some instruction connected with her clothes. No, as she toyed perpetually with her necklace – sometimes fondling the apple, sometimes gently swinging it by its chain – she gazed, apparently unseeingly out of the window or at the portrait of herself by László – horribly glossy and slick I always thought it, although undoubtedly 'a good likeness' – which hung above her desk.

Once the telephone in her bedroom rang, and she leaped to her feet and dashed in there, slamming the door behind her. I had never seen her move so unselfconsciously – usually her actions were so controlled. She stayed away for about five minutes and, on her return, sank back into the same state of abstraction from which the ringing of the telephone had roused her.

I finished my tasks. She gave a little start as I brought the cheques and letters over to her. I felt that she examined them without her usual concentration, signed them rapidly and perfunctorily – and she hardly even glanced at my punctilious entries on the counterfoils of her chequebook. Perhaps, I thought, she was beginning to trust in my efficiency.

Everything completed, the envelopes neatly stacked for collection by one of the servants, the typewriter put away in its cupboard, I said, 'Is there anything else you'd like me to do?'

'Hmmm?' Once more she roused herself, but only to say, 'No, there is nothing else, thank you.'

I almost asked if something was worrying her. But she looked so remote, lost in her thoughts, that I lacked the courage. I left her staring blankly at her portrait.

Time hung heavily on my hands for the rest of that

morning. What I should have done, of course, was start work on my father's manuscript. As always when one avoids a duty, guilt seems to drag at the hands of the clock. I lacked the energy to walk, or to plan an expedition farther afield.

I gave up *Emma* entirely, visited the library, and collected a pile of books. Upstairs, I dipped into one after another. When I went down to lunch, a solitary footman on duty informed me that Madame and Herr Udo were lunching and dining out, would not be back until late that night. I ate my lunch alone, in state, wishing Magda had told me of her plans. I would far have preferred a tray, on the terrace or in my room, to three solemn courses in that gloomy dining-room. I told the footman that, in the evening, I would have a mushroom omelette in my room.

The afternoon stretched ahead of me - and I went to the trunk, removed its chintz cover, opened it. But it was my mother's manuscript, not my father's, that I took out. Slowly, I began to transcribe it, correcting the grammar, the spelling, the punctuation, as I went along. How quickly the rest of the day passed - I could hardly believe it when the maid arrived with my supper. As I ate, conscience appeased, I found myself able to enjoy my meal - and *Emma*. But soon I felt drowsy. I put the tray outside in the passage, locked the door and went to bed.

I was awakened by a terrible scream - piercing, agonized, suddenly cut off. Sitting up in bed, I wondered whether I could have dreamed or imagined it. No - the physical horror of it still rang in my ears.

I remembered all too well the outcome of that other venture of mine by night. My impulse was to lie down again, curl up in a foetus-like position, pull the bedclothes up around my ears. But the human anguish that had rung out in that desperate cry prevented me from doing so.

I switched on the light, got up, put on my dressing-gown and slippers. I looked at my watch. Half after one - surely

Magda would be back now? Well, I must go and find out.

If she weren't back – might the dog, Karl, have attacked someone in her absence? That thought held me back, made me sit down abruptly on the bed, but I forced myself to stand up again.

Surely the dog would not be running loose in the house – and I felt certain that it was from within the house that the scream had come.

I unlocked the door, opened it, and moved quietly in the dimness of what I thought of as 'my' corridor. When I turned into the passage that led to the landing, I saw a light at its end.

I crept along by the wall. I had seen people do this in movies, and had thought it looked unnatural. But now I realized that I'd been wrong – I desperately wanted something solid beside me, something I could feel against my body, and touch with my hands.

I hesitated as I reached the balustrade which, starting at the end of the passage, ran along the landing to the top of the stairs. I peeped around the edge of the passage wall, saw something, and drew back. What I saw was Magda. She was wearing her white chiffon robe, and was standing half-way down the stairs. What made me draw back, stopped me calling to her, was the strange, fixed way she was staring out across the hall.

Cautiously, I edged just a little bit forward, so that I would be able to glimpse what she was looking at. Again I peered around the edge of the wall.

They were moving towards the front door – Emil and Udo. They were half dragging, half supporting, the woman who was propped between them, her arms draped over their shoulders. The dog Karl followed behind, nose to the ground.

The woman's head jerked back, lolled, and I saw her face. Even upside down, with eyes staring open – only the whites were visible – and mouth gaping slackly, I could see that this was the face of the woman whom I called 'Elizabeth'.

She's drunk, I thought. *She has passed out.* But then I saw that, from her body, a trail of red drops was leaking to the floor. It did not stay there long. As he followed, Karl was lapping at it with his tongue.

{12}

Should I have intervened – cried out, rushed forward? I am still utterly convinced that to have done so would have been mad, that it was my instinct for survival that took charge of me, made me step back into the passage, turn, and tiptoe to my room.

There, my first action was to lock the door – but I had to unlock it again, at once. I dashed into the bathroom, and was violently sick.

Afterwards, sitting on my bed, getting up, pacing over to the window, going on to the balcony – it was a very hot, still night – I tried to make up my mind what to do.

One thing I knew. They were all involved. Udo, Emil and – yes! – Magda were all responsible for that agonized scream I had heard, for the slumped, bleeding figure – whether alive or dead I did not know – that I had seen borne across the hall.

And, of course, what they had done to her, to Elizabeth, must be connected with some activity of Nick's – just as, I was now wholly convinced, the breaking open of the filing cabinet had been. *Roquebrune.* What had happened to Elizabeth must be related to whatever the people I had seen in the village that day were engaged in: she herself, the old man, Edwrads, the man with the crooked nose – and Nick.

Nick – off to Germany again, with Edwards, visiting Magda's 'beloved *Vaterland*,' which he so disparaged. Nick – staying with Magda's 'dear Papa', whom he spoke of with such contempt. Mightn't the reason for such journeys be something entirely different from anything he had said or suggested?

But what?

There was only one answer I could think of. Politics must be what lay behind it all. Politics – a subject of which I knew practically nothing, and in which I had never taken an interest. But now all sorts of memories – clues, should I call them? – were stirring, surfacing in my mind.

I remembered Nick's words, that first day, about catastrophe and war, and that bitter comment he had made later on Europe's 'death agonies'. I remembered the angry frown on his face as he flung his newspaper aside.

All that had meant nothing to me, had aroused no curiosity in me at the time. And there were other things, too. I recalled how the Graf and Gräfin had reacted to what I had said about Thomas Mann. And there had been that awful luncheon when the Graf had spoken of 'Jewish pigs'. Magda had yawned, and Nick had said something about how that expressed her attitude to politics. Perhaps he had been wrong? Perhaps he had been dissembling? Or had her very yawn been a deception? 'Strength is the noblest of all qualities.' '*Alles in ordnung.*' Little as I knew of Nazism – those words of Magda's corresponded with what I had heard.

If that were so – if Magda were a Nazi – and on the evidence of what had happened to Elizabeth, Nick, in Germany, could be in extreme danger. But what was he *doing* there? What did 'politics' involve? Spying – with Magda's 'dear Papa' as the perfect cover? Could Nick really be a spy? It sounded terribly unreal to me. And yet what I had seen in the hall had been real. 'I really do not think she cares for anything but *boiled* pork.' *That* was reality – no, it wasn't. But now my mind was wandering. What was *I* going to do? I hadn't the slightest idea.

The police – of course they were the people one turned to in preposterous circumstances like these. But the idea of going to the local *gendarmerie*, telling them what I had seen, overwhelmed me with a sense of utter hopelessness.

SCENARIO: French police confronted by nineteen-year-old American secretary with a story about her employers, the wealthy, respected inhabitants of a magnificent local villa. She denounces Mrs Nicholas Forrest, wife of the famous playwright and daughter of a leading German industrialist. Two other 'criminals' are involved: Herr Udo von Eisenspach, son of the Graf and Gräfin von Eisenspach, and – the butler.

She says that she has seen a woman – dead or alive? – being dragged, in the middle of the night, across the hall. What woman? Elizabeth. Elizabeth who? No answer. How does she know the woman was called Elizabeth at all? *Hair as black as ebony . . . lips as red as blood* –

Abruptly I abandoned my 'scenario', possessed by a sudden vision of myself incarcerated in a French asylum. Yes, efficient Magda might well be able to 'organize' that.

But in whom, apart from the police, could I confide? Wildly I thought of Marie – the only person at the villa with whom I had any kind of friendly relationship. She had saved my life. But why on earth should *she* believe my story? She worked for Magda. Mightn't she feel obliged to tell her, *for my sake*, because I ought to see a doctor.

She had saved my life. That was when I wondered, for the first time, whether Karl's attack on me had been an accident. After all, it had happened on the day after I had discovered Magda and Udo opening the filing cabinet. Couldn't they have feared – groundlessly, alas! – that I might tell Nick after all? Couldn't they have wanted to make quite certain that I didn't? I was suddenly cold with a new fear: overriding, instinctive terror – on my own behalf.

Don't say a word to a soul! Don't get involved! Keep quiet while you plan your escape from the villa! Shrill little voices in my head enjoined me to be silent, to do nothing – *and to let Nick go unwittingly to his destruction.* No – that was the one thing in the world I couldn't do.

It was when I acknowledged that, acknowledged it in my heart and mind, that the solution came to me. Tomorrow I must go to Roquebrune. I must go to the little house from which Nick and the others had emerged. I must seek out that tall man with the crooked nose, and tell him everything.

I cannot say that my decision brought me peace, or that, having reached it, I sank into a tranquil slumber. Far from it!

First of all, there were the practical aspects to consider. The bus to Roquebrune left at a quarter of twelve - there was not another one until late in the afternoon. What if Magda had a lot of work for me to do in the morning? I must check up on the afternoon bus. But mightn't my setting out on an expedition late in the day seem strange? And would there be a suitable bus back? *Perhaps the man with the crooked nose would not be at home.* It was no use brooding on that. All the same, I did so.

I was distracted, but only by a fresh anxiety - about whether I would be able to manage to behave in a normal way in the morning. I tried to picture myself ordering breakfast from Emil and - even more important - entering Magda's boudoir with a natural-looking smile on my face.

So, then, there were the Roquebrune problems, and there was the 'act' I would have to put on at the villa. And there was something else - there was my fear.

The fear was the worst - as ruthless an enemy as Magda or Udo. It kept me pacing to and fro, from my bed to the balcony and back again. Every time I lay down and tried to sleep, the fear made my heart thump and my head throb. Tired though I was, I was glad when morning came - a heavy grey day succeeding the hot, still night - and it was time to bath and dress and go downstairs. The black and white tiles of the hall had their ususal unblemished sheen - I pushed a vivid image from my mind. 'Yes,' I said to the footman - Emil, thank goodness, was not on duty - 'I'll have my breakfast now, please - on the terrace.' I wasn't hungry but I forced down a croissant, not knowing when I would next have a meal.

I cannot say that I was 'glad' – but I felt as one does in the dentist's chair, when there is no alternative to 'getting it over' – as I knocked on Magda's door, and she called 'Come in'.

After what I had seen the night before, I felt she was bound to look different in some way – worried, exhausted – but her calm loveliness was quite unaltered. However, for only the second time in my experience, she was not yet dressed. She did not wear last night's ruffled chiffon robe, but a different white one of crisp broderie anglaise, threaded with blue satin ribbon – and her wonderful hair hung like a gold cloak around her.

It horrified me that she could look so beautiful, that she could smile at me so serenely – but my worries about the practicality of my expedition were immediately dispelled by her first words.

'Ah, Annabel, you are a fortunate girl. I have no work for you to do – or nothing, anyway, that cannot wait until tomorrow. And I am feeling a little tired – after being so busy with the party, and having many late nights. Every now and again, I have a day of complete rest, for my health's sake. That is what I intend to do today. I shall have massage, and then sleep, and shall take nothing but a little mineral water.'

I wondered when she took anything else. She must eat *sometimes* – it had always baffled me. And, I thought, I had never seen anyone look less tired. Now, as she twisted her necklace – suddenly I detested that crystal apple – she said, 'And what will you do with your free day?'

'Do? Oh – oh I'll probably go on a trip somewhere, d-d-do a little sight-seeing – if that's all right.' How furious I felt with myself for stammering.

'Of course it is "all right". I am sorry that Edwards is away – he could have driven you somewhere.'

'Oh – thank you. But I can easily take a bus.'

'I have not ever been in an omnibus,' Magda said

reflectively. 'You do not find that they are filled with dirty peasants who smell of garlic?'

'Oh,' I said, yet again, 'no – I rather enjoy travelling by bus.'

'Well, that is good, then. You will go to Cannes perhaps? To Nice?'

'I – I'm not certain yet. I must check on the buses.'

'One of the servants will be able to help you. Shall I ring for Marie?'

'No. Don't bother.' How emphatic I had sounded. 'I'd like to have a look at the guide-book before I decide where to go,' I added hastily.

'Yes, that is sensible. To plan. Enjoy yourself, little Annabel.' I was dismissed at last.

I was so relieved at the way things had turned out that even my fear stayed in abeyance while I filled in the time until the bus left at 11.45 for Roquebrune. I only felt a momentary flicker of it when, just as I was getting on to the bus, Udo's Mercedes flashed past. He and Emil were sitting in front. I glimpsed Karl, stretched on the back seat, and shivered. But neither man, I thought, had noticed me. Surely it wouldn't matter if they had?

The bus made its winding ascent to the village. The sky was still overcast, and heavy clouds were massed behind the mountains. I felt that there was no point in rehearsing what I was going to say. I must, as my father would have put it, 'play it by ear'. Anyway, it was fortunate that my French was fluent. *But what if the man weren't there*? That was a possibility I refused to contemplate.

The bus deposited its passengers in the dusty square. I took my previous route through the village – today, walls and sky were the same colour – and recognized the house easily enough. But how my heart pounded as I lifted the gleaming brass knocker, shaped like a hand, that hung on the door. How loud its rat-tat-tat sounded in that quiet street.

After a moment, I heard slow footsteps. Then the door was opened – and my spirits fell. For it was not the man with the crooked nose who stood in the dark little hall. It was a plump old woman in a shapeless black dress. She looked at me with surprise.

I took the plunge. I said, in French, 'Good day, Madame.'

'Good day,' she said, but she did not return the smile I gave her.

'Excuse me, but I am looking for a man, Madame.'

How ridiculous it sounded. Evidently she thought so too, for she raised her eyebrows. 'A man, Mademoiselle?'

'Yes. I – I have seen him here. He is tall. His nose is – not quite straight.' I felt that 'crooked' would sound rude.

She studied me. 'You do not know his name – this man?'

'No,' I said. 'But I must see him. It is urgent – most urgent.'

She must have heard the desperation in my voice. She hesitated. Then she said 'And he does not know you?'

'No. No. But I come from the Villa Aurore. And I bring most important news. I know that he will want to hear it.'

Again she studied me. Then she said, 'Come in.'

I entered the dark little hall, and she ushered me into a small stiff parlour on the left.

'Sit down, Mademoiselle.' I obeyed, sat down on a sofa upholstered in black horsehair. 'I will have to find out,' she said, 'about the person you speak of. What is your name, Mademoiselle?'

'Annabel Lee. But he won't know my name, I'm sure. Tell him I'm Mr Nicholas Forrest's secretary.'

For the first time, I felt she relaxed a little. 'Ah, Mr Forrest's secretary. You are English?'

'No, American.'

'I will go and find out.' After a moment, she added, 'You may wait here.'

She went out, closing the door of the parlour. A minute or

two later, I heard her open and shut the front door. I heard her footsteps on the cobbles. Then they died away, and I became conscious of the loud ticking of a clock – the only feature of my surroundings of which I was aware.

At last I heard returning footsteps – yes, surely, this time, those of more than one person. They stopped at the house, and, a moment later, the latch of the parlour door was lifted. Here was the man whom I had come to see.

His face was expressionless, as he said, 'My mother tells me that you wish to see me. Can that be possible?'

'Yes, yes, Monsieur. I have to speak to you – there's no one else I can turn to. I have most urgent news for Mr Forrest, and about – Elizabeth.'

Now he was frowning. 'Mr Forrest? Elizabeth? Why should you come to me about these people?'

'I saw you in the courtyard of the villa – with Nick and Edwards. And here in Roquebrune another time.' He was still frowning. I said, 'Oh please be patient, and I'll tell you everything as best I can.'

Once I had started, the words poured out, as if I could not wait to be rid of them. When I came to the episode of the filing cabinet, his expression changed. '*She*?' he said in a tone of surprise. 'His wife? The Boche? I know, of course, that she is *putain*. But Nick has always said that politics are of no interest to her.'

So Nick had really believed that. But *putain* – prostitute – what an extraordinary word to have used for Magda! However I had no time to puzzle over that. I hurried on, came finally to what I had seen the night before.

'Elizabeth,' he said. Then he added, 'I am quite certain that she must be dead by now, even if she were not when you saw her. Poor girl.' He had clenched his fists, I saw, but his face, his voice were controlled. A hard man, I thought. He said, 'It is Nick we must think of now.'

He stepped towards me and, to my surprise, took my hand in his, and shook it firmly. 'You are courageous,

Mademoiselle,' he said. 'And you did the right thing when you came to me. We can only hope that we shall be in time. I must get news to Nick at once. Strange - I was doubtful about this rendezvous, but I let Nick convince me that it was genuine. Now I feel certain that it was a trap.'

'Rendezvous?' I said. 'Trap?'

He hesitated. Then he said, 'Nick is engaged in getting people out of Germany and Austria. Jews and others. Scientists - people whom the Boches cannot afford to lose, even when they are Jewish. There is no time, no need to say any more. I must act at once.' His tone changed. 'You came here by car?'

'No, by bus.'

'Hmmm. I would drive you. But I have no time, and it would not be wise. You must wait here until it is time to get the bus back.'

'*Back?*' I said. I had not dreamed, or imagined, that I would have to return to the villa now: return to Magda, to Udo, to Emil - and to Karl.

He said, 'I am afraid that you must go back. I understand your feelings, but - think if you were to disappear. They would surely suspect something, might close in on Nick earlier than they had planned, before I had time to get word to him.'

'I see,' I said.

'You have no reason at all to believe that they doubt you, have you? They must know that you said nothing about the filing cabinet. And you told the Boche woman that you were going out today, and she made no objection.'

'No,' I said. 'No, I'm sure they don't suspect me.'

'Well then!' His tone was bracing. 'You have no need to worry. Return to the villa. No harm will come to you. By tomorrow everything will be decided. Come back to Roquebrune then, and all will be arranged. Nick will see to it - if . . .' He broke off. 'Anyway,' he said, 'remember that you have friends, good friends.'

'Yes,' I said dully. 'Yes.'

'I must go now. My mother will entertain you.'

Entertain me! But I managed to smile as I said, 'Goodbye, Monsieur.'

'Don't call me "monsieur",' he said. 'Call me "Guillaume". That is my name – Guillaume Renard. And it is "*au revoir*", not "goodbye".'

'*Au revoir*, Guillaume.' He was gone. And soon I must go too – must return to the Villa Aurore.

13

Madame Renard entertained me to the best of her ability. Too well, in fact - unceasingly she pressed me to coffee, *marc*, home-made cookies, olives, slices of a local cheese. I had eaten nothing since my croissant that morning, but I was still not hungry. My stomach felt hollow, but not with a hollowness that demanded to be filled - more as if it would reject anything that was offered it. However, I remembered all I had heard of the sacred laws of peasant hospitality - as binding on the guest as on the host - and, determining not to be rude, I managed to get down a cup of coffee, a few olives and a cookie.

Our conversation didn't flow. It largely concerned the weather, and I asked her a few questions about Roquebrune. All the time, she knitted a sock, at great speed, and I wished I had some mechanical task to occupy my hands. But then I was visited by a sudden image of Magda, twisting, fondling her crystal apple.

All the same, I had no wish for the time to pass more quickly - dragging me remorselessly back to the villa. When the moment came for me to leave, and I had thanked Madame Renard, and was alone in the cobbled street, I found myself trembling. While I had been in the house, the sky had become much darker. Even up here on the mountain, the air was heavy. I was sure that there was going to be a storm.

The village seemed even quieter than usual. The sound of my own footsteps on the cobbles unnerved me. I imagined that I was being watched from between the slats of the shutters, that figures lurked behind stone arches – as, indeed, I myself had lingered on my last visit to Roquebrune.

I felt less menaced in the spacious square but, as the bus started on its journey down to Cap-Martin, it was as if a chain were being fastened around me. It was bound more and more tightly until, by the time I had reached the villa, I was almost breathless. The heat was much greater down here. I heard a faint rumble of thunder as I opened the iron gate and started to climb the steps to the terrace.

In the hall I met Emil, who told me that Mrs Forrest and Herr Udo would not be dining. Were they both going out, I wondered, or was Magda still resting in her room? How I hated the presence of Emil near me. I had always disliked his appearance – after last night it repelled me. *Had it been Emil who had set Karl on me* – under instruction from Magda – and been foiled when Marie had appeared?

'Fraulein will have her usual omelette?' he was asking me.

Magda's chef made the best omelettes I'd ever tasted – light yet moist – and I never tired of them, though I varied my choice of filling. What should it be tonight – *fines herbes*, tomato, mushroom, cheese? It gave me an unreal feeling to be considering that with Emil standing before me: Emil who had dragged along the bleeding Elizabeth, who might have set Karl –

'Yes, a cheese omelette tonight, please.' *Say cheese.* I had a sudden piercing memory of Nick's voice and smile.

I was about to turn away when Emil said, 'The Fraulein enjoyed her expedition?' He was not normally given to social exchanges – with me at any rate. I was surprised.

'Oh yes,' I said quickly. 'Yes, I went to Antibes.'

'Ah, to Antibes,' he said. Did I see a flicker of surprise on his face? I remembered the Mercedes speeding past as I boarded the Roquebrune bus that morning. But neither Emil nor Udo had noticed me – I was sure of that. Well, almost sure – then suddenly uncertain. How stupid of me to have told such a pointless lie. But I had done so automatically, instinctively, because I had not wanted to mention that name of Roquebrune. What might *they* know of Roquebrune? What might they have forced from Elizabeth? That scream, the blood . . .

'A cheese omelette then,' I repeated unnecessarily. 'Good night.'

'Good night, Fraulein.' Surely it was imagination that made me feel his eyes were on me as I crossed the hall, started up the stairs?

The omelette was delectable as ever – I managed to eat more than half of it, but when the maid came to fetch my tray, she commented on my lack of appetite.

'It is the weather, I think,' she said. 'Later there will be a storm, and then it will be better.'

Indeed, the oppressiveness of the air had intensified. I felt no urge to go on to the balcony. I stayed inside, in my little armchair. I did not even attempt to read. I just sat there, tormenting myself. If only I had told Nick about the filing cabinet in the first place. Would Guillaume be able to get a message to him?

Eventually I fell asleep in the chair – I had had such bad nights recently. I was violently awakened. A crash of thunder made me start up with a shudder. The wind was blowing in little sporadic gusts.

I looked at my watch. The time was just after eleven. The sensible thing to do was get into bed and try to sleep properly, be fresh for whatever the next day brought. I undressed, but did not go to the bathroom to wash. I had locked my door as soon as the maid had left, and I did not want to leave my room. I even thought of closing the windows and the shutters, but that would be crazy on such a hot night – I'd never get to sleep, wouldn't have the benefit of the coolness the storm would surely bring.

In bed, I felt reluctant to switch off the light – forced myself to do so. I would sleep much better in the dark.

Instead I lay, listening to the coming of the storm, and thinking about Nick.

I love him. Surely, now, I could allow myself that thought – now that I knew of Magda's treachery? But Magda was not the only obstacle to love. There was a far greater one – the fact that Nick cared nothing for me. A brilliant flash of lightning illuminated the room. I started to count slowly: 'One, two, three, four.' I had reached 'five' when the crash came.

Five miles away. It was my father who had told me that, if one counted after lightning, each number before the thunderclap represented a mile's distance from 'the eye of the storm'. One of his little items of information. *The eye of the storm* – what a strange phrase. I imagined a giant eye blazing in the sky, but the thought of my father brought a vague sensation of the comforting, the familiar. It was then that I heard the handle of my door being turned.

It was turned, and then it was rattled. Yes, I must be right. It couldn't be just nerves – there was the rattling again. I lay rigid, unmoving. Another flash of lightning. 'One, two, three,' I automatically counted before the crash – even louder this time; two miles nearer.

Who had been at my door – was there still? I listened, but the sound was not repeated. Didn't I *know*? Udo had followed up his earlier threat, and come to my room – perhaps he had drunk too much again.

Minutes passed, and I decided that my night visitor had gone. Gradually the beating of my heart slowed down, and the tension in my limbs relaxed slightly. In a moment I would turn on the bedside light. Why did I lack the courage to stretch out a hand?

Another brilliant flash. 'One, two.' The eye of the storm was nearer now. I saw it vividly, that eye: huge, dark and staring, giving sudden murderous glances of white fire. How the wind was battering. I wished I had closed my window. But to get up and do so was, at this moment, quite beyond my power. It was then that I became aware of a new sound – not a rattle, and it did not come from the direction of the door. It was a scrabbling – and it came from the balcony.

The effort which it cost me to turn my head, infinitesimally, in that direction seemed enormous. The scrabbling persisted – and now, oh surely, I was imagining the dark crouched shape which rolled over the rail on to the balcony? The lightning lit Udo's face as he came through the window. I tried to scream, and couldn't – the sound would have been obliterated by the thunder. My hand went out, fumbled desperately for the light switch – found it as he reached my bed. He blinked startled. I was sitting up. Then he smiled. '*Der Jäger* has come for the rabbit,' he said.

Wildly I looked around for some kind of weapon, grabbed the mineral-water bottle from my bedside table, grasped it, crouched, facing him. If I could break the bottle somehow . . . But, with one lunge, he snatched it from me.

He was wearing no jacket, but dark evening pants, an evening shirt open at the neck, no tie. This strange attire suddenly seemed more frightening than a Dracula cloak, a Hallowe'en mask. He put the bottle down on the table, and leaned forward and seized my arm. He dragged me off the bed – yes, as I had found before, he was extremely strong. Suddenly I was conscious of the thinness of my white cotton nightdress.

I struggled – uselessly. He twisted my arm up behind my back in that grip of his. Then with his full strength, he ground his heel down on my bare foot.

'Two can play at stamping games,' he said. There was a smile of enjoyment on his face. The pain I felt was excruciating. Tears came to my eyes, but I didn't want him to have the satisfaction of seeing them. I shook my head, and drew in my breath in a great gasp.

He was twisting me around now, so that I had my back to him. Then, to my surprise, he started to push me towards the door. Where could he be taking me? But surely nothing could be worse than being trapped in my bedroom with him? Rape – that was what I had thought of all along, but perhaps that wasn't it at all. The Roquebrune bus. I heard Elizabeth's scream in my head as he unlocked the door.

The passage was dark. He did not turn the light on. What if *I* screamed? No one would hear me – any more than they had heard Elizabeth. All the servants, with the possible exception of repulsive Emil, would be in their quarters on the other side of the big yard beyond the courtyard. Anyway, my mouth was so dry that I didn't feel I'd be able to scream.

Once, as he pushed me ahead of him, down the corridor, he groped with his other hand, found my breast, and twisted it viciously. The certain knowledge flooded my body at the same time as the pain did. No, he didn't want me – or only for cruelty.

We were in the second passage. Light shone from the landing ahead, as it had done the night before. And then we were there, with the potted palms and the stupid little gilt chairs. He stopped outside Magda's bedroom, next to her boudoir. He flung the door open, and pushed me inside. All I could do was stare.

Karl beside her, she lolled on the great white bed. Black Karl – and Magda's satin nightdress was black. Her golden hair tumbled around her shoulders, but she did not look beautiful.

Her face and neck were flushed in mottled patches, as I had seen them once before. But, that other time, her cheeks and chin had not been smeared with grease. She was holding a chunk of meat in her hand. It looked like liver – cooked rare. I saw that there was bloody juice, as well as grease, around her mouth. A trickle of it had run down her neck, under the chain of her crystal apple.

'Ah, it is little Annabel.' Her voice, normally so clear, so calm, was thickened and slurred. Still holding the chunk of meat, she stretched out her other hand to lift a bottle of

Kirsch from the floor. She raised it to her lips, and gulped from it.

I must have been gaping at her – mouth open, eyes wide – for she looked at me, and then started to laugh. A great peal of laughter that I recognized. That abandoned laugh I had heard long ago in the night. The last person I would ever have associated it with was Magda.

Udo, I realized, had released my arm. As I brought it down to my side, I was conscious of how it ached, and also of the pain in my foot.

Udo moved over to the bed. He stood looking down at Magda with a curious smile – indulgent, almost affectionate. I would *try*. Blindly I wheeled towards the door. Udo had closed it. I reached for the handle. I heard a low growl behind me; and turned.

'I would not try to run away,' Magda said. Karl stood on the bed now, teeth bared. Magda's hand was on his collar. 'Karl will not fail twice, you know,' she said, and smiled.

I made myself stand stiffly upright to disguise the trembling which I felt starting all over my body. My eyes took in the tray of food on the table beside the bed. Lumps of the bloody liver, fat slices of sausage, cold roast potatoes and a mound of sauerkraut were piled in a massive heap on a great serving dish.

She was eating now. I had never seen anyone eat so ravenously. The piece of liver gone, it was one of the cold potatoes that she was cramming between her lips. She had not finished chewing before she scooped up a handful of sauerkraut, and, dripping brine over the sheets, carried it to her mouth, shovelled it in. Her cheeks bulged. A crash of thunder shook the room, sounding as if it were directly overhead. In this room, with its heavy curtains drawn, one could not see the lightning. As the thunder crashed, Karl made a sound that was half a whimper, half a growl. Magda took a piece of liver from the dish, and fed it to him. I noticed that he did not eat as savagely as she.

Magda raised the bottle of Kirsch again, drank. The flush on her cheeks deepened. Suddenly, uninhibitedly, she belched.

'And now, Annabel,' she said, 'there are some questions we must ask you. What were you doing in Roquebrune this afternoon?'

'Roquebrune?' I said. Should I try to deny that I had been there? But they must have seen me getting on to the bus. And then I had told Emil that I had been to Antibes. Silence – was that the answer? No, surely silence would seem conclusive evidence of guilt.

'Why do you want to know, Mrs Forrest? I really can't understand any of it. Herr von Eisenspach climbs into my room in the middle of the night. And he hurt my foot . . .' Surely this would be the reaction of someone innocent – indignation and bewilderment?

'Spare us your protestations, Annabel. We are not interested.' She was not smiling any more. It was almost abstractedly that she stretched out her hand for another chunk of liver, and started to chew it. 'We know that you went to Roquebrune. You were seen to do so. I repeat: *What were you doing there?*'

'Why Mrs Forrest, I just went to look around. The village is famous.'

'But you have been to Roquebrune already, with my beloved husband.' She almost snatched the bottle of Kirsch, this time.

'We didn't see the castle, that time. I've been planning to go and look at the castle, as soon as I had the chance.'

'And yet, when I spoke to you this morning, you said you had made no plans. But this is not what I am wondering about the most. I am wondering why you told Emil that you had been to Antibes.'

That, of course, was the question to which I had no answer. 'Oh,' I said, 'well, I d-d-didn't think it was any of his business.' It sounded extraordinarily lame – and there was my stupid stammer.

'Hmmm. And perhaps you did not think it any of *my* business?' she started on another cold roast potato.

How I strove to sound natural. 'Oh no really, Mrs Forrest. I'd be delighted to tell you anything you want to know. But you must admit, at this time of night, and the way Herr von Eisenspach has behaved . . .' My voice trailed off into silence.

She ignored what I had said. 'You went to Roquebrune. And we know all about Roquebrune. We learnt about Roquebrune last night, from your colleague, Elizabeth. I must admit I am surprised. We thought that she had told us everything – eventually. But she did not tell us about you.'

I was in deeper than I had dreamed. Now they imagined that I was an active part of what had been going on.

'Elizabeth?' I said. 'I haven't even met any Elizabeth. And I certainly haven't any "colleagues".' It was odd. Now I was speaking the truth, and yet, even to me, it sounded false.

'It is time for you to stop this lying, little Annabel. Do you know what happened to Elizabeth?'

All I could manage was to shake my head.

'To make her talk, we had to hurt her a little. Then she told us everything except, as I say, about you. It was naughty of her to leave that out. I shall tell her so if I see her again. But I probably shall not do so. After she had talked to us, we set her free, of course – and I have no idea where she has gone.'

Set her free! I remembered how she had looked, and how Guillaume had said that she must be dead. No, I was certain that Elizabeth had not been 'set free'.

Another gulp of Kirsch – those greasy lips, that mottled skin: how could I ever have thought Magda beautiful? She said, 'And we shall set you free, too, Annabel. Just as soon as you tell us what you were doing in Roquebrune today.'

'Nothing,' I said. 'I only looked at the castle. I don't know what you're talking about.'

'Fool!' she shouted, but then her voice became soft again. 'What do you think you will gain by refusing to speak? Are you, perhaps, expecting to be rescued. Do you, by some chance, think that my husband will come to save you, like a brave knight on a tall white horse? Of course I realize now that you must be his mistress, as so many others have been. I would have thought you would be a little young, a little simple for his tastes – evidently they are changing as he grows older. Anyway, Annabel, my husband will not come to save you – that is something he will never do again. Why, as you know, he thought he was to save someone this evening – another filthy Jew, he supposed. But the man he is to meet is a loyal subject of the Führer's. Your lover – my husband – has made his last journey. Is not that so, Udo?'

She looked up at him, and he smiled. 'Yes Magda. The trap has closed on Nicholas tonight.'

I had felt a pang when Magda spoke of Nick's mistresses. But now that seemed so silly, so childish. His life was in question.

'This evening,' Magda had said, and Udo had spoken of 'tonight'. Guillaume could have been in touch in time. I saw a glimmer of hope. Magda's next words extinguished it.

'He has no chance at all. The frontier guards have been alerted, should he become suspicious and miss the rendezvous, though there is no reason why he should. We are efficient, Annabel, we Germans. *Alles in ordnung* – as I have so often said to you. And we are devoted to our country, to our leader, in a way that you soft Americans and English could never understand. Soft, soft – Nicholas is soft. About the Jews, about all inferiors. We are different. I would die for my Führer.' Her tone changed: 'It was he who gave me my jewel, you know – my dear apple.' Why, her tone was almost loving, as her fingers caressed the pendant. But then her hand seemed irresistibly drawn to the great dish beside her. It hovered, pounced on a slice of sausage.

'I still don't know what you're talking about,' I said. 'About Mr Forrest, I mean. But he can't just disappear. He's a famous playwright. People will want to know what has happened to him.'

'He will not disappear, Annabel. Do you really think that we are so stupid? He will be killed in a motor accident – he and the chauffeur, Edwards, who helps him. Mountain roads are dangerous, especially in bad weather. It is easy for a car to skid on a sharp bend. Now, Annabel, talk to us. Tell us why you went to Roquebrune today.'

I must not let them know that I was aware of what had happened to Elizabeth, or tell them that Guillaume was trying to get a warning to Nick. As long as they didn't know that, there was hope, wasn't there? I must believe so, anyway. I must hold on. I thought of Elizabeth, and I wondered when my breaking-point would come. But that was just what I mustn't think of.

'If you do not talk at once, things will be harder for you, much harder. Elizabeth made things hard for herself, at first. But then she became sensible, as you must.'

I said nothing. I let my eyes travel up to where the white draperies were caught in their silver coronet. *A bridal bed*, I had thought. Lounging against the white satin headboard in her black satin nightdress, Magda had nothing bridal about her now.

She looked at her watch. 'Where is Emil?' she said to Udo. 'He should be here by now. All the servants will be asleep. There is no more need for him to keep watch. We may need his help – but first he must go and pack this girl's things.' She turned to me. 'If you do not talk, Annabel – but you will; I am sure you will – no one will ever see you again. You and all your possessions will disappear.'

How strange the human mind is. Words came from my lips: 'Not the tin trunk. Not my father's book.'

'Book?' She looked at me as if I were mad – I suppose most people would have thought I was. Up to her mouth came the

Kirsch bottle again. As she put it down, she said, 'I do not know what nonsense you are speaking of. We will make you talk. If you do not, or if we have to hurt you too much, so that you are disfigured – that would be a pity, Annabel – you and all your things will vanish as if they had never been.'

'There are people who will want to know what happened to me,' I said. My voice sounded higher than usual, shrill, and I tried to make it calmer. 'I have relatives in the States. And there's my mother.'

'Your mother in the sanatorium? But of course I would answer when she next writes to you. I would tell her how shocked I was when you vanished, and in the meantime I would report your disappearance to the police at once.'

'Won't they think it strange – two secretaries disappearing from your house?'

'Two? But Elizabeth was never reported as disappearing. I was always sure that Nicholas knew where she was. And, this time, Nicholas will be dead. I might suggest to your mother, even to the police, that you had a *Schwärmerei*, a young girl's love, for him—' She broke off, turned back to Udo. 'I really think that you must find Emil,' she said. 'I cannot understand where he can be. Annabel will be quite safe here, with me – and Karl.'

'I will go,' he said. It was strange, but I was almost sorry to hear the door close behind him, as I looked at Magda, drinking again from the Kirsch bottle. Now, with her other hand she beckoned to me. She smiled – her smile had a loose lopsided look. I did not move.

'Come here, little Annabel. Or must I send Karl to fetch you?'

I could hear heavy rain falling outside, as slowly I moved across the room towards where she lay sprawled on the bed. She put the Kirsch bottle on the floor.

'Sit down,' she said, and patted the edge of the now grease-stained silk sheet. I glanced at Karl, on her other side, eyes fixed on me. Oh, my old, hopeless terror of the dog! Mesmerized, I sank down next to her, smelled sweat and food, aniseed and jasmine. Nick had said, 'I loathe the smell of jasmine.' And her greasy hand came forward to cup my breast. Her face, smeared with blood and fat moved close.

I shrank back. 'Karl,' she said, but very low. The dog stirred, and I kept still.

'I will play with you just a little,' she said. 'You are so innocent, with those wide eyes. And then Udo will come back, and you will talk and then go free. Otherwise we will hurt you very badly, and then Udo and Emil and Karl will take you to some beach a long way off, and Emil will sink your baggage in the sea. And when Karl has finished with you, no one will ever recognize you, even though your body may be washed up one day.'

So I knew now exactly what had happened to Elizabeth – and what was going to happen to me. I felt icy cold. Her hand slowly started to move down my body. Food was stuck thickly under the rosy nails.

In that moment, I made a decision. I was going to die anyway, so I would do it in my own way. I struck out at Magda's face with all the force I could summon; it must have been quite considerable, for I felt her head jar on her neck. I leaped up, turned and ran towards the door.

'Karl,' she called, and then I felt the dog's breath on my neck. Its paws were on my shoulders, bringing me down. The door in front of me opened. I heard a little popping sound, and the dog's weight fell violently from me.

I looked up. Guillaume stood in the doorway. He had a little gun in his right hand. He held out the left one, and helped me to my feet. I staggered.

Then I turned. Karl lay on the floor, flung back by the impact of the bullet which had made a red hole between his eyes. Magda, on the bed, was staring, her mouth open.

Now Guillaume was pointing the gun at her. 'Do not make any noise at all, Madame,' he said. 'If you do, I will shoot you.' He hesitated. 'Or rather Mademoiselle will.'

He handed the gun to me. 'Point it at her. Here - like this. Pull the trigger - so - if you have to.'

My hand was shaking wildly. To steady it, I gripped my wrist with my left hand. *My father and his cup of coffee.* Guillaume had pulled a handkerchief from his pocket. He tied it over Magda's mouth, and tightly behind her head. Then he dragged off the top sheet and started to wind it around her. *Was that what one did with a winding-sheet?* He knotted it, at her shoulders and at her ankles. She looked like a mummy, except that, above the handkerchief, her blue eyes bulged.

A dressing-gown, of black satin like her nightdress, lay tumbled in a heap on the floor. Guillaume picked it up, handed it to me as he took back his gun. I was glad to be parted from it.

'Put this on, Mademoiselle. We must hurry.'

I thrust my hands into the sleeves of the robe. I went through the door, in response to his gesture. I did not look back. I did not want to see those bulging eyes again.

We were on the landing. I was conscious that I was limping. I tried to gather up the dressing-gown, which was far too long for me, as Guillaume hurried me towards the stairs. 'Emil and Udo,' I muttered. 'Don't talk now,' he said.

Down the stairs, across the hall, through the open door on to the terrace. It was raining torrentially. Half-way down the steps, I heard feet behind us, and stumbled. Out came Guillaume's hand to stop me falling. The iron gate, like the front door, was open. We were through it, and I glanced round. Udo stood at the top of the steps. Guillaume raised his gun, and Udo ducked, ran back into the house.

A small Renault was a little way up the road. At last we were inside it, and, at last, he started the engine.

'They're going to kill Nick, and make it look like an accident,' I said. 'A motor accident.'

'I have sent a message to him, Mademoiselle. Be calm.'

'But the guards on the frontier have been alerted.'

'There are more places than one at which to cross a frontier.' I wondered if he could possibly feel as confident as he sounded. 'I have to make one telephone call now,' he said. 'Just to check up. There is a place in the village.'

He was driving, fast, down into Cap-Martin. He stopped outside a café. It was closed, but there was a light on inside. He knocked, and a man let him in.

Alone in the car, I was suddenly taken over, possessed, by an extraordinary terror. The smell of jasmine rose from Magda's dressing-gown. I felt Karl's breath on my neck. A greasy hand moved over me. Perhaps Udo had run to his Mercedes, had followed us, with Emil. They would find me alone, defenceless. I locked the two doors. I strained eyes, ears, but saw and heard nothing except the driving rain.

At last Guillaume came out of the café. I opened his door, and he got in. 'The lines are down,' he said. 'It is the storm. I cannot check up now. You locked the doors, I notice,' he said, and smiled.

Nick, oh Nick. I said, 'I was afraid Udo and Emil might follow us.'

'Emil will never follow anyone again, Mademoiselle.'

'I – I don't understand.'

'He is dead. I will tell you all about it. Naturally I was not pleased that you had to return to the villa, after what you had told me. When I had succeeded in getting a message to Nick – the telephone was working then, of course – it preyed on my mind. So tonight I came down to Cap-Martin. I met Emil at the back of the house. I had to kill him, and conceal his body – it will be removed before the morning. Then I watched in the courtyard, and saw that other Boche climb over the balcony. After a few minutes, I followed. I saw an empty bed – yours, I guessed. I went along the passages until I heard voices. I listened outside the door. Then the woman told the man – Udo, you call him, yes? – to go to look for Emil, and I concealed myself behind a column, while he went on his fruitless errand.' Guillaume gave a little, dry laugh. 'I knew that I must act soon. Then I heard a blow, and she called to the dog. You know the rest.'

'Yes,' I said. I found that I could not feel any horror at Emil's death. 'Elizabeth,' I said. 'That poor Elizabeth. The dog killed her, down somewhere by the sea, last night.'

'Poor Elizabeth. Beautiful Elizabeth,' he said.

Even now that she was dead, her beauty lived in people's minds. Perhaps, if Nick were capable of any kind of love, he had loved her. '*Intolerably stupid.*' But that could have been a deception. How vile, hateful, I was to feel jealous of a dead woman.

Nick. I said, 'I wonder what they will do with my trunk now.'

'Your trunk?'

'Yes – there's something in my baggage that I want very much.' I did not feel like embarking on the subject of my father's book with Guillaume. I felt he would be as puzzled as Magda had been. 'She said,' I went on, 'that they would sink all my things in the sea.'

'Well, if you have escaped, I imagine that they will hardly bother to dispose of your baggage.' He paused, then he said, 'I suppose that they will leave for Germany as soon as possible.'

'But – Elizabeth. Aren't you going to tell the police?'

'There are times when one has to weigh one's priorities. Please do not concern yourself with that now, Mademoiselle. And there are Nick's views to take into consideration.'

What a strange man this was, I thought. He did not express himself at all like a peasant. And yet his mother was obviously one.

We had left Cap-Martin by a different road from the one that passed the villa. 'Where are we going?' I asked.

'To Roquebrune. There, my mother will look after you. She has lodged other guests for us.'

I remembered the old man I had seen emerging from the

house. Obviously he had been one of those whom Nick had rescued.

'When shall we know about Nick?'

'Tomorrow, I would imagine, Mademoiselle.'

'Please call me Annabel,' I said. 'You have no idea of what time tomorrow?'

'No – Annabel. You must be patient. There is nothing else you can be. Have courage. You are fond of Nick?'

I glanced at him. He was smiling. 'Naturally, I'm worried about him,' I said.

'Oh yes, very naturally. All the ladies are concerned about Nick.'

In the circumstances I thought his comment callous – whatever the truth behind it. 'Are we nearly there?' I asked in a cool tone. We had been winding upward for some time now.

'Yes, very nearly,' he said, and it was only a few more minutes before we were parked in the square. The rain was still falling heavily, and I was soaked by the time we had climbed the winding street to Madame Renard's house. My foot ached, and the cobbles were painful to my bare toes.

As she opened the door, holding a candle, and wearing an overcoat over her nightgown, she gave an exclamation of astonishment – which was hardly surprising. My dripping hair was plastered to my head, and I clutched the sopping black satin robe around me. In a moment, though, she was fussing over me, bustling me into the little parlour. Guillaume lit an oil lamp, and she stumped off to return with a towel and a calico nightgown like the one she herself was wearing. Vigorously she towelled my hair – then hustled Guillaume from the room.

'Sleep well,' he said. 'I promise to let you know if there is any news.'

'Thank you for everything,' I replied. With a shrug, a smile, he was gone. I heard him leaving the house – so he did not live with his mother. Perhaps he was married. He was a most mysterious man.

When I had thankfully taken off that black robe, dried myself and put on the calico nightgown, Madame Renard brought me a cup of lime tisane. I was shivering, and I gulped it down thankfully. Then she led me up a tiny flight of stairs, showed me into a little bedroom, furnished only with a big wooden bed and a painted dower chest. She waited until I got into bed. Then, wishing me goodnight, she departed.

She took her candle with her. I lay in the dark. The coarse linen sheets smelled of lavender. I felt I would never sleep. I wished she had left a light for me. Magda's greasy lips, the dog bearing me down – I shivered again. But the feather quilt under which I lay was warm and comforting. My foot throbbed. Nick was driving along a mountain road. Warmth was spreading through me, and my eyes were closing. Could I really be falling asleep?

14

I awoke in a dim light. Then I saw that glints of sunshine were piercing between the slats of the shutters. My foot was swollen. I limped over to the window, and flung the shutters open. Water from last night's storm was gurgling along the open drain on either side of the street, and diamond drops glittered on the leaves of a plant which grew in a pot at the bottom of a steep flight of steps, but it was a brilliantly fine day. I looked at my watch - the time was just after nine.

By now there might - oh surely would - be news of Nick. Down the narrow stairs I hobbled. Hearing voices behind a door, I opened it, and found myself in a small, dark but very clean kitchen where Madame Renard was sitting with Guillaume.

He told me that there was no news. The telephone was still out of order. Lines brought down by the storm had not yet been repaired.

Madame Renard hurried me out of the kitchen - I could see that she thought my calico nightdress unsuitable wear in male company: not at all *convenable.* Once more I was confined to the parlour. I heard Guillaume go out. In a few minutes, Madame Renard reappeared, bringing me calico underwear and a black dress - all far too large; the dress came nearly to my ankles, and hung about me like a tent. She offered me a pair of clogs, but my foot was too painful for me to wear them. She noticed its condition properly for the first time, and exclaimed. When she heard that a *sale Boche* was responsible, her sympathy doubled. Now that Guillaume had gone, I was allowed into the kitchen to wash, and she lent me an almost toothless but clean comb with which to wrestle with the tangles in my hair. Then I was firmly returned to the parlour, where she brought me a pail of some hot herbal infusion in which to soak my foot. Soon after came *café-au-lait*, bitter with chicory, and a roll – I could have eaten two. Unhappy though I was, this morning my body craved food.

How well I came to know the parlour that day. Madame Renard did not want me to show myself in the village – and I certainly had no desire to do so with my bizarre appearance. Anyway, at any moment, news of Nick might arrive.

There were no books – I wished that I could have tried to lose myself in one, though I would probably have been unsuccessful. Instead, perforce, I learned every detail of that room.

There was the small stiff sofa with its horsehair seat. There were the upright wooden chairs around the table in the centre of the room, which was covered with a bobble-fringed cloth of dark red velveteen. The only piece of furniture I really liked was an armoire, primitively but charmingly painted with flowers and leaves. Sometimes I counted: the bobbles on the tablecloth, the uneven flagstones on the floor. Tiring of that, I stared back at the plaster madonna, robed in blue, who simpered at me from a little carved shelf. But most closely of all I got to know the wall clock of bleached wood, with its big round face. How I came to hate that clock – its loud, remorseless tick, its slow-moving hands, its swinging brass pendulum and the tinny notes with which it recorded the passage of the hours.

At midday, Madame Renard brought me bread and a bowl of 'Ratatouia', as she called it in her Provençal dialect – a ragoût of aubergines, tomatoes, peppers and zucchini, simmered in olive oil. With the food came wine, which I refused, although she pressed it on me as 'good for the nerves'. I asked for water – we had only drunk bottled mineral water at the villa, but surely, here in the mountains, it would be safe? How absurd it seemed to worry about *that*, today, I thought as I drank it.

In the morning, there had been steps and voices in the street outside, the shouts of children playing. But after the midday meal, the hush of the siesta descended. Madame Renard went up to her room to rest, suggesting that I should do the same. I shook my head. Oh, I was tired, achingly tired, but not in the least sleepy. I sat on, in the parlour. Now I understood the full meaning of the phrase 'watching the clock'. Why didn't Guillaume come to put me out of my misery – or even, I thought once, to plunge me in it more deeply, to let me know the worst, if the worst had happened? But no, no – I would rather watch the clock, and hope.

When the village stirred into life again, at around four, every sound was an agony to me. With the shutters closed, as Madame Renard had insisted that they should remain, the parlour was quite dark by six, when she came in and lit the oil lamp on the table.

The lamp cast a circle of light on the red cloth. I could hear Madame Renard moving about in the kitchen. The clock ticked, and its pendulum swung to and fro, to and fro.

At seven, she brought me bread and soup. When she came to clear the table – she would not allow me to do anything – she told me that she would be going to bed shortly. I asked her if I might stay up. She shrugged and nodded, showed me how to turn off the oil lamp – I had never encountered one before. She left me a candle and matches to take upstairs when I went to bed.

But that was precisely what I did not want to do, to go upstairs, lie down in the darkness, straining my ears for a footstep. No I preferred to continue my lamplit vigil in the parlour, sitting at the table with my elbows on the red cloth.

The clock struck nine. It was only a minute later that I heard footsteps in the silent street outside. Roquebrune retired early – I had not heard anyone go past for half an hour. I took my elbows off the table, sat upright. Would the footsteps continue up the village street? But no, they halted – and then there came a tap at the front door.

It must be Guillaume with news – at last! I could not, would not wait for Madame Renard to awaken and come downstairs. Out into the hall I moved, as fast as my limp allowed me. I fumbled with the bolt of the front door, dragged it back, turned the curved iron door handle.

I peered out. From behind me, the light in the parlour filtered out into the street. It was Nick who stood there.

Neither of us said anything for a moment. Then I exclaimed, 'Oh – oh, I can't believe it's you.'

He stepped into the hall, and closed the door. 'Then I must prove it,' he said. He put his arms round me, and then he kissed me – oh, that kiss! I couldn't help it – I gave myself up to it entirely. It was he who, hearing a sound on the stairs before I did, drew away. Madame Renard stood there, once more in nightdress and coat. She was smiling.

In a moment, he had crossed the hall – in two strides – to meet her, was wringing her hand, thanking her, in his beautiful rapid French, for her kindness. She looked delighted – more animated than I had ever seen her. Obviously he was a favourite of hers. *A favourite with all women*, I thought. But, all the same, how happy I was. The dark little hall seemed transformed. Even Madame Renard's wrinkled features glowed for me like a face in a painting by La Tour, lit by an almost other-worldly radiance. And Nick – my eyes could not see enough of him; they followed his every movement.

She was offering him refreshment. 'A glass of wine, perhaps,' he said, 'and one for Mademoiselle Annabel.'

Of course I would not drink it, but I said nothing then. She ushered us into the parlour, went to fetch the drink. He took my hand, then stood back, gave a happy laugh. 'Annabel, you look like an orphan child in that strange dress. No, don't be embarrassed. It's most appealing.' But, to my annoyance, I was blushing.

Madame Renard returned, carrying a tray on which were a bottle of red wine, two glasses and a plate of the same little cookies she had offered me - could it only have been yesterday? She beckoned to us to sit down at the table. He moved the lamp aside. We sat facing each other.

'But won't you join us, Madame?' he asked.

She beamed, but shook her head. 'No, no, Monsieur. I see that you and Mademoiselle wish to be alone. I shall return to my bed - and leave you together.'

I felt embarrassed by the complicity of her smile. My mind was working again now. That kiss had been - an aberration. Why should Nick and I wish to be alone? Well - to talk, of course. All the same, as Madame Renard turned to go, my eyes were drawn at once to him, facing me across the table. I would have expected him to look exhausted, but, in the lamplight, his face shone with a vitality, an energy I had never seen on it before.

He was pouring two glasses of wine. 'No, not for me - you know that,' I said.

'Tonight I won't let you refuse me, Annabel. I insist that you take a glass of wine with me. Please!'

So, for the first time in my life, I raised a glass of wine to my lips, took a sip. The taste was strange to me, but no - to my surprise, I did not dislike it.

We put our glasses down simultaneously. He stretched across the table, and took my hand in his. I did not remove it - told myself that it would have been ungracious to do so. Our linked hands rested on the red tablecloth as we talked.

'So Annabel,' he said. 'It seems that you've saved my life.'

'Oh no,' I said. 'It was Guillaume who did that.'

'I'm certainly in Guillaume's debt. But according to him, I owe still more to you. It was you who told him of the trap I nearly fell into. The message only just reached me in time, in fact - just before I left to meet that man I thought I was going to rescue.' He paused. 'Then, of course, when I knew they were on to me, Edwards and I had to abandon the car, cross the frontier at a special place that had been arranged.' His eyes were fixed on me. 'Guillaume told me,' he said, 'that you were very worried about me.' He raised his eyebrows.

'Oh yes, naturally one would be,' I said, looking away. 'I'm so glad it all went well. I did wonder a lot, today. I remember you saying, the time we came here for the procession, that one could find Roquebrune claustrophobic. Well, I know what you mean.'

'I wish I could have come here earlier. But first I had to go to the villa.'

'To the villa!' I exclaimed.

'Yes, indeed.' He laughed - that cold laugh I remembered. 'There can seldom have been a more unwelcome caller - or a more unexpected one. Although you had escaped, they had no idea that I had - as you know, the telephone has not been working since last night. I found them packing up to leave for Germany - your escape and Guillaume's appearance had really put the cat among the pigeons. And Emil was missing - you know why, I gather. Magda had dismissed all the other servants, but I was in time to stop them leaving. I told them to stay in their quarters until she and Udo had gone. I left Edwards in charge.' His face twisted in distaste. 'Clearing Magda's room will be an unpleasant task - but our servants have faced such tasks before. Guillaume tells me you were a witness to one of those unspeakable scenes.'

'Mrs Forrest. Of all people. I'd never have believed it.' And indeed, all day, in fearful counterpoint to my anxiety for Nick, last night's Magda had haunted me.

'I can understand your surprise. *Mrs Forrest*! Anyway, she won't be my wife for much longer. She and I went through our marriage ceremony in Germany. With her connections there, a divorce can be arranged very quickly and easily - and will be. I made sure of that today. By now, they should have gone. And I'll send all her possessions after her - her hideous furniture, her bad pictures . . . everything. Only the villa itself is mine and that Boudin you admire' – he smiled – 'and the other things in my study. Oh, if only you had told me about that filing cabinet. But why should you have suspected her when I didn't? We'll talk about that later. Meanwhile, I hope never to set eyes on her again.'

He was silent for a moment, then he said, 'The one thing I can't bear to think about is Elizabeth. Poor girl – though she knew all the risks involved in our work. Oh, I should like to bring them to justice for that. But it's impossible. I must face the fact – as I know Elizabeth would have wanted me to. There are too many things at stake: people, new plans for the future – everything has changed now. I must let them escape – but poor beautiful Elizabeth!'

Beautiful Elizabeth – those words I had heard, and thought, so often. Had he loved her? His voice had been so gentle when he said her name, and now slowly, reminiscently, he was shaking his head. 'Beautiful,' he said – again – 'and brave, and patriotic in a very simple way. At first I found it hard to believe that anyone so lovely could be so stupid. As I've said before, she was a terrible secretary.' Again he shook his head, smiling sadly. 'Though, of course, I only gave her the job as a cover. But Magda never stopped complaining about her inefficiency, so I thought it better for her to leave the villa, to work from Monte Carlo where she would be freer. I still don't know how Magda first became suspicious of me – she would have learned about Elizabeth and her whereabouts from papers in that damn filing cabinet. How could I have been so silly? But though there were so many things I hated about Magda, I never associated her with politics. I thought her other interests were her only ones – although Udo always seemed to me to be an obvious Nazi.' His tone was a little dry when he spoke again. 'Your admirer must have proved a sad disappointment to you, Annabel.'

'My admirer?' I said.

'Yes, Udo. Don't pretend that there was nothing between

you. I saw it with my own eyes at that appalling party.'

'You saw nothing of the kind,' I said indignantly. 'He was holding me by force. I detested him – and, after that evening, it was mutual. I stamped on his foot – that was how I got away. Well, last night he paid me back.' Defiantly I extended my bruised and swollen foot which had been under the table.

'Oh, Annabel,' he exclaimed. He stood up, then suddenly knelt on the floor, and took my foot in his hand. He stroked it. Then he raised it to his lips, and kissed it. I had not bargained for the shiver that ran through me like an electric current.

He looked up at me, smiled. 'How jumpy you are, Annabel. No wonder – after all you've been through.' He rose from his knees, sat down again, picked up the wine bottle. I put out my hand to cover my glass – empty now, I saw with surprise – but he brushed it aside, and filled both glasses.

I must be detached. I must distance myself from that shivering creature. I said, 'So you never suspected Mrs Forrest was active in politics?'

'No, not for a moment. Though I admit that I didn't spend much time thinking about her at all.'

'One could imagine that,' I said, 'from the way you treated her. You were always so horrible to her.'

'Horrible, Annabel? That's a strong word. Though I suppose it's not inaccurate. Horrible. But Annabel, have you forgotten what you saw last night?'

Those greasy lips, that hand on my body. 'No,' I said. 'No, I think I understand.'

'I can make certain that you do. But it's quite a long story, and I wouldn't want to bore you.' There was that old irony I didn't like – but I wanted so much to hear his story.

'Please tell me,' I said.

'Very well. If you like – though you won't like the story.

Where shall I start? When I met her, I suppose. That was twelve years ago. You've often commented on her beauty yourself, and though I can't appreciate it any longer, I must accept the fact of its existence.' He took a sip from his glass, went on. 'Well, I can assure you that her looks now are nothing to what they were then. Magda von Kronenberg – everyone was stunned by her snowy skin, her blue eyes, her golden hair, her perfect features, her wonderful figure, her youthful, radiant health.' Again he paused for a sip of wine, before continuing.

'I was a comparatively young man then – twenty-six. I was tasting great success for the first time, and I was excited by it. International society, lavish parties, gambling and dancing all night: everything, in fact, that I now find absolutely tedious – but I didn't then. And you must take into account that provincial background of mine that I think I once told you about.'

I nodded.

'I had just emerged,' he went on, 'from an *affaire* with an English actress who had been in my first play – an extraordinarily attractive creature. Not beautiful – but fantastically sexy. Small, dark, vivid, lively, a most amusing talker – which was lucky as she chattered from morning till night. Her nights were otherwise occupied.'

I picked up the edge of the tablecloth, started to fiddle with part of the fringe.

'I was wild about her,' he went on. 'When I found out – the last to know, of course! – that she was being unfaithful to me, not just with one man, but with three – she was compulsively promiscuous – I reacted violently. Not, as I would now, by retreating into myself, by becoming the hermit who used to irritate Magda so much, but by plunging into those pointless activities I've just mentioned. It was in the Twenties, all this, you must remember, Annabel – that hectic decade your father wrote about so well. I had a great many *affaires*, too, but all of them, at that time, left a bad taste in my mouth, didn't bring me any real happiness. And then, at a terribly grand, stuffy party in London - not my usual style, and I can't remember how I got asked to it or why I went - whom should I meet but this Rhine maiden, this pure, golden goddess - for that was what I thought she was.

'She was silent in those days - dazzling Magda von Kronenberg. After my chattering actress, I imagined that her silence concealed hidden depths - instead of dreadful shallows. She gazed at me with her blue eyes. She smiled or she nodded gravely as she listened to me - and I was terribly flattered. She seemed gentle to me and shy, appealingly nervous. In those days it was a string of pearls that she fingered - she hadn't bought that crystal apple yet.'

'She told me that Hitler gave it to her,' I broke in.

'Indeed! Well, that doesn't surprise me now - though it certainly would have earlier. Anyway, Annabel, the things I'm talking about all happened before he came to power - and before I myself was at all a political person. But, like all my generation, I hated the waste and chaos of the last war - which I'd just missed fighting in - and thought it rather specially fine to fall in love with a German, particularly as my parents were horrified. "Fall in love," I say. Yes, I suppose I "fell in love" with Magda. And do you know why? After all those *affaires* of mine, a puritan streak was emerging. And beautiful, shy Magda seemed to me the personification of virtue, in her white dresses - really almost an angel! Why, she didn't even seem to need to eat and drink as ordinary humans do.

'What did she see in me? I've often asked myself that. My success was at its height then, of course. And a playwright - for her that was something new, different. She hadn't met anyone like me before. Definitely, too, in those days, she found me physically attractive. But, looking back, I think my main advantage, from her point of view, was the last thing I ever dreamed of. She thought that she would be *free* with me. I was what she would call a "bohemian", not some rigid German Graf. She would be able to live her own life, with all that that entailed, all that I had absolutely no idea of. Oh, how I wish I'd taken her to bed instead of marrying her. But I never thought of suggesting such a thing to my chaste goddess.'

He gave his little cold laugh then, and drank some more wine.

'We had a vast, elaborate wedding in Berlin. Her family thought me a very odd character, but she overcame their opposition with that iron will of hers. I can't say that I much cared for them, either – by the way, that was the first time I met Udo, whom I later learnt that she'd seduced when he was a boy of fourteen. Anyway, I wasn't marrying her relations. I was marrying her – the dazzling snow maiden in white satin, whose blue eyes shimmered through the mist of her veil as she came up the aisle to me on her father's arm. Hilarious!

'However, I didn't think that at the time. That was why our wedding night came to me as such a surprise.' He laughed again. 'It's traditionally the bride, of course, who's amazed by the revelations of the marriage bed. Not in this case! Delicately I approached my virgin bride – and found myself in the clutches of an expert at every sexual trick you can imagine – or, of course, can't, my dear Annabel. I'm sorry to talk to you like this.'

My eyes on the fringe of the tablecloth, I murmured something inaudible such as 'It's all right.' But it was true that I didn't really know what he was talking about. He filled our glasses. Caught up in his narrative, I had emptied mine – this time I didn't try to stop him pouring.

'Anyway, my London actress was an innocent in comparison to Magda. How did I react? With shock, at first.

But then I told myself that, after all, I was a man of the world - and, having had so many *affaires* myself, could I really sit in judgement on her? And I must be honest - I enjoyed her at first. A really accomplished whore who's also a radiant beauty can give a man a lot of pleasure. And yet there were times - and they became more frequent - when I felt a sort of nausea, as if I'd been gorging on rotten meat. Which leads inevitably to the first occasion - about six months after our marriage - when I found her satisfying her other appetites. There'd been days when she said she had a headache and didn't want anyone to disturb her - but this time I caught her in the act. Gulping some liqueur, cramming food into her mouth with her hands. Like an animal, I was going to say, but that would be unfair - animals have so much more dignity than my wife.'

He paused, then he said, 'And she wasn't alone. She had a girl with her. Oh - that has been a persistent anxiety. Why, there was even a poor little girl who worked as a maid at the villa whom she made advances to. I had to sort that out as best I could, give the girl money - what else was there to do! Innocence appeals to Magda - she wants to corrupt it. She didn't . . . ?' He left a question unfinished.

'No,' I said firmly. I wasn't going to discuss *that* with him - the greasy mouth, the exploring hand. But the repulsive memory was swept away by the rush of joy I felt at hearing the true explanation of that scene I had witnessed between him and the little maid.

'I'm thankful for that,' he said. 'When Guillaume told me you were running madly for the door, with that dog after you, I was haunted by what you might have been running from. Anyway, to go back to my story, that first time I found her with a girl, she wasn't in the least bit taken aback. In fact, she suggested that I should join them. Do you know, I went away and was violently sick. After that night, I never touched her. It was like what often happens when you're poisoned by a bad oyster - you can never eat the things again. Even if I had wanted to have her, which I never did, I don't think I'd have been capable of it. Of course that made her furious - she's very vain. From then on, we grew to hate each other, more and more. We lived our separate lives under the same roof. She had her *affaires*, with both sexes - sometimes both together - and her orgies of food and drink. What a mixture of emotions I used to feel, looking down that dreadful Jacobean dining-room table at her - talking so graciously, twisting her apple, sipping her Vichy. Loathing, contempt, bitterness - sometimes I even took refuge in a sort of incredulous amusement.

'I know what you're wondering, Annabel. You're wondering why I stayed married to her - to a woman who revolted me physically, and with whom I had nothing whatsoever in common. I detested her friends and relations. I deplored her taste. Oh, what appalling situations I've been obliged to accommodate myself to. *Obliged.* Annabel, that word is the key. At the very beginning, I couldn't bring myself to think about the marriage at all, let alone do anything about it. I was suffering from a sort of paralysis. I'd lost the power to act. I was being poisoned, my work, my character - the lot. And then came the Nazis' rise to power, and I began to feel again. I was no longer numb. In short, I became involved.

'That, Annabel, was where the obligation to stay married to Magda came in. You've no idea how useful her connections, her appalling family and friends, have been to me in my work over the past five years, the work which has given my life its only real meaning. What a perfect disguise my association with the von Kronenbergs provided. Or so I thought, for I had, as you know, no idea of Magda's own political development. Would you say I underestimated her? No, in view of the frightful creed she adopted, I think I'd almost say the opposite. Anyway, I was a fool.'

He sighed. He had finished his wine, and he poured what little was left in the bottle into his glass - mine was still half full.

'Oh I don't know,' I said. 'Why should you have suspected her? You were busy. You had your politics, your writing. And I expect you had *affaires* too, just as your wife did.'

'Just as she did - I hope not!' He raised his eyebrows. 'But yes - I had *affaires*. A few. There was a French woman.'

'Madame Marèchal?' I asked in a detached tone.

He burst out laughing. 'No, *not* Madame Marèchal - what a tedious idea. Someone far more attractive and amusing, who lives in Paris.'

I could feel depression coming down over me, like a yellow London fog. *Attractive and amusing.* 'And there was Lady Sarah, of course,' I said.

'Sarah? Well . . . But why do you say "of course"? Did you think my manner indicated a great devotion to her?'

'No, not at all.' I heard my cool little voice going on. I couldn't stop now. 'But I looked through your window. It was by mistake. I was going to swim in the courtyard. It was the night after the Roquebrune procession.'

Now he glanced away. 'I see - what a distasteful experience for you.' But he laughed again, abruptly. 'Not much better for me. Really almost a rape, if you will forgive my being so unchivalrous. I'd tried to tell her for weeks that what there'd been between us a few years before was over - but these hunting women won't take no for an answer, from fox or man. She appeared in my room, and stripped off all her clothes. I was thankful I was leaving next morning - I'd had a message confirming it from Elizabeth during the procession.'

'I see. No, you aren't very chivalrous, are you? And I suppose you had an *affaire* with beautiful Elizabeth.'

'Beautiful Elizabeth,' he said. 'Poor, silly, beautiful Elizabeth. Well, there was something but it became embarrassing. She took me too seriously.'

'That *must* have been embarrassing,' I said, and added, 'I really can't imagine how we got started on this subject.'

'How? Why you started it, of course. It's not a subject I would ever have gone into so deeply – well, it's hardly a deep subject, is it?'

'No,' I said, flat and low. How I hated him and his 'little *affaires*'. I decided that I couldn't bear the situation another minute. I stood up, wincing as, forgetful, I put my weight on my injured foot.

'I'm tired. I must go to bed,' I said. 'Well Nick, I'm very glad that you escaped from those awful people. I'll come to the villa tomorrow, if I may, to collect my things and make arrangements.' I hesitated, but I knew I could not afford false pride. 'Perhaps,' I said, 'you'll be very kind and help me to find another job. I'm sure you know lots of people, and a reference would be most useful.'

He was staring at me, first looking astonished, then positively scowling. 'Sit down again at once,' he said. I hesitated, and he added, 'This minute, Annabel.'

I sat down. Now it was he who stood up. He took two paces. The room was so small that this brought him to the door. Obviously frustrated, he swung round, made the two steps back again, and stood looking down at me. I put my hands on the table. In a moment I would stand up again, go upstairs.

'What on earth are you talking about – another job?' he said.

'I can hardly stay alone with you at the villa,' I answered.

He was silent for a moment. Then he said, 'Bourgeois nonsense. But, if it bothers you, I'm sure something can be arranged. A – a chaperone.'

'A chaperone for the secretary!' I said. 'I've never heard anything so ridiculous. Anyway, what I said may seem "bourgeois nonsense" to you. But I can't afford to think that way. I have to earn a living. My reputation matters. You, of course, don't have to worry about yours.'

As soon as I had uttered that last sentence, I regretted it. It had sounded bitter and malicious - horrible. Worse than that, even, it had sounded so *personal*, exactly the note I most wanted to avoid now. I glanced up at him quickly.

Characteristically, his eyebrows were raised, but his mouth was folded in a narrow line. I looked down at the tablecloth again. That was when he laughed, laughed warmly, heartily - the last reaction I had ever expected. Startled, I raised my eyes. His expression was as warm, as happy as his laugh.

'Annabel, you've never made a truer remark. My reputation is certainly the least of my worries. As for yours - I shall certainly never harm it, I promise.'

How could I trust such a promise, from him? - but I couldn't help returning his smile. That was the fatal moment, the moment when I felt the hard shell in which I had been trying to encase myself crack open. He picked up my hands from the table, and gently pulled me to my feet.

He was kissing me again, on and on. His lips were on my mouth, then on my neck. I was shivering again, and the shivers multiplied till they were running all over me. A phrase I had read somewhere, 'a bundle of sensations', came into my mind. That was what I was. Then the phrase was gone. He was drawing me over to the sofa. We sank down on it together. Another long kiss. I was absolutely limp in his embrace, lips raised and parted, eyes closed when - suddenly, amazingly - he pulled me to my feet, and stepped away from me. If he hadn't put his hands on my shoulders, I would have fallen.

I opened my eyes. He was staring down into my face. For a moment we were absolutely still.

He started speaking, rapidly. 'Annabel, your pupils are enormous. They're filling your eyes, so that they aren't grey any more - they're black, like velvet. And your face is flushed. And your lips are blurred, where I've been kissing them; they're melting into your skin.' He rubbed his mouth across my hair. 'Such soft hair, incredibly soft. I noticed that long ago.' I was trembling. He took my hand, led me over to the table, pressed me down in my chair – and returned to his.

'No,' he said. 'No, I absolutely refuse to do this. I'm taking advantage of your innocence and sweetness. You were right. You must go upstairs – and I must leave, at once.'

I was possessed by an utter recklessness. I was wild and quivering. 'No,' I said. 'No, don't go. Stay here with me.'

'You're what they call "carried away",' he said, 'and that's all my fault. I'm sorry.' He added, 'You'll probably be surprised to learn that I have some principles.'

'Principles?' I said.

'Yes, Annabel. Be sensible. Why, only a few minutes ago, you were talking about your reputation, and about how impossible it would be for you to stay alone with me. Well, you were right.'

'That's different,' I said.

'Different? You mean that I should make love to you now, and that tomorrow, or in a few days' time – spent in a *pension*, perhaps; the conventions must be observed – you'll go off in search of a new job, with a nice little reference from me. "I much regret that personal circumstances over which I have no control compel me to dispense with the services of Miss Annabel Lee. She is a most efficient secretary, competent and punctual, with a typing speed of" – what's your typing speed, Annabel? Anyway, is that what you had in mind?'

No, of course it wasn't – but wasn't it better than nothing? I loved him so desperately, and I would be leaving him soon. He didn't love me, of course, but for just one night I might pretend he did.

'Don't you want me?' I said.

'Want you? Ridiculous girl – can't you tell that I do?' His tone was fierce, but now, suddenly, it became cool and dry. 'Oddly enough, however, there's one thing I've never done – and I don't propose to start now. I've never taken a girl's virginity.'

I blushed then. So that he wouldn't see it, I looked down at the tablecloth. When I raised my head, I said, 'But I'm not a virgin.'

He was frowning. Then he smiled. 'I'm afraid I don't believe you.'

'It's true.' Then I had an inspiration. I said, 'There was a man in Paris, someone called Tom Storey. He was the first.'

Nick was expressionless now, silent. Then he smiled again, but his smile was different. Something that had been in his face before had gone: something I knew immediately, with a dreadful sense of discord – as if a rough hand had been dragged across the strings of a guitar – that I missed appallingly.

'Tom Storey?' he was saying. 'Oh yes, I know whom you mean. The versifier – I can't call him a poet.' He paused. 'But he's been dead for years,' he said. 'You started young, Annabel.'

He was looking me up and down, measuringly. *Everything had gone wrong.* He was standing up, coming round the table, raising me again to my feet.

Suddenly I wanted to escape. He was taking a box of matches from his pocket, lighting my candle, which stood, in its brass candlestick, on the table. Next he put out the oil lamp. Though the candle's light was gentler, it did not soften his face. *Victorio*, I remembered suddenly – I hadn't thought of that for ages. He was handing me the candlestick. 'Hold it carefully,' he said, 'though we shan't need it for very long.'

He picked me up. He carried me into the hall and then up

the stairs. My hand was trembling, and the candelight flickered wildly on the walls. It went out when we reached my room and he put me down on the wooden bed with its sheets that smelled of lavender.

{15}

I was the first to wake. Cautiously I raised myself on one elbow, and studied him. I noticed for the first time that his eyelashes were short but thick. I saw the shadow on his jaw, and a tiny scar above his left eyebrow. Sleeping, how peaceful and remote he looked.

'Liar,' he had exclaimed, as I cried out in pain. 'Liar, dreadful little liar.' He had been moving fiercely, and now he was absolutely still, on top of me. Then I felt him lifting himself away from me, across the bed.

He lay on his back. When he spoke, it was in an icy voice – a voice even worse than that changed look on his face had been downstairs. 'How could you have done that – told me that you weren't a virgin? What exactly was the plan you had in mind?'

'*Plan!*' I exclaimed, baffled for an instant, but then I saw what he thought, what he imagined – that I was trying to trap him in some way, into marriage perhaps. That was when I burst into uncontrollable tears.

I'd never cried in this desperate way before. I had wept when my father died, but that had been different, welling from a deep aching sense of waste and loss, mingled with grief. This was an agony of shame and despair.

I couldn't stop. I sobbed on and on. Then, out of the darkness, he spoke again. His voice wasn't exactly kind, but it was no longer cruel. 'Now Annabel, stop crying, and answer my question.' But I still couldn't stop. He put his hand on my shoulder, left it there.

'Stop now,' he said. 'Stop, stop.' He spoke slowly like someone trying to soothe a child. Then, 'I'm sorry if I sounded harsh,' he said, 'but life has made me very suspicious. And I simply can't understand why you said what you did.'

Then out it came - the truth. The words broke through my sobs: 'Because I love you.' I was so shocked at myself for saying it - another trap, I supposed he would think - that my tears dried up. I gave little gulps and shudders.

The hand on my shoulder stiffened. Then, after a second, it relaxed, and I heard him give a deep, deep sigh. There was silence - broken at last by another sigh. Then the hand on my shoulder started to move to and fro, stroking it. 'Do you know,' he said, 'I think I believe you.'

I couldn't help it. My body, of its own volition, turned towards him, rested against him. Then he put his arm around me. My head rested on his chest, as his hand stroked my shoulder. Yes, my body felt peace and joy, but in my mind I was still deeply unhappy. '*Think* you believe me,' I said. 'Do you imagine I'd lie about such a thing?'

He laughed, but very gently. 'You can hardly expect me to accept your word automatically, after what you said earlier this evening.'

I had to admit it. 'Yes, I can see that.'

'Remember the women I've known, Annabel, the experiences I've had. Wasn't I bound to consider the possibility that you might feel that, as your first lover, I would be under an obligation to you? An obligation, as they say "to make an honest woman of you". Oh, don't flinch like that, please. I don't believe it any more.' He paused. Then he said, 'And, of course, I *am* under an obligation to you, anyway. After all, I owe you my life.'

I jerked up into a sitting position, casting his arm aside. 'No,' I exclaimed passionately. 'No, no, no. You don't owe me anything at all. You don't ever have to see me again, after tomorrow. It was just that, because of what I told you'

– I wasn't going to repeat that I loved him – 'I wanted to be with you tonight.'

Quite roughly, he pulled me down beside him again, held me to his side. 'Silly, silly girl,' he said. 'One night of love, indeed! Do you really imagine that life is like that, especially where a person like yourself is concerned?' He was silent again – and then there was another of his unexpected laughs. 'Tom Storey indeed! Why did you pick on such a dreadful, pretentious fellow? It almost put me off you.'

Irresistibly, I smiled in the dark. 'But not quite,' I said.

'Ah, your spirit is returning. That tongue of yours is sharpening up again. What can we do about that, I wonder? Hmmm – my first virgin. Very strange. A unique sense of possession, possibly. Though, in other respects, far from ideal. From your point of view, particularly. I think we must definitely do something about *that*.'

Now, looking down at him as he slept, I half smiled, dreamily shook my head. He had certainly kept his word in that regard. I had loved him before – now I loved him so very much more. *How would I be able to bear to part from him?*

He moved. He opened his eyes. He blinked – one of the rays of sunlight that came through the slats in the shutters was on his face. He turned his head, and saw me. 'Annabel,' he said, 'oh, Annabel – what a delightful sight to wake up to.' Smiling, he pulled me towards him.

Afterwards, when we had been lying in happy silence for several minutes, he said, 'You know, I've reached a decision. I'm not going to let you go.'

I made myself smile. 'Oh, yes you are. Just as soon as we reach the villa, I shall make you sit down and write me that reference.'

'Be quiet, for heaven's sake. Annabel, you told me a lie last night. And then, later, you told me what you said was the truth. Was it?'

He was holding me tightly, looking right into my face

from only inches away. 'Yes,' I said.

'Say it then. Say it again - what you said last night.'

'I love you.' I murmured it, tried to turn my head aside, but he held my chin, and wouldn't let me.

'You love me - God knows why. But yes, it's true. I still believe you. Things often look different in the morning - but not this time. And Annabel, I think I might be able to say those same words one day. But I'm not going to say them now. And, though you may not think so, that's a reason why you should trust me. Trust me, Annabel - and stay with me, while I get all this business with Magda sorted out. Oh, you needn't stay at the villa. You can move to that *pension*, if you want to. In fact, you can move to the Negresco, if you like. No don't look so horrified - the *pension* it shall be. And Edwards shall fetch you in the car each morning, so that you can perform your secretarial duties, in your usual efficient manner - though perhaps you ought to increase that typing speed a little.'

I couldn't help laughing, but . . . *'I might be able to say those same words one day. Trust me Annabel'*. I felt that what he had just said had transformed my life. But I was determined not to be 'intense'. He was looking so happy.

It was hard to describe the mood of wild gaiety that possessed us then - and to which I surrendered myself as wholeheartedly as he did. We laughed at my absurd black dress. We laughed at the way I limped down the stairs - my foot was much better, but not fully recovered - yet refused to let him carry me. 'Carrying's not done in the daytime, hmmm? Why, Annabel, you're more English than I am.' I was surprised at the aplomb with which I could face Madame Renard's ribald glances and little jokes - 'Monsieur, no doubt, has an especially good appetite this morning' - when she brought us our breakfast in the parlour. 'Mademoiselle is as hungry as Monsieur,' I declared when she had gone.

Only after breakfast, when he said we ought to be getting

back to the villa, did a shadow cross my mind. It must have darkened my face, too, for he said, 'Darling, you mustn't be afraid to go back there. They are gone - and with them everything hateful, everything ugly. We shall take undisputed possession of our kingdom by the sea.'

We said goodbye to Madame Renard, and thanked her profusely. She tried to give me back my nightdress and Magda's black robe, which she had washed and ironed, but I wouldn't take them - the very sight of them repelled me. She waved from the doorstep as we set off down the village street. There were not many people about, though those that there were gave us curious glances.

'Goodbye, Roquebrune,' I called out as he started the car in the square - little Roquebrune where I had spent some of the most anxious hours of my life and, now, the most perfect.

Yet, as we traversed the Moyenne Corniche, and took the road to Cap-Martin, I was conscious of a growing sense of dread, a recognition that, no, I did not want to reach the Villa Aurore. I told myself how stupid I was. He had called it 'our kingdom by the sea', quoting from the poem after which I had been named. But, at the back of my mind, the nagging anxiety remained, rose to a peak as we drew up outside the iron gate.

Hand in hand, we climbed the steps to the terrace. The front door was open, but none of the servants was about. He strode into the salon, stared around at its pompous furnishings, at the dark, varnished paintings on the walls.

'My God,' he said, 'what a clearance we're going to have here.' Over to a window he went, dragged savagely at one of the heavy curtains, actually pulled it to the ground, where it crouched in a heap. He flung open the shutter behind it, and sunlight streamed into the room. 'Light and air,' he said. 'Annabel, there will be light and air everywhere.'

But suddenly I was feeling tired and dirty. I was conscious of my bare feet, of my ridiculous dress.

'Nick,' I said, 'I think I'd like to take a bath and change my clothes now.'

'So I'm to lose my little orphan girl?' he said. 'I'll miss her. But I need a bath myself. I'll come upstairs with you.'

Up on the landing, he exclaimed, 'Oh, how free I feel. I need never see her again. She's gone - gone for ever.'

Here was the door of Magda's room. 'Shall we exorcize her ghost?' he said, and flung it open.

All the debris of that night had been removed - the food and drink, the body of Karl. The bed was white and fresh again - except for the bright blood that stained the sheets.

They lay together side by side - Magda and Udo. The bullet had been aimed at her heart - there was a great patch of blood on her white nightdress, and her crystal apple, shattered into fragments, glittered on her breast. Her eyes were open, glazed, in her white face - but Udo's head was a mess of blood and bone. His hand had flopped over the side of the bed, and a gun lay on the floor beside it. Through my horror, I found myself thinking, *It's like a scene from a play*, and the words planted a seed in my mind.

I heard myself making a little whimpering sound, and Nick saying, 'My God,' under his breath. He drew me from the room - my body was quite rigid - and closed the door.

'So he killed her, and then himself,' Nick murmured. 'Extraordinary!'

Extraordinary. *Like a scene from a play.* The seed in my mind sprouted, grew into a poison tree, put down deep, twisting roots, spread clutching branches. Extraordinary. Oh yes, extraordinary.

'I must go to the police at once,' he was saying. 'Best to go there. Can't face getting involved with some half-witted *gendarme* on the telephone. You'll come with me, darling, of course.'

I took a step back. 'No,' I said. 'No.'

'You'll stay here alone? You feel you can do that?'

'Yes,' I said. 'I'll stay.'

'Brave girl - yes, perhaps it's best for you to be involved as little as possible. But what will you do while I'm gone?'

'I'll take a bath,' I said mechanically. 'I'll change.' Then I added, 'I must look respectable when they arrive.'

'How sensible. What presence of mind.' He put his arms around me briefly, and I tried to relax my rigid limbs. He kissed my forehead, and I closed my eyes.

He crossed the landing, paused at the top of the stairs. 'Stay in your room,' he said. 'I'll decide how to handle things.'

'Yes,' I answered. I waited, my fists clenched at my sides, until I heard the car start. Then I moved.

I couldn't go back into that room of Magda's again. So the nearest telephone was the one in the hall. Down the stairs I hobbled, desperately fast, and clinging to the banister. By the table in the hall, I snatched the local directory from a row of them, all bound in stamped leather folders. I scrabbled through the Cap-Martin section, and found the number of a taxi. The man I spoke to said that he would come in ten minutes. Up the stairs again, and along the passage to my room.

Yes, everything was in order - Guillaume had been right; they hadn't given another thought to my baggage.

No time for a bath. I dressed in wild haste, and I doubt if anyone has ever packed faster - or worse. Last of all, I took my little hoard from under the carpet by the wardrobe, put it, with the modest amount of French money I possessed, in my purse. Then, dragging my travelling bag behind me, I set off.

Along the passages, and across the landing. Down the stairs, the bag bumping behind me. I had just reached the hall when I heard the taxi draw up. I hurried out on to the terrace, and called to the driver. He came up the steps, and I gave him directions for fetching my trunk.

At last - all was accomplished. My trunk was in the taxi,

and now the driver was going down the steps ahead of me, carrying my travelling bag. A voice called 'Mademoiselle!' and I turned.

It was Marie, pale and anxious-looking, gazing at me in astonishment. 'But Mademoiselle, where is Monsieur Forrest? And where are you going?'

'I'm sorry Marie, I can't stop. Goodbye.' I hurried through the iron gate after the driver, and got into the taxi.

'To Nice please – to the railway station,' I said.

{16}

Although it was November, the air of that small town in Georgia was still soft and balmy. I sat on the porch in a dilapidated rocking-chair which creaked every time it moved. A dog barked in the distance. A boy rode past on a bicycle. Nothing else disturbed the quiet street. It was only just after eight, but my grandmother had, as always, gone to bed half an hour before, and my uncle was out playing cards with two other elderly widowers and a decrepit bachelor. We always had our supper early, at half after six.

How warm and still the night was! There were days on which I fancied that I felt a hint of sea breeze from the coast, twenty miles away – from Savannah, the city after which my mother had been named. But that was seldom. Most of the time, the weather was slow and drowsy – like the town in which I had been living for the past two months.

It seemed to have been longer than that. I lived according to a routine. There were no starred occasions on my calendar to make the days speed by – and, at the moment, I didn't want any. Oh, the time must come when I would do what I thought of as 'going out into the world' again. But not yet, not now.

In the mornings I rose early, and spent an hour or two working on my mother's manuscript. I had finished transcribing and correcting it, and had just started to type it, on an old machine which my uncle had lent me. During the day, at my insistence, I helped in his law office – a small return for my board and lodging, and anyway I couldn't have borne to do nothing, to hang about the house, brooding on the past. In the lunch break, I ate a sandwich and drank a cup of coffee before taking a short walk. I went on longer walks at weekends - walks which, I believed, made people think me strange. Friends of the family would stop their automobiles to offer me rides to wherever I was going, and look puzzled when I refused. Nobody in the town seemed to go for walks.

There was one cause for excitement, On my arrival in New York from Cherbourg, before I set off on my journey south, I had visited my father's agent, and shown him my father's manuscript. His response had been one of tremendous enthusiasm - he was, as he put it, 'quite bowled over' - and my father's publisher's reaction was the same. My intention of typing the manuscript myself had never had to be carried out - they wanted it done immediately, in New York. The book would come out in the Spring, and the publisher was already talking of the prospect of a 'Lee revival'.

I'd done my duty to my father; now there remained what I owed my mother - all that I could do, the preparation of her book. How many hours I'd spent, on my walks, in bed at night, meditating on the discoveries I had made about my parents. How often I'd gone over my father's treachery and my mother's pain. Now, slowly, I was moving towards some kind of reconciliation and acceptance,

My father, I recognized, had put all that was best in him into his books - and, having done so, had really had nothing left to spare for life. What pain, what labour it had cost him to produce his work. What bitter unhappiness he had suffered when, as his novels became better, their success had declined. And how many years had gone into the creation of his last published book. Yes, I could see that my mother's work, which she had dashed off at such speed, must have seemed a mockery of his efforts, a taunting caricature.

Could he really have predicted the terrible results of first the rejection of her book, and then the reading of his? Well, perhaps he could have, if he had thought more deeply about her - but he had lacked the capacity for that kind of thought. *He had had nothing left to spare for life.* Yes, that was what it came back to. Toiling at his real work, grinding out his bright little stories - who would guess, skimming through them in magazines, that they'd been born in hell? - and battling with his alcoholism: all of that had drained him to a bloodless shadow.

A shadow - that was what, these days, I felt *I* was: a shadow that walked, listened to family reminiscences, worked, ate, slept - and awoke each morning to renew its pale existence. So I, a shadow, was becoming reconciled to my shadowy father, even though the process was a slow one. But, after my experience in Zurich, it was bound to be.

It had been to Zurich that I went from Nice. And, as the train brought me nearer and nearer my mother, each moment I longed for her more. It was true that Dr Zeiss had told Nick that he did not think it advisable that I should see her yet, had repeated this to me in our correspondence, but he had also said how much better she seemed to be getting. Surely he might change his mind about my seeing her, if I told him of what I planned to say to her and convinced him of how careful, tactful, gentle I would be.

As the train bore me on, I imagined myself entering her room, carrying a great bunch of the flowers she loved. She would look at me, and her face would light up. After we had embraced, I would tell her how I had found her novel, read it, and thought it beautiful, and that I was convinced that I would be able to get it published. Of course I would not mention to her the part my father had played in its initial rejection, but I would suggest to her most vigorously that a refusal by one publisher meant nothing - would remind her of how many successful authors had been through just such an experience.

I reached Zurich the following morning. I left my baggage

at the station. The shops were just opening, and, from a florist, I brought three dozen fresh red roses – the dew was still on their petals. Carrying them I walked to the clinic. It was a brilliant morning, with just a hint of crispness in the air.

A new receptionist – not the one I'd seen before – greeted me in the lobby. I told her that I wanted to see Dr Zeiss. She asked my name, and when she heard it, I thought that a puzzled look crossed her face. She went through the door behind her desk, and, only a few minutes later, returned, accompanied by Dr Zeiss himself.

I smiled at him, greeted him warmly – and could not account for the astonished expression on his face, the startled glance he gave my armful of crimson roses.

'So soon!' he exclaimed. 'I would not have thought it possible.' He took my hand, then put an arm about my shoulder – a gesture which surprised me, as in the past I had found his manner rather formal. 'Let us go to my office,' he said.

'So soon!' – what could he mean? We went into his office: chairs, a desk, a green carpet, a strange picture of a woman – by one of his patients, I guessed – over the mantelpiece. He showed me to a chair in front of the desk, and went to sit behind it.

'I cannot believe,' he said, 'that you could have got here so soon. Why, I only sent the telegram a few hours ago.'

'Telegram?' Under my bewilderment, I felt a sudden chill.

'You did not receive it? Can you have arrived here today by chance?'

'I didn't get a telegram. I wanted to see my mother. I thought you might allow me—'

'Oh, my poor child.' Abruptly he got up from his chair, and came around the desk. He put his hand on my arm. 'You are too late.'

'Too late?' I repeated. My heart was thudding dully, and

there was that old hollow feeling in my stomach.

'Yes. Something very bad has happened. Yesterday evening, your mother took her own life.'

'Took her own life,' I said flatly. Now I felt entirely numb. I heard myself say, 'I thought she was so much better.'

'Yes, indeed. We were all convinced of it. Her mind was so much clearer, although her skin disease was still causing her great pain. We think that must have been what precipitated the crisis.'

There were grey hairs in his neat little dark moustache. He took off his glasses, and they left a red mark on his nose. Without them, his face looked bare. He wiped the lenses with a handkerchief, and put the glasses on again.

'What did she do?' I asked.

'You wish me to tell you? She hanged herself, Miss Lee.' He went on rapidly: 'We had no idea of such a thing happening. She seemed so calm. In the afternoon, she sat in the garden for a little while. And then, in the evening, a nurse went to her room – and found her. There was nothing we could do. All methods of resuscitation were attempted.'

Oh, yes, he was sympathetic, but I could see that he was also worried – worried for the reputation of his clinic, worried perhaps that I might make a fuss of some kind. What would have been the use of that? He had nothing to fear. Making a fuss was the last thing on my mind.

When he realized that, he went out of his way to be helpful, made all the arrangements for me, organized the transport of my mother's body to Paris, dealt with all the formalities involved. For I was determined that she should be buried beside my father. He said that there was money, spoke of the sum that had been left with him by 'that charming man, your employer'. 'Yes,' I said.

I telegraphed to my grandmother, but I was the only person present at my mother's funeral. Anyway, it would not have been possible for my grandmother to come. She was too old, not very well, and could not have afforded the journey.

My grandfather, who had died three years ago, had lost all his money in the Wall Street crash, and my uncle's law business was a small and struggling one.

After the funeral, I went and sat for a long time in the Luxembourg Gardens, where I had walked so often, as a child, with one or another maid or governess. I was staying now in the same small hotel, in that district, where I had stopped on my way from London to Cap-Martin. When I returned to the hotel from the Gardens that afternoon, I wrote a letter to my grandmother. I asked her if I might come to visit her - as she had asked me to do after my father's death. I felt that she was my only link with my parents - more than that, my only link with life. Her house was my only approximation to a home in the whole world.

Now, in the gently creaking rocking chair on the porch, I looked at that word, 'home' - measured it, questioned it, studied it first from one angle, then from another.

How warmly my grandmother had renewed her invitation to me to 'make my home' with her; how kindly she and my uncle had welcomed me. How hard they tried, despite their limited means, to distract me, to entertain me, to find 'company' for me. And how ungrateful I felt, how guilty, about the resistance - passive but intense - with which I responded to their efforts. I couldn't seem to find anything in common with the boys and girls of my own age whom I was introduced to - their pleasures, their concerns seemed meaningless to me, and alien. Now they were beginning to abandon their attempts to involve me in their activities - attempts which had never been all that enthusiastic; I must have seemed as odd to them as they did to me. In the same way, people were no longer offering me rides when I was on my solitary walks.

One thing that I enjoyed was to hear everything my grandmother could tell me about the beautiful, restless girl - undisputed belle of the town - who had been my mother.

My grandmother's stories were all of the years before my mother's marriage, of the admirers who had courted her before she met my father. Of him she hardly ever spoke, and it was evident how deeply she disapproved of him: the writer of 'light' books, the drinker – she had a horror of drink – who had trapped her lovely hummingbird daughter, and destroyed her.

How pleasant, although shabby, my grandmother's old house was – its big porch, its well-tended yard, its big high-ceilinged rooms. And yet – I had to admit to myself that I didn't think of it as home.

There weren't very many books in my grandmother's house: a shelf of Victorian novels and, in my mother's old bedroom – now mine – a bookcase of the fiction of her teens and a few volumes of poetry. It was in one of these that, in a poem called *Renouncement*, I found two lines that haunted me:

> *With the first dream that comes with the first sleep*
> *I run, I run, I am gathered to thy heart.*

For I didn't only grieve for my dead mother, and brood over my dead father. A third person was always appearing in my dreams and creeping into my thoughts – a person who, as I constantly told myself, might, as far as I was concerned, just as well be dead. And yet he lived in my mind all the time.

At my grandmother's, I allowed myself one extravagance – an order for the *New York Times*. I had two reasons. After all that had happened at the villa, I felt I must learn more about what was going on in Europe – the Munich crisis gave me my first real understanding of what might lie ahead. And also – oh, of course, primarily, if I told myself the truth – I had wanted to follow the Forrest case. Nick's fame, Magda's wealth, the element of 'illicit love' had ensured it international coverage.

From the first, I found that the case was regarded as 'open-and-shut'. *He killed her and then himself* – those had been

Nick's words, and they expressed the view of the police and of the press. No one questioned the facts, although the motive was discussed exhaustively. Reference was made to that old French favourite, the *crime passionel.* Had Udo been motivated by jealousy, by possessiveness, even by some dark Teutonic yearning for a *Liebestod* – a love-death like Tristan's and Isolde's? Whichever motive was suggested, the truth was clear: *He had killed her, and then killed himself.*

That scene was photographed on my mind. *Like a scene from a play.* Magda and Udo arranged on that bed, on those sheets whose freshness was only defaced by their blood. *Like a scene from a play* – and never, I thought, had there been a more improbable one. Udo kill Magda – and she not struggle? Udo kill himself? Everything that I'd seen of those two savage creatures told me that they'd both cling to life with all their strength. No, I had known immediately that the scene was false – and then I had guessed the truth.

Nick had come to me straight from the villa. *Trust me, Annabel,* he had said – but how could I trust him? He'd lied to me. He'd talked and laughed and made love to me, with their blood fresh on his hands. However vile Magda and Udo had been, I couldn't love their murderer – couldn't love the cold calculating man who had come to Roquebrune to lie to me. And after what had happened that night, next morning he had taken me to find their bodies.

At that moment I was distracted from my all-too-familiar line of thought by a car pulling up outside the gate. Surely, I thought, it was too early for my uncle to be back from his card game? Then I saw that the car wasn't his. A tall man got out, and I stiffened in my chair.

He paid the driver, and the car drove off. Now he was opening the gate, and I saw his face.

I rose as he came up the path towards me. I felt an impulse to run into the house and bolt the door. But I knew I couldn't do that. All the same, I retreated behind the rocking chair. I gripped its curved bentwood back with both hands. He came up the steps to the porch, and stood facing me, the chair between us.

'Well, Annabel,' he said, 'so I've found you at last.' Those words could have expressed satisfaction, but they didn't. I'd never heard his voice sound colder, or seen a colder look on his face.

I said nothing.

'I'm not here to ask you to come back to me,' he said. 'You have no need to worry about that. I've travelled a long way, Annabel, just to ask you some questions, and I'm going to stay here until you answer them. That should spur you on. I'm sure you'd like me to leave as soon as possible. Well, I shall - but, this time, I'm not going to be fobbed off with your habitual lies.'

'*My* lies!' I exclaimed. He really couldn't expect to get away with *that*, unchallenged.

He raised his eyebrows. 'Yes, Annabel, your lies - who else's? Your endless, tedious, inexplicable lies. The charade of pretending not to be a virgin - now why did you go in for that? At the time I was stupid enough to believe your absurd story about "loving" me - but not afterwards. Not after you pretended that you were happy, that you were going to stay with me - and then rushed off, without a word, at the very moment when I'd made that ghastly discovery and had to cope with its aftermath. Now come on, Annabel, what I want you to do is calmly, quietly - no dramatics or faked tears this time, please - give me your reasons for the whole performance, if you can face them, that is. Cruelty, would you say? Cowardice? A twisted mind? Who knows, if I help you to recognize them, it might do you some good.'

'How *dare* you?' I said. 'How *dare* you?' My voice rose. 'When it's you that's the liar, you that's putting on an act? The only reason I can think of for your coming here is to torture me - and you call *me* cruel!'

He took a step forward. Suddenly I was glad of the chair between us. I said, 'How could you possibly expect me to stay after what you'd done?'

'What can you mean?' His voice, unlike mine, was low, but the rage in it almost frightened me – almost, because I was too angry to be afraid. '*Done*?' he went on. 'What have I *done*? Is it possible that you're blaming me for what happened between us at Roquebrune? Is that it, Annabel? Is the "wronged woman" your latest role?'

'Don't sneer at me!' My fingers were gripping the back of the chair so tightly that the wood gave a little creak of protest. 'Yes,' I said, 'yes, I do blame you for what happened at Roquebrune, but not in the stupid sense you're trying to imply. I don't know why you bother. You must know what I really mind – that I let myself love a cold, callous, brutal murderer.'

Neither of us spoke. We stared at each other. My hands relaxed their grip. I was conscious of that dog, barking again in the distance. Perhaps Nick would go now, but he just went on staring. Then he repeated my last word: '*Murderer*?'

He sounded quite dazed, as if with astonishment. But I *knew* – I'd known all along. 'You may not like the word,' I said. 'I suppose you'll say it was all for politics. Well, perhaps it was. But I still don't know how you could do it – kill your wife and Udo, and then come and make love to me.'

He raised his hands, clasped them together, pressed them under his chin. Above them, his face was first blank, then creased into a frown. And, at last, the frown faded. His hands dropped to his sides. He laughed.

I had noticed his tendency to laugh at quite unexpected moments before – but this time it really shocked me. I looked at him with horror.

He stopped laughing. Slowly he shook his head. When he spoke, his voice was reflective. 'You know, Annabel, I can't decide if you're better than I thought, or worse. At least, now, I have some understanding of why you left. But I really find it hard to accept that you could believe such a thing of me.'

I plunged on. 'I know she wouldn't have let Udo kill her without a struggle – everything so neat and tidy. A suicide pact, really. But she'd never have entered into one, and neither would he. They just weren't like that. I've never been more sure of anything.'

He nodded. 'Yes,' he said. 'Yes. As it happens, you are perfectly right about that. Most perceptive of you, most intuitive.' He paused. 'I only wish,' he added, 'that your perception and intuition had been just a little deeper, and had been applied to me.'

A moth brushed against my face. I started violently.

'Udo didn't kill her,' Nick said, 'and he didn't kill himself. But I had nothing whatsoever to do with their deaths. I'll tell you who was responsible, although I didn't tell the police. It was Guillaume.'

'Guillaume!' I exclaimed. It was like that moment on a chilly grey day when a fire catches, and one stretches out cold hands towards the first flame.

'Yes. Let me explain. He saw himself as an executioner, felt himself justified by what they'd done, most especially by the murder of Elizabeth – and, of course, also by the fact that they had planned my death, and were prepared to kill you. He also thought that they presented a permanent danger to everything we'd been working for – he was right about that, too. God knows how much poor Elizabeth told them, when they tortured her.

'Guillaume's a very ruthless man. He is passionately political, and he also has connections in the underworld. All the people of Roquebrune and of Cap-Martin are afraid of him, in awe of him, aware of his power. If it hadn't been for that, of course, he would never have been able to carry out his plan.

'He had disposed of Emil's body already when I came to the villa. And, Annabel, when I came there, everything was as I told you that night. I talked to Magda and Udo, in that pigsty of a room where she was packing up her things. And then I came to you at Roquebrune. Guillaume had told me when I saw him in the afternoon that he had private business to attend to that night. It was when I left the villa that he put his plan into operation.

'He locked Edwards in one of the garages, and he sent the other servants to their rooms, except Marie. Everyone obeyed him – all those who worked for us, apart from Edwards and Emil, were local people. He made Marie help him – oh, not with the actual killing, but with clearing up the room, changing the sheets, and so on, while he held Magda and Udo at gunpoint in the boudoir. He knew that Marie would never give him away – partly from fear, partly because, apparently, she detested Magda; it's difficult for a woman to keep many secrets from her personal maid.

'I don't really want to talk in detail about how he shot them, forcing Magda to wash and change and so on, and then making them lie down on the bed in the positions he required. But you don't really need to hear any more, do you? Or perhaps you don't believe me, even now?'

I came around from behind the rocking chair to stand in front of him. I said the only thing I could: 'Oh Nick, of course I believe you. I'm so terribly sorry. Do you think you can ever forgive me?'

I could not read his expression. He didn't move towards me. He said, 'Do you know, I wonder if I can. I wonder if I can forgive you for believing what you did, for thinking me – how did you put it? – "a cold, callous, brutal murderer". And quite apart from that, of course, there's the intolerable dance you've led me. One thing, at least, was lucky. On my way to the *gendarmerie*, I decided that I definitely wasn't going to mention your presence at the villa – I already had that in mind when I asked you to stay in your room. And of course I didn't mean to mention our night in Roquebrune. At that stage, of course, I felt, as the police did afterwards, that the case was a perfectly simple one. I believed the evidence of my eyes in that bedroom, Annabel. I'm glad I did. It made my interview at the *gendarmerie* much more convincing than it would have been otherwise – and my behaviour afterwards, when I went back with them to the villa. And it wasn't until after they'd gone, that Marie told me of your dramatic departure – I don't know if you can imagine how *that* news affected me.'

'I'm sorry,' I said again.

'Yes, Annabel. Anyway, after the police had gone, I got my first clue to what had actually happened from Edwards. So then I went and tackled Guillaume. Oh, he admitted it at once – he knew I wouldn't give him away, because of our work. In fact, I got the impression that he expected me to slap him on the back and wring his hand. Well, I didn't exactly do that. All the same, you know, I think he did the right thing, the only thing – though I could never have done it myself.'

He paused a moment. Then, 'You know,' he said, 'the police enquiries, the inquest, the hideous publicity – it was strange, but none of those things mattered to me as much as your disappearance did. It obsessed me. Even the Munich crisis didn't affect me as it would have at any other time.' He gave a dry little laugh – cut off abruptly as he said, 'How could you have done that – left me without a word, without even a hint of where you'd gone? Couldn't you, at the very least, have discussed your suspicion with me?'

He was waiting for an answer. I said, 'I think I felt that if I saw you I might weaken. You might even have been able to persuade me to stay – but I knew I'd never be able to forget what I was convinced you'd done.'

'I see. Well, one thing did soften me, Annabel. When I opened the telegram that arrived for you the day after you left, I was horrified to hear what had happened to your mother. But how was I to get in touch with you? I felt sure Dr Zeiss couldn't know where you were – or he wouldn't have sent his telegram to the villa. And by then I was in the thick of the police investigations. So I did nothing. But it was through Dr Zeiss that I tracked you down in the end. At last I wrote to him, and he gave me your grandmother's address. I thought I'd write to her, but I tore up about twenty of my attempts at a letter. So I decided I'd go to that revival of *Meringue Chantilly* after all. It opened last night. A success – for what that's worth. I was glad to escape down here in search of news. But oh, I felt mad with rage at you when I saw you on the porch.'

'Are you still m-m-mad with rage?' I asked. That was when he opened his arms.

'You know,' he said, a little later, 'there's one problem. Can I afford to marry – yes, for us, Annabel, it would have to be marriage – a girl who jumps to such outrageous conclusions about me, who decides, without a moment's hesitation, that I'm a double murderer? The risks are really quite appalling.' Then he smiled. He said, 'But I've always enjoyed a gamble.'

My grandmother and my uncle were the only witnesses at our wedding in the church where my parents had been married twenty years before. It was sentimental of me – but, as Nick put the ring on my finger, I felt that Delaney and Vanna blessed us. Just as their bodies rested, side by side, in that quiet corner of Paris, so now their turbulent spirits, assuaged, merged together in tranquillity.

EPILOGUE

It was a gusty December day when Edwards met us. The palm trees on Promenade des Anglais swayed wildly in the wind, and the sea was grey.

But I didn't care about the weather. I was too happy. I remembered the last time I had arrived at Nice and how lonely and nervous I'd felt. Now Nick was with me, and my hand was tightly clasped in his.

I had one bad moment. Just before we drew up by the iron gate, the past came over me in a wave. Then I saw Marie waving from the terrace, and noticed that the shutters of the villa had been repainted – in that French blue which has always been my favourite.

'Ah, Mademoiselle,' Marie exclaimed as I embraced her.

'She's not "Mademoiselle" any more,' Nick said as we went into the hall. 'She is "Madame" for ever.'

The villa had been transformed. The Boulle and marquetry, the gloomy dark oak, the commodes and credenzas, the brocades and velvets were gone. So were those chandeliers – so massive that, in spite of their stout chains, I had always avoided walking directly underneath them. The elaborate curtains no longer draped the windows. The dim landscapes and sombre portraits had vanished.

There will be light and air, Nick had said. Now, all the walls were white. The heavy carpets had been replaced by a few oriental rugs, scattered on the tiled floors.

The furniture was sparse, as I feel furniture should be. There were a few old painted chests and *armoires.* A weathered slab of marble on pine trestles was our table – surrounded by rush-seated chairs. Matisse prints hung on the walls. Over the fireplace in the salon was a little Marie Laurencin – a blonde girl with a blue scarf, a pink-cheeked girl holding a pink rose. Nowhere in the house did I feel, as I had feared I might, a shadow of its former mistress.

In the early spring of 1939, my father's book was published to tremendous acclaim. The 'Lee revival' became an undisputed fact. My mothers's novel, published two months later, blossomed briefly, faded – then died. The critics who reviewed it, although some of them found it 'touching', devoted their attention to the fact that it was written by the wife of Delaney Lee. I recognized that her memory would, in the end, be preserved through his.

Oh those months of 1939, those months with Nick – I shall never forget them. We made love, we walked, we read, we made love. We ate the light meals we both liked, and, in the evening, I drank a glass or two of his wine. We talked, too, talked about everything – and soon I came to share his political interests and convictions. It was fortunate that I did for there was always one cloud on my horizon.

It was a very short time after our return to France that he said, 'I shall have to go away next week, for a few days.'

'Oh,' was the only response I could manage.

'You trust me, don't you?' he asked lightly, and it was with perfect truth that I answered 'Yes.' For nowadays I was as sure of his love for me as I was of mine for him.

We had been walking. We were standing on that same rocky outcrop where I had stumbled on my first afternoon at Cap-Martin. We were looking out, over the olive grove and past the villa, to a rough white-crested sea.

He put his arm around me, and then he quoted again from that poem of Poe's which bears my name – the poem I had always disliked until that morning at Roquebrune:

But we loved with a love that was more than love–
I and my Annabel Lee –
With a love that the wingèd seraphs of heaven
Coveted her and me

And this was the reason that, long ago,
In this kingdom by the sea,
A wind blew out of a cloud by night
Chilling my Annabel Lee

'Yes,' Nick said. 'There's a cold, cold wind blowing, Annabel. But, one way or another, we must face it.'

One way or another. He went away – I stayed behind. 'I've always enjoyed a gamble.' Those words were always in my head every time he went away. For he went away several times – but each time he came back to me and I was happy again.

What he did not do at all during those months was resume the writing of his play. 'That will have to wait until after the war,' he said. *After the war* – it was the first time I'd heard those words spoken with such utter certainty. And of course he was right to be certain.

It was a few weeks before war was declared that Nick and I went to England. Tonight the German bombers are overhead, and Nick is in occupied France. I know that only because the work I do – in a London office – is linked with his.

I am in a crowded air-raid shelter, and I am thinking of him. '*I've always enjoyed a gamble.*' Gambling is a serious trade, these days – it was only two months ago that Guillaume was tortured to death by the Gestapo. '*I've always enjoyed a gamble*' – but always, in the past, Nick came back to me.

He will again. Now, in this huddle of pale exhausted people, I close my eyes very tightly for a moment. Using every ounce of will-power I possess, I conjure up another person and a very different scene. Together, he and I return to our kingdom by the sea.

After the war . . .